POSSESSION

Eve sighed and turned to the task of searching the professor's bedroom for the secret formula. But the moment she put her hands to her hips in readiness to begin the guileful chore, she was knocked dumb when the door to the bathroom en suite shot wide open and Theo, standing tall and majestic like an ebony god, emerged and stared blankly at her.

He wore a blue towel around his waist, and his hairy chest and muscular body were wet—an indication that he had just stepped out of the shower. Eve was aghast. She absorbed Theo's beguiled expression with nervous embarrassment. It was obvious from the way his face began to change to one of sheer amazement that he had not expected to find her there.

Her wayward, primitive instincts were tangibly aware that the towel was the only impediment that concealed his naked flesh. That same subconscious also took the rare opportunity to assimilate his athletically structured physique—his rounded shoulders, medium-size biceps, sturdy arms, and lean torso, which tapered amiably to an equally trim waistline.

"When . . . When did you get back?" Eve asked.

"About a half hour ago," Theo said softly, glancing at his watch. "I'd b̶e̶t̶t̶e̶r̶ ̶g̶e̶t̶ dressed. We're still on for dinner?"

Eve nodded, too̶ her ̶feet had regained ̶e to-ward the door. She̶ ̶her, yet no sooner had ̶ ̶ bed than he took hold of her ̶ ̶ her toward him.

Other books by Sonia Icilyn

ROSES ARE RED
ISLAND ROMANCE
VIOLETS ARE BLUE
INFATUATION

Published by BET/Arabesque Books

POSSESSION

Sonia Icilyn

BET Publications LLC
http://www.bet.com
http://www.arabesquebooks.com

ARABESQUE BOOKS are published by

BET Publications, LLC
c/o BET BOOKS
One BET Plaza
1900 W Place NE
Washington, DC 20018-1211

All Kensington Titles, Imprints, and Distributed Lines are available at special quantity discounts for bulk purchases for sales promotions, premiums, fund-raising, and educational or institutional use. Special book excerpts or customized printings can also be created to fit specific needs. For details, write or phone the office of the Kensington special sales manager: Kensington Publishing Corp., 850 Third Avenue, New York, NY 10022, attn: Special Sales Department, Phone: 1-800-221-2647.

First Printing: June 2002
10 9 8 7 6 5 4 3 2 1

Printed in the United States of America

*For my darling daughter Parissa
and her remarkable patience*

Prologue

"This is the new guy on the scene," Assistant Commissioner Humphrey Brown said quite discreetly, handing the small color photograph to the woman sitting beside him on the hard wooden bench in St. James's Park. "We don't know how involved he is. I thought maybe you could get close and flush him out."

Eve Hamilton glanced at the photograph. "Handsome."

"Careful," Humphrey Brown warned sternly. "He may be lethal. We know he was the last person to see your brother before he died."

Assistant Commissioner Brown was a large man, Caribbean born with a black mustache that decorated his top lip like an unruly and offensive caterpillar. The hairy appendage was as much a part of his identity as his walnut-brown, sharpish face. His abrupt manner reminded Eve of her brother, Paul Hamilton, student medical researcher for the De Cordova Institute of Plant Genetics. That was his last place of employment, the assistant commissioner—a close friend of the family—had told her. He had been like an uncle to her and her brother before her brother's untimely death.

"Do you think this guy killed Paul?" she asked, looking closely at the snapshot in her hand.

The face that looked back at her had a striking, but more mature, resemblance to Craig David, her favorite

British pop singer. *Number one suspect,* she thought of the tawny-brown skin, designer stubble jawline, broad nose, cornrow braided hair, and enormous chocolate-brown eyes that reflected a roguish face.

"He's the godson of the Brazilian ambassador." Assistant Commissioner Brown added the information casually. "And we don't have intelligence on who killed your brother. What we do know is that something is going down and this guy is involved."

Eve reluctantly tore her gaze from the photograph to visualize how such a handsome man could be caught in a state of affairs that called for Humphrey Brown, the only black assistant commissioner at the Metropolitan Police responsible for specialists' operations in England, to telephone her office and arrange this secret meeting. When she returned her attention to Humphrey, the question was on her lips, the words spilling out with plumes of cold breath that mingled with the dew of the dawn.

"What's going on?"

"Look, Eve," he began, searching her expression, making a mental note that her eyes were identical to the shade of brandy he had downed earlier. "What I'm about to tell you is confidential. You're not really part of our operation, so I'm going out on a limb clueing you in."

The assistant commissioner folded shaky hands between his knees and peered ahead at the yellow streak in the sky. It was nearly the end of April. The rising sun did very little to calm his nerves. His eyes roamed to catch a glimpse of up-with-the-lark joggers making their way through the park before he eventually spoke. "I want to get the bastard who killed your brother, and this guy right here is the main man I'm holding responsible." He indicated the photo Eve was still holding between her cold fingers.

Humphrey Brown had never looked this unsettled before, and she felt the shiver of some impending truth tickle through her veins. "Go on," she whispered softly.

"Her Majesty's Customs and Excise Office discovered that his godfather owned a building in Piccadilly Circus," the assistant commissioner continued. "Their head of enforcement checked the records and thought it was an abandoned warehouse . . . until last year."

"What happened?" Eve was hooked.

"The whole place got torched and no one saw a thing."

Eve nodded, digesting the information carefully, wondering whether she should get involved. At thirty-two, she was attractive, fairly accomplished in her own career, and well traveled. She was accustomed to living well, enjoyed dinner parties with her friends, spoke mild French, loved watching classic movies, and was quite abutted to the elite of the London social scene. Her face on occasion would be snapped by the paparazzi who, in recent times, speculated about her love life.

Recently, she made a point of keeping her image out of the spotlight by becoming more involved in the charity side of her work. A self-empowered woman, she came to the decision that her *Hamilton Connections* could open doors and be made more useful for helping and supporting others than for being gossiped about in the latest society column.

A short stint in Malawi, a tiny part of Africa where she had gone on a sabbatical to find inspiration for her work, had shown her that she really could make such a difference. Paul's death was an unexpected distraction while supporting her mother and dealing with the problems in her own personal life. Now she was back in full form and in agreement with the assistant commissioner that her brother's murder should be quietly investigated following a disappointing inquest into his death.

Paul was a tall, mildly handsome man, a scholar whose lips always twitched when he was nervous. She had kept heartwarming memories of him as someone shy and slightly sensitive, certainly no one who was threatened to be wanted dead. The few articles that were tangible evidence of his existence were housed in a box in her spare bedroom. She needed answers.

"Were there any witnesses?" Eve asked, recalling Paul's memorial service, her mother's face, and the fact that she had refused to cry for her brother.

"There was a guard who was found lying on the floor knocked out," Humphrey continued. "It turns out the whole warehouse had a fail-safe security system, X-ray detection devices, laser beam surveillance, motion alarm, and an eight-combination, push-button lock to an upstairs office." The assistant commissioner shook his head, completely baffled. "The guard swears he did not know that the building contained a walk-in vault. He was just paid hourly to look after the place."

"Did he say anything?" Eve asked, curious.

"The only thing he could tell us was that he heard a lookout go upstairs to the roof and the pop and crackle of a blowtorch."

"And the vault?"

"Empty."

"Fingerprints? Clues?"

"None." Humphrey's expression was dismal. "It had all the hallmarks of a professional heist. That's why our special operations branch was called in. Forensics vacuum-searched the place and found microscopic traces of coca leaf, but diagnostics doesn't think it's for cocaine manufacture."

"Why not?"

The assistant commissioner's heavyset eyebrows fur-

rowed. "We know the place was used as a secret lab.
There's something about the coca leaf that's got us
spooked." He paused. "We've been hearing rumors that
a major Brazilian drug trafficker has been funding experiments on a new drug to monopolize the market.
I'm not sure the ambassador is in on it, but this new
guy . . ."

"His godson," Eve reminded him as she looked at the
photograph again. "He may be running the show."

"Exactly." Humphrey offered her a meaningful
glance. "Do you still want to do this?" His mild Jamaican
accent held steel.

"Yes," Eve said, determined, deciding that every
woman deserved an adventure. "I need to do it for
Paul."

One

The man seated at the side of the podium while Lola Henriques was addressing the seminar drew Eve's eyes immediately. It was difficult to concentrate on what the speaker was saying for she had seen this man's face before.

She recognized the assertively masculine angles in its lean strength of feature, the well-shaped profile, and the hint of sensuality about the pink, rounded mouth. *Handsome,* her mind recollected as she watched his gaze search the room, his chocolate-brown eyes giving very little indication of what he might be thinking.

We can't offer you any protection, the assistant commissioner's voice echoed in her head, as Eve followed the man's gaze toward the overhead projector which Lola Henriques was using to display a variety of disturbing facts. He was engrossed in Lola's findings on toxic chemicals and pollutants, uncontrolled consumer waste and burgeoning landfills, poppy crops replacing cornfields, but Eve's mind had strayed momentarily. *I respected your brother,* Humphrey's voice infiltrated.

Eve grimaced as a picture of Paul's smiling face flashed through her head. He had been killed much too early in his career. He was the oldest child of their Jamaican father, a civil servant who had died when Eve was a young girl, and their Dominican mother, an English teacher, now retired and still trying to come to terms with her son's death.

Paul would have been proud of you. Those were the last words the assistant commissioner had spoken before he disappeared through St. James's Park in London, swallowed quickly by the early morning fog. He had headed back to the Metropolitan Police headquarters, fondly known as the Met, to report that he had covertly enlisted her help to flush out a suspected menace that lived in the country, a successful Afro-Brazilian scientist.

Eve unfolded the paper she had kept in her hand since entering the lecture hall in Sommerville College at the University of Oxford and again looked at the details the assistant commissioner had written down for her to memorize. Professor Theophilus de Cordova was expected to address the seminar. *Careful,* Humphrey Brown's words played again in her head. *He may be lethal.*

The piece of paper was duly replaced in her handbag as Eve tried not to let her reactions show in her expression. She refocused her attention on the man still seated close to the podium. He looked arresting in a superbly tailored navy suit and pale blue shirt which defined his broad shoulders and sturdy build. He was facing her with a room full of students and fifty other delegates. Lola Henriques's wide brown eyes twinkled as she introduced the next speaker with a sudden girlish grin unusual for a woman in her sixtieth year and which did not go unnoticed by Eve.

Devotion, she thought with uncustomary cynicism, gazing at the woman, a short matronly kind, very Old Brazilian in appearance. She had been told that at the age of forty-two, Theophilus de Cordova was a respected entrepreneurial scientist: a regular Midas with the golden touch. It was alleged that his turnover in women was equally rich, many of whom were of notoriety, and, as the assistant commissioner pointed out, had not one ill word to say against him.

"Ladies and gentlemen," Lola Henriques began, her tone holding a faint hint of an accent. "May I present our main sponsor, Professor Theophilus de Cordova." The room applauded as he strode toward the podium. "He has already pledged £90,000 toward our South American Ecological Project in São Paulo," Lola continued, "and will be available to answer any of your questions after his talk."

The professor glanced around the lecture hall full of delegates, his gaze falling on Eve before roving on. The first thing that struck her was his height. She had not expected the man to be so tall, at least six-two. But, of course, his photograph could never have given her any indication on that score. She had thought the assistant commissioner had given her an old snapshot, but his cornrow styled hair, broad nose, and enormous chocolate-brown eyes with their long, thick generous eyelashes, were reminiscent of what she had seen.

Now his eyes were wide with curiosity and gleaming with keen intelligence. His very persona indicated a man possessed with a wealth of knowledge and charm. It reflected in the chiseled profile, in the roguish hard angles of his unshaven jawline. Professor de Cordova looked fascinating. Eve swallowed, desperately gathering her thoughts as to why she was there, but it was hard to compile any meaning to her presence when she was facing such a sinfully handsome man.

"Good afternoon," his speech began, his Brazilian accent filling the lecture hall as he moved toward the overhead projector. "I am here because I want to clean up Brazil."

Eve was surprised by the depth and timbre of his voice. It was in perfect harmony with his appearance. She quelled the twist his vocal cords made on her anxious stomach muscles as he continued. "My foundation has one objective and that is to help implement the South American Ecological Project through cultural outreach, educational programs, and community projects," he said. "The project is dedicated to promoting and teaching sustainable community systems that meet the economic, political, and social needs of people without compromising the environment. The first stage of its objective, headed by Lola Henriques, is called Green Light," he continued. "Healthy seeds, plants, and soil."

And with an irrepressible grin that told everyone in the lecture hall just how much he loved what he was doing, Professor de Cordova whipped off his jacket, moved over to drape it on the chair where he had been seated and picked up a black marker. "Suppose genetic transformations took place in bacteria whose speed of multiplying is several million times faster than what it would be in animals," he addressed the audience with ease as he returned to the overhead projector. "Then animals developed immunity and protection systems that were able to kill the bacteria. What sort of hybrid would we be left with? And could this process be applied to plants?"

The hall was gripped. A delegate immediately debated the prospect. "Are you suggesting an intelligence in plant life?"

Eve stared as the professor's eyes lit up. "I could just as easily ask, Does God think?" he went on. "Thinking is our way of moving from one arrangement of knowledge to a better one. But our supreme force is all knowing. Therefore to suggest that He thinks is an—"

"I have not come all the way from Rio to listen to Hegelian views," another delegate advocated strongly. "A clash of thesis here and antithesis there is not going to help solve the problems in Brazil. What about our crops and land cultivation?"

"Just like the mind is self-organizing," the professor answered, "plants have patterning systems, too. It is my intention that project Green Light will become a great asset to our country and to our bordering neighbors. You have been invited here today to hear my views. Please let me explain."

"Explain what?" A delegate at the back of the lecture hall suddenly ejected himself out of his chair and caused Eve to turn her head. He had a French accent and was not much older than the professor, only shorter, with an arched back and fiery eyes beneath the rim of steel-framed glasses. Foreign looking. From one of the African states, Eve presumed. His eyebrows were furrowed in agitation suggesting he had had very little sleep. "Your guarantee is not worth a hell of a lot, now is it? I read the paper that you published on the Internet. It's baloney."

"Ah, Dr. Henri Da Costa," the professor introduced the delegate loudly.

"I know about Piccadilly, how it blew out the bag," Da Costa yelled. "Has the ambassador been informed about what you're doing?"

Eve immediately noticed the professor beckon to two security officers stationed nearby who discreetly closed in on Da Costa. "Tell them the truth," Da Costa went on. "What about Phoebe?" The doctor was immediately manhandled, and Eve's mouth fell open as she watched the guards forcibly remove him from the lecture hall.

"I'm sorry for Dr. Da Costa's outburst," Theophilus de Cordova apologized quickly. His gaze fell on Eve for one brief moment, and she was able to see clearly the hurt in his eyes. "I do not have the political nous nor the diplomatic awareness to deal with my godfather's office."

"But does the ambassador support project Green Light?" a delegate could not resist inquiring.

"The problem with Brazil is that there are doers and there are describers," Theophilus answered in his defense. "The vigor of a nation is measured by those who *do,* not those who *describe.* The ambassador knows that I like to do things and that is a positive he wholly supports."

The hall was instantly captivated, as was Eve. She was in awe of the professor as she marveled at how quickly he took command of the situation. Within seconds, she had turned to the person sitting beside her, a bespectacled brown man with alert dark eyes and a wide smile. "Is he always so forthright?" she could not help asking.

"The professor?" the man asked, his Middle-Eastern accent pitched in complete amazement, as though it surprised him she had not realized this truth for herself. "He is . . . How you say? . . . an institution. He is very good speaker. He fires the blood. I want him do talk in my country, the United Arab Emirates. We promise pay him very good fee."

Eve nodded and returned her attention to the podium. She tried to remember more of what the assistant commissioner had told her about Theophilus de Cordova, but nothing came to mind except the revelations she was witnessing firsthand. The professor was proving himself to be someone of remarkable character. More so than she could ever have imagined. She could hardly believe that Humphrey Brown could think this man a threat. Perhaps he was a master criminal. A dupe at disguises. Whatever he was, Eve felt intrigued to discover more. The man standing at the podium had her one hundred percent attention.

Two hours later, the talk was over. Professor Theophilus de Cordova had begun to circulate the room, dispensing handshakes and chatting among the guests who congratulated him for taking time out to promote a fund-raising campaign for the host project he actively sponsored.

Eve assessed him carefully, never allowing him to meet her gaze and often keeping a discreet distance so as to eavesdrop on the tidbits of comments she had heard him make. But it was not long before he eyed her with speculative interest, his gaze running a swift, comprehensive glance down her shapely, chestnut-brown body clad in a well-fit lilac suit, before he waded through the small crowd, making steadfast strides in her direction.

"You look familiar," he said upon arriving within inches of her. "Miss . . . ?"

"Ms.," she corrected quite levelly. "Eve Hamilton."

His smile reached his eyes. "And your . . . company?" He waited patiently, expecting a timely answer, thick, dark brows drawing together just a fraction when Eve failed to produce one. His gaze narrowed. "You are here because—"

"Curious," Eve interrupted, suddenly pulling her thoughts together. A little voice in her head was suddenly alert. *Don't blow this,* it told her. *Stay calm.*

The lines between his brows deepened. "You're a . . . student . . . junior researcher?"

"No." *Not far from the mark,* she thought, at least on reminding herself that she was indeed on a mission. "Just business."

His eyes slanted. He appraised the vibrant face before him with its doe-shaped brown eyes, well placed cheekbones, secretive lips, and the tumble of shoulder-length brown hair that formed an exceptional picture of beauty to him. "What kind of business?"

"Sponsorship," Eve returned with an unsteady voice, an obvious betrayal of how she was feeling. Such male interest—the very potency of it—was very distracting and certainly not what she had expected. Theophilus looked like the kind of male you knew existed, but except for an act of God, would never meet except in dreams. It felt daunting to her now to be up close.

"Are you looking to invest?" His eyes widened in meek approval, admiring the cool dexterity of her behavior.

Eve was more than aware of the stare. It seemed to penetrate to her nerve endings, and she could only pray that her initial hesitation had not been picked up by those piercing chocolate-brown eyes. "I think I need to be more convinced," she said calmly, though she was alarmed to discover a certain restriction in her throat. She deplored it in herself because it was a clear sign of nerves.

"Then it is my job to persuade you that we are worthy," he said, his tone becoming slightly husky. "You are representing . . . ?"

"Myself," Eve confirmed quite harshly, aware that his level of interest in her had intensified. She felt wary of it.

On the one hand, this was exactly what she had planned when she had combed through her wardrobe for the brightest colored suit she could find; had worn her hair loosely because it was a more becoming complement to her rounded face; had dressed in the sheerest panty hose in her possession to accentuate her long, curvy, brown legs. But, on the other hand, her innards resented the professor's close scrutiny of her. She knew it was because she found him attractive, but that was a secret the professor could never know about her. Eve was in that lecture hall for a purpose, one the assistant commissioner would want her to follow through.

"Excuse me?" The professor was puzzled by her tone.

"I'm the one looking to sponsor," Eve explained, aware that she was facing her number one suspect with no real notion of what that purpose was. This man had no idea that she was on his case, that she had been sent to discover why he was conducting his scientific affairs in Britain. Eve blinked. With it came the awful realization that she could not handle this mission. It was beyond anything she was used to. Humphrey Brown should never have asked her. "Perhaps I've caught you at an inopportune time."

She turned on her heels quickly, attempting to quell the sudden rush of feeling that caught her unawares. It was a combination of antipathy for the loss of her brother and sheer unadulterated attraction. The feeling was instinctive, yet oddly disturbing. Eve felt compelled to take in some air. In fact, she felt more compelled to leave.

Her mind was swimming with a myriad of thoughts. The professor was a matter between the Met and the Home Office, and she ought not to be involved after all. But now that she had been asked, how was she going to admit herself into this man's life when she had no idea what she was doing or how she was going to proceed.

It had been a month since Eve had last seen the assistant commissioner, and it was on his recommendation that she attended the seminar. A lucky acquaintance with Lola Henriques had happened to gain her an entry pass. But what Humphrey Brown had not told her was on what basis she should be there, other than to glean information about Theophilus de Cordova.

"Are you all right?" he suddenly asked. Eve felt a firm grip on her arm.

"I'm fine." She broke free and eyed the exit doors, thinking it was time to hightail it out of there. She could not do this. Short of throwing herself at the man, her conscience, and in fact her very breeding, could not permit her to make the first move, especially on a man who seemed so worldly. Her plans disintegrated the moment she turned her back and felt the rush of disappointment course through her veins.

Professor de Cordova made no attempt to detain her as she moved purposefully through the thinning delegates, some of whom had already departed. The encounter had ruffled her. Eve felt sick and angry. She also felt aroused. She had not expected the face in the photograph to affect her so traumatically. Eve questioned it. She questioned herself. Could this be the very person who was responsible for her brother's murder?

"You forgot to leave me your card," the Brazilian accent behind her suddenly demanded as she felt the grip on her arm once more.

Eve turned to find herself instantly weakened by the dark, brooding gaze that met her. Having always considered herself a strong woman by nature, she could not quite comprehend what was happening to her. The professor certainly had not affected her in this way when he was addressing the seminar, so she was baffled as to why she should be trembling by his close proximity.

"My card?" Even her voice had weakened. Eve was not aware that she had even reached into her handbag to produce the common courtesy of a business card until she watched herself hand over the simple item into the large extended hand that retrieved it.

"A mobile number?" he objected, wrinkling his nose.

The childlike gesture snatched a thread on Eve's heartstrings and tugged it, causing her mouth to twitch by the shockwaves that spiraled throughout her innards. "I'm never in one place long enough," she mumbled, desperately goading herself to remain calm. "I travel a lot."

"Are you allowed to travel to a little cocktail party I am having tonight in honor of the foundation?" he offered quickly, assessing her reaction. He liked the look of her. Her adorable, innocent expression appealed to him.

It was the opening Eve needed to acquaint herself with the professor, yet she felt nervous to accept. The assistant commissioner had warned her to be careful, but she had not thought she should have taken him literally. How could she possibly conduct an investigation against such a mild-mannered, handsome man?

"I don't think I can be there," she forced her excuse politely, convincing herself that she had made a dreadful mistake coming there.

"You can tell me more about why you'd like to sponsor our cause Ms. . . ." He glanced at her card again, then his eyes widened in alarm.

"I'm a fashion designer," Eve wavered, affecting a smile seconds before it fell from her face.

She could see that the professor had suddenly adopted forced courtesy, and she was able to register that he had a perfect set of teeth, designed for charming. "I'm not sure why you're here." He extracted a card from his inner breast pocket and offered it to her, his attention distracted. "But if it's for what I think it is, you're wasting your time. I'm not fooled by this little camouflage."

Eve took the card and stared. He was fobbing her off with the name and address of his attorney. Professor Theophilus de Cordova had decided that she was not of the correct caliber to be of interest to him after all. Was this how he also dispensed with his employees when they became surplus to requirements, as he had done her brother?

"Excuse me." Eve was rattled by his highbrow manner.

His eyes penetrated, flashing his impatience. "Yes."

Eve took a breath, her assessment of him totally revised. "I did debate whether I should come here tonight.

I thought a man of your importance might be arrogant and dismiss my ideas because of what I do for a living," she began, totally clueless on where she was going with the conversation. "Unfortunately, I was right. I had hoped you would be more sympathetic toward a fresh, innovative approach to raising funds for your foundation. It seems I've made a terrible judgment call. I'm sorry to have wasted your time."

Theophilus de Cordova stood motionless, then asked, "How old are you?"

Eve was thrown. "Thirty-two."

He pondered the information with veiled disbelief as though he, too, had reassessed an earlier decision. "You mean twenty-two," he scoffed, sardonic. "I don't entertain young, fly-by-night, fair-weather girls on the chase the moment they graduate and hang up their university degrees," he continued. "They expect put-down one-liners, and I don't crack jokes. I'm not outrageous either."

"But you're Mr. Self-Knowing and wisely happy with it," Eve reproved, judging the change in his opinion of her.

"I know most things," Theophilus de Cordova stated tersely. "And what I know is that I resent this little air-head performance of yours to suss me out."

"What you don't know," Eve began, slightly shaken that he may have latched on to her motive, "is that I'm a full fledged, grown woman with an educated mind, which I have no wish or need to prove to any man. I'm here—"

"Because?" Theophilus goaded.

"I wanted . . . I wanted to sponsor a fund-raising project under your foundation," Eve lied, conjuring up the first thought that entered her head.

Theophilus leaned on his heels and narrowed his eyes in confusion. He contemplated Eve with a scrutiny which unnerved her as he detected some semblance of the inner defiance she was sending in his direction. "Who are you really, and who are you representing?" he asked suspiciously.

"I told you," Eve insisted. "Myself."

"At your tender age?" Theophilus mocked, his chocolate-brown eyes blazing as he took hold of her wrist. He applied no pressure, yet the firm grip was filled with tension. Eve felt the effect of it rush up her veins like the pumping of red hot blood from an adrenalin rush. It shook her. She wanted to pull back, but Theophilus kept his hold.

"Let me go." She kept her tone discreet so as not to attract attention.

"Before I call security," Theophilus demanded, "how much are you being paid?"

Eve's eyes widened. "What?"

"It's Dr. Keltz, isn't it?" Theophilus spat out, his hot breath fanning Eve's face with fury. "I got the letter."

"I'm not on anyone's payroll," Eve admonished, maddened by the insinuation.

Theophilus's eyes narrowed. His grip tightened. "So who arranged your student entry pass to this seminar?"

"I've never heard of Dr. Keltz," Eve stated. "I gave you my card."

"Which tells me you're unqualified to be here," Theophilus derided. "You're passing yourself off as a fashion designer which incidentally has nothing to do with habitat conservation, the topic of our discussion tonight. Not very original, are you?"

"I'm not a student." She tried to break herself free.

"Just tell me who sent you, and I'll—"

"Hello again." A voice suddenly infiltrated as a sturdy woman approached, a smile mirrored across her features as she hastened to refasten a well cut jacket, one of Eve's most recent creations.

Eve nodded her greeting, too overawed to speak.

"February at the London Fashion Week was wonderful, wasn't it?" Lola Henriques asked, instantly enthused.

"Yes," Eve murmured, placing in her mind their initial meeting at the National History Museum where she had conducted her last show. She felt Theophilus's hard hand release her.

"Your new line was fascinating," Lola commented with gaiety. "I'm looking forward to seeing you at *Style Paradise*. I'm not usually so frail as to drool over fashion when I should be working," she added, "but even we conservationalists need a little fantasy once in a while."

"**Fantasy** is just an illusion that lies in the cut and sway of the fabric," Eve said, forcing a smile.

"How poetic," Lola crooned. "I see you've received my entry pass and met our illustrious professor." Her smile widened as she turned her direction toward Theophilus. "If I were twenty years younger, he'd be in trouble."

"You know this girl?" Theophilus asked.

"She's Eve Hamilton," Lola informed immediately. *"The* Eve Hamilton, winner of the Rover British Fashion Award."

"She's for real?" Theophilus was dumbfounded.

Eve nodded, gratefully picking up the gauntlet with the usual finesse which belied her *Hamilton Connections,* where she often chance met people who became useful much later whenever she needed a favor. A fund-raiser was the perfect explanation to get her into full swing.

"Lola's familiar with my work in Africa," she babbled in explanation. "I called her and asked if she knew you. She told me that you were doing a talk, and I wanted to come. Your foundation sounds very interesting."

"So you really are—"

"Who I say I am." Eve made no mention of who had asked her to be there.

"Is something wrong?" Lola inquired, plunging her long fingers into lace gloves.

"I think the professor decided I needed a reference." Eve chided.

"I apologize," he immediately conceded, almost shyly. "You don't look old enough—I mean . . . how could I tell?"

"With language," Eve countered on a mild note. "You asked, I answered, and you didn't believe me."

"That's because . . . never mind," he said.

"He usually only gives anyone five minutes of his time," Lola warned softly. "You're lucky."

"Low boredom threshold?" Eve asked, curbing the impulse to touch the professor's throat. His protruding Adam's apple instinctively reminded her of his male potency, so much so, she was forced to recede her womanly nature. "How does a girl change that?"

"A woman can tell me more about her ideas over cocktails tonight," the professor offered immediately.

Innate stubborness swayed Eve from accepting so easily. She felt that she needed to consider the situation more carefully. Theophilus de Cordova had accused her of working for someone. A man named Dr. Keltz. It suddenly threw a different complexion on things, certainly outside what the assistant commissioner had disclosed. Would she, for instance, be putting herself into any danger when he recalled what he had accused her of?

Eve could not assess that answer from his stance. The professor's face had warmed and she could see the genuine affection of his invitation in the depth of his eyes. At his age, she naturally expected someone over-the-hill, gray-haired, wearing bifocal spectacles, with a few teeth pulled, and badly dressed. Equally, she imagined Humphrey Brown to have shown her a dated picture as an old clue to go on.

It was quite something to find such a man standing

in front of her, not like what she had expected, putting
her on edge. It was hard to even liken him to the title
he held, for Theophilus de Cordova looked more like
he had walked off the cover of *Ebony Man* than someone
steeped in the sort of knowledge that coaxed students
and delegates from far and wide to pay money to hear
him talk.

And she had not yet formulated in her mind on what
basis she wanted to support his foundation. The idea
had sprang from her brain out of desperation. She could
hardly be expected to think up avenues of how she was
going to proceed with her fund-raiser without giving the
matter some processing time first.

"I really am busy tonight," she said finally. "But if
there's a way of reaching you without going through
your . . . attorney." Eve happily returned his card. "I'd
gladly like my personal assistant to arrange an appoint-
ment to meet with you."

"Of course." The professor straightened his shoulders and pulled an imitation crocodile skin wallet from
his back trouser pocket. Eve watched him pluck another
card from its interior and hand it over. "I'm leaving for
Scotland tomorrow," he added, his voice adopting a purposeful professional tone. "My company is based there."

"Scotland!" Eve breathed, glancing at his card which
read: THE DE CORDOVA INSTITUTE OF PLANT GENETICS,
LTD., listing his name and title.

"The professor has a lovely cottage in the Lothians,"
Lola enthused lightly. "In a little place called Cramond
near Edinburgh. You'd love it. I had the privilege of
staying there last summer with some colleagues from
the botanical institute when he relocated there. You're
doing some wonderful work, professor," she added smiling widely before turning to Eve. "You must visit and
have him show you his laboratory."

"That sounds like an excellent idea," Theophilus de

Cordova suddenly intervened. "I'm leaving in the morning from Gatwick Airport. Why don't you join me, as an abject apology for thinking so badly of you?" he cajoled.

Eve shook her head, overawed by the sudden proposition. It was tempting. The assistant commissioner, if he were with her now, would no doubt be applauding her speed for initiating access to the professor's home so quickly. But Eve felt a shudder at the revelation that she would be visiting the place where Paul had died.

Though his body had never been recovered, and a memorial stone had been placed next to their father's grave, she still had to remind herself that Theophilus de Cordova was the man her brother had worked for. The professor was also the one person who had not attended her brother's memorial. It was this lack of respect that did not go unnoticed by Eve. Such ragged thoughts running havoc in her head could not allow her to accept his request so readily.

"I'm sorry," she said, fancying that she had seen Humphrey Brown's dismal face flash before her very eyes. "I have things to do in London for an upcoming show. My personal assistant will call you." That would give her thinking time, Eve mused, convinced. She would also be able to call the assistant commissioner and have him do a computer check on Dr. Keltz.

"I'm sorry to hear that," Theophilus declared. "But if you change your mind, you're welcome to stay at my home. I promise I won't discuss the scent of the *pyrenaicum aureum* as opposed to the odor of the *tenuifolium pumilum.*"

"Two varieties of lilies," Lola Henriques divulged with a chuckle, facing Eve with the same girlish grin she had thrown the audience earlier. "He likes you."

"I like anything that is a picture of beauty," the professor said quietly. He made no secret of it as his dark eyes reappraised Eve, this time appreciating that he was not facing a young girl, but a woman in full bloom. "Lily of the valley."

Eve's eyes widened as she touched her neck. "My perfume."

"My mother still wears it," he said, his gaze burying into Eve with such intensity she was made aware that it was really time she left.

"I'll be in touch," she mouthed, affirming a clammy handshake with both Lola and then the professor before leaving the lecture hall.

The violet-orange night sky indicative of an evening in May was fading into black when Eve hit the sidewalk. To her chagrin, she realized that she was shaking as her thoughts faded to reality. It had all been too much, she realized now, confronting the enemy. She would have to call the assistant commissioner immediately and tell him that the case would not be simple at all. There were all manner of complications, a convolution of difficulty she was not prepared to face. And the first one was the unsettling pounding of her heart. Eve was not certain the organ, even though well exercised, could withstand a second meeting with Professor Theophilus de Cordova.

Two

"This is better than I expected," Humphrey Brown said with mirth, taking a sip from his brandy glass. "When are you leaving?"

Eve knew she should be feeling inordinately pleased with herself that Professor Theophilus de Cordova had invited her to his cottage in Scotland. But it was hard to share her victory with the assistant commissioner when the impulse to touch the professor's manly throat was still with her two days later. She wore her bemusement like a cloak, aware that Humphrey Brown could see something in the depth of her brown eyes, only he was unsure what lay beneath them.

"I don't know if I can do this," she told him uneasily. She had nervously glanced at herself in the tall, narrow mirror in her bedroom that morning, seeing a troubled face staring back at her before she left to meet the assistant commissioner.

Her midcalf white skirt and short-sleeve top in soft white cotton were just right for a day in May, and although not one of her designer creations, she looked more confident and chic than she felt. She wore the minimum of jewelry—a simple Cartier watch, pearl studs in her ears, a signet ring on her right middle finger—and her hair was up in a knot on the top of her head with the odd short strand dropping about her face and neck, making her appear like she had not had enough sleep. It was evident in her eyes, which she had tried to disguise with dusky beige eye shadow and brown mascara. Only a thin layer of foundation was applied to her chestnut-brown skin and a touch of gloss to her lips. She looked presentable. If only she felt as assured.

"Yes, you can do it," Humphrey affirmed just as quickly. "You're just having a flutter of nerves, but the moment you're up there, you'll be thinking of getting justice for Paul."

"That's just it," Eve said, confused, the disorientation etched across her features as she momentarily glanced around the small interior of the bar situated on Baker Street. "The professor looks too nice to be responsible."

"I don't believe I'm hearing this," Humphrey Brown spat out his anger while shaking his head vigorously. "Professor Theophilus de Cordova killed your brother, and all you can talk about is how nice he looks. What happened back there?"

Eve only wished she knew. She stared at her tea cup and wished she had ordered something as strong as what the assistant commissioner was drinking. "He was more interested in someone called Dr. Keltz," she told him, still immersed in her distraction. "I distinctly got the impression that he's an enemy of some sort. He received a letter from the man."

"Dr. Keltz." The assistant commissioner pondered the name while studying Eve's bemused round face. "Never heard of him. I'll have the Met make some inquiries." He watched her sip her tea. "Did he recognize you in any way? I mean—"

"He thought I looked familiar," Eve nodded, still wrapped in the maelstrom of their brief introduction. "But I don't think he's cottoned on that I'm Paul's sister. In fact, he hadn't even heard of me until two days ago."

"And there I was thinking you were renowned the world over." Humphrey ejected a wry chuckle before getting serious. "Fact is, you're a good-looking woman. He'll remember you. Professor de Cordova likes to keep discreet affairs and always ends his brief interludes on good terms. You have nothing to worry about. Pack your bags and keep in touch."

Eve's brows rose. "You're really suggesting that I should do this?"

Humphrey stared at her closely, finding that her brandy-colored eyes were suddenly enormous in her amazement. "I thought that's why you wanted to see me," he said, confused. "To get your instructions."

"I don't work for the Met or the Home Office," Eve proclaimed, annoyed.

"But you agreed to help," Humphrey reminded, assessing her more closely. "What is this? You backing out?"

She dipped her head. "Maybe."

"Now look." Humphrey tried to adopt a sympathetic tone, but Eve was more than aware of the aggression that came out in his words. "We can't do this alone. I thought I'd made that clear a month ago. Paul was your brother. You both were like my own children—the kids I never had. I owe it to your dead father and your mother to bring that man to book. If you want to be a lame duck and back out, fine. I'll find another way of doing this job without you."

"Don't talk to me like that," Eve whimpered, feeling the sting of tears in her eyes at the painful reminder of the loss of her father and brother. "I loved them both."

"Then prove it," Humphrey Brown concluded, making direct eye contact. "Don't sit there like some dried-up prune waiting for the legal system to catch up with what we both know. Move your butt. Go up to Scotland and nail that man."

"You make it sound so easy."

"He wants you there," Humphrey reminded harshly.

"That means he likes you. Take advantage of the opportunity and squeeze him to a pulp. I want every juicy bit of information. In fact," he reached into his briefcase and pulled out a manila-colored file, "here's a dossier." The assistant commissioner handed it over. "It's not much, but it's all we have to go on."

Eve reared back in her seat and considered crying. Humphrey Brown was not being lenient, but rather was using armylike tactics as though he were talking to one of his brigade of police officers. She was not used to this kind of briefing. Her world was more romanticized, an average day spent in the back room of her studio designing the latest ladies' wear or presenting a show at one of the four leading cities of fashion. What did she know about covert operations or frisking a man down to his bare essentials?

That was what the assistant commissioner expected of her. It was as though he had developed a one track view; that she had suddenly become an umbilical extension to his department's case study on Professor de Cordova. It made her feel unusually like she were standing on the precipice of the white cliffs of Dover. Below she could see the water's edge and the sea beyond. If she fell over, her demise would be as that of her brother. But if she stayed very close to the edge, there was still a chance of surviving.

Being anywhere near Professor de Cordova was that edge. Humphrey Brown was asking a lot from her. If he had not known her since childhood, she would have considered his behavior to be grossly out of order. But he had been born in the same parish of Jamaica as her father, had arrived in England on the same ship in the same year, 1956. He had shared the same overcrowded room in the same rented house in Notting Hill, and then when Paul was born, moved on to make room for her parents and their baby. Two years later, after she had arrived, the family moved to Forest Gate, where, at the age of five, she had watched her father die.

She had always felt Humphrey's presence in her life. He was often a regular visitor to the house in the difficult years that followed and made sure her mother had been able to cope with having lost her husband. He was also the solid rock her mother needed when Paul had been killed. Like the father figure he was, the surrogate uncle he became, Humphrey Brown organized everything.

Eve knew she could not deny that the assistant commissioner cared. His was the face that always sang lullabies to her as a child—the man whom she had often fantasized about becoming a permanent fixture in her mother's life. Naturally, Eve did not want to deny him her help. But while caution reigned, she wanted to be certain that she was doing the right thing. That she was not going to put her mother to further grief should anything happen to her.

"I'm due a holiday," Eve told Humphrey, accepting the brown file he offered. Folding it and placing it into her handbag, she added, "I'll try and get you all the information you need."

"Good girl," Humphrey smiled. "What about your studio? That's a loose end."

"I've got that covered," Eve explained. "But I can only give you two days. I have to prepare for a show next week. In the meantime, Jasmine, my personal assistant, can handle my business commitments until I get back."

"And what about your fiancé?"

"Tyrone?" Eve shrugged away the deep sense of loss with flippant despondency. "He's an ex-fiancé now."

Humphrey's face measured a good degree of surprise. "Since when?"

"I don't want to talk about it," Eve quipped.

"Does your mother know?" He was concerned.

"No. And I don't want her to find out, either."

"I don't want any slipups," Humphrey warned. "There's a lot at stake here."

Eve immediately grew uneasy. "Like what?" Her eyes narrowed. "What are you not telling me?"

Humphrey shook his head. "It's nothing for you to worry about."

"So?"

"The Met likes to see results," he said. "Targets have to be reached, costs evaluated, officers vetted with a fine-tooth comb. There's pressure to keep our noses clean."

"You've been in the job too long to be worried about getting the boot now," Eve debated.

"When you get to my age"—Humphrey wavered, re-calling that the only things that had changed about Eve were her long curvy legs and the advancement in her years—"you start to worry about things like your pension. If I can just link this professor to the Cali Cartel, then I know I've got a good few years left."

Eve leaned forward and held Humphrey's hand. She rubbed his palm with her thumb, an adolescent attempt to reassure the one man who had been the closest person to a father she knew, that everything would be all right. "I want you to promise me something," she said. "I don't want you to tell my mother what I'm doing. And," she heaved a sickly breath, "if at any time you think I'm going to be at risk or in danger, I want you to tell me, okay?"

"I've got your back," Humphrey avowed. "You can count on me."

"I know I can count on you," Eve agreed, putting the assistant commissioner's hand to her cheek where the warmth of it transported to her skin. As long as he was in her life, she never felt fragile or weak. Like him, she had been the hard rock for her mother over the years, too. "I won't let you down."

* * *

The humid air outside the train was misty and infused with the smell of fuel as Eve departed and stood on the platform. She pulled her suitcase from the carriage and closed the door, looking around aimlessly. It was not long before her eyes fell on the tall man who approached, his enormous eyes flickering as he caught her expectant gaze.

"Typically British, twenty minutes late," Theophilus de Cordova said of the train that had pulled into Waverley Station in Edinburgh. "Did you have a nice trip?"

"I thought I would never get here," Eve said, the aching of her limbs protesting at the seven-hour journey. "I could do with a hot soak."

"The car's just around the corner." He picked up her suitcase from the platform and began to lead the way. Eve dutifully followed, mentally adjusting herself to the knowledge that she was now on Scottish territory.

As she entered the black Land Rover and sank herself into the cream-colored seat, she could not help feeling like she had entered the gateway to a devious adventure. It was the kind of escapade she felt certain only happened once in a lifetime, and Professor Theophilus de Cordova, she was sure, would be more of a phenomenon than even she deserved.

There was still a lot to learn about the man. What his tastes were, who was close to him, where he got his strengths—and his vast knowledge, she was certain, would probably reach an area that could intimidate her. But these thoughts were at the back of Eve's mind, along with the agenda she had yet to keep when she turned toward the professor. What was most important to her at that precise moment was to be fed and bathed.

"You must be hungry." he said as he slammed the driver's side door and ignited the engine. He tried to redirect his mind to what food he should give her, but Theophilus could not escape the smell of Eve's perfume. Nor could he take his eyes off the long, shapely, brown legs that stretched themselves in the passenger seat and the pastel lime-colored dress he glimpsed lying beneath her white mackintosh.

"I am." Eve nodded as she thought of her appetite, then stared at the array of digital equipment in front of her. "What's all this?"

"Standard turn-of-the-century navigational system, CD stereo, temperature control, in car telephone . . ." Theophilus pulled away from the station. "Don't you drive?"

"No," Eve admitted.

"Fashion designers are not into gadgets I take it," he intoned lightly, appreciating the delicacy of her chestnut-brown skin that seemed more nubile than when he had last seen her.

Theophilus had never known any woman to look much younger than her actual years until he had met Eve Hamilton. It was an attraction he could not quite explain, except that he had known he had wanted to see her again. And now that she was in front of him, within six days of their initial introduction, he wasn't quite sure how to take her. That thought puzzled him in more ways than he cared to imagine.

"I outgrew gadgets a long time ago." Her voice filtered into his thoughts.

He believed it, too, but he could not relate. She wore her hair down, as it was the first time they had met, and it was making him quiver trying to guess whether she had always worn it that way. Was her hairstyle the secret to her youthful disposition? Or was it her flawless complexion and the way she applied her make-up with such precision; well-marked brows, color to her cheekbones, a nice pink gloss to her secretive lips, and eyes that were made more dusky by a faint brush of sultry brown, Yves Saint Laurent, no doubt? He wasn't sure.

The car sped on. It was dark. It would be another thirty minutes to his home. The professor wanted to talk. "First time in Scotland?" he asked, noting Eve's attempt to glance through the tinted windows where she failed to get a decent view. He had his headlights on and was going slow, but he knew she would not be able to see much of the scenery around her for the time of night.

"I've never had occasion to come before," Eve told him. "Given the time it took me to get here, I doubt I shall visit again."

He chuckled. It was a nice sound. Eve was awed at how delighted she felt to hear the ring of it. "I'm glad you came, especially so soon after I'd invited you," he said. He could not resist offering a friendly pat on her knee before changing into gear. "You'll like it here."

His touch stirred Eve's blood immediately. She felt its heat singe her heart as the blood piped its way through her veins like hot lava on a journey down to the potent area between her legs. She instinctively crossed her ankles and squeezed her thigh muscles to dispel the feeling.

Theophilus was affecting her again. He was casually dressed in a black polo neck sweater and dark corduroy trousers, with a worn suede brown jacket thrown over. Though it was almost nine o'clock in the evening, his jawline hardly seemed rugged but was smooth as though he had, for the first time in the last few days, undergone a fresh shave. She could also tell that his short hair had been recently redone, the fresh rows of braids making his entire ensemble totally agreeable to her.

His appearance was making things more complicated. She could already feel the small lingering sensations she had felt for him on their first meeting. This was not good. Eve immediately thought about Paul. About the assistant commissioner and his job at the Met. About the official inquest into her brother's murder that had substantiated, with little known evidence, that his death had been unlawful and caused by misdemeanor by person or persons unknown. Her reason for being with this handsome man suddenly flew into perspective. Eve was not going to fall under his spell.

"I can only stay the weekend," she warned immediately. "I'll be taking the six o'clock train into London on Sunday."

"I'm surprised you're here at all," the professor commented with an even tone. "The last time we spoke, I was given the distinct impression you had a rather busy schedule. What made you change your mind so quickly?"

Eve swallowed at the reminder of her motive. "I'm doing a show next week," she began, forcing a convincing note. "This weekend was the only time I had available to see your work."

"And what of *your* work?" the professor asked, his Brazilian accent raised a notch in curiosity. "It must be quite interesting."

"It's what I've always dreamed of doing," Eve responded casually. "From when I was a little girl and my mother bought me my first sewing machine. I used to make clothes for all my friends' dolls."

The professor chuckled. "Did your own dolls go neglected?"

Eve eyed him quickly with narrow, well-plucked brows. She wasn't sure whether Theophilus was making fun of her, but decided to sensibly override the remark. "I figured out that I liked designing and studied at the Central Saint Martin's College of Art and Design."

"Then you became a fashion designer," Theophilus concluded.

Eve again noted the chortle in the professor's tone. This time she chose to nullify his manner. "I believe you think I'm talking about something else."

He turned and faced her briefly before redirecting his attention to the road. "I'm behaving a little insensitively, aren't I?" he gauged from the expression on Eve's face. "I'm sorry. I'm guilty of sometimes attaching too much importance to the idea of the creative process which, in my view, does not include fashion designers."

Eve's eyes widened, her brain refusing to accept what her ears were hearing. "I'm not sure what you mean," she relented, not wanting to appear rude, but taking offense all the same. "Creativity is synonymous with freedom, which means a person's behavior is very much dependent on what they wear."

"But don't you think designing clothes produces way-out ideas that are impractical?" the professor drawled dryly. "I mean, I understand the nature of creativity because for me it's about opening the mind to other ways of doing something that has always been done a certain way."

"That's map-type thinking," Eve debated suddenly. "Creativity is all about imagination. Yes, a dress may be done in a certain way, but there are a thousand other ways of changing the style of that dress."

"That's the kind of concept that emerges at a relative stage of ignorance and becomes frozen into permanence and limits thinking," Theophilus suggested. "Does a dress, for instance, have to be designed for a woman to wear? Couldn't the mind open to ways of creating a dress for a man?"

"You're being pseudo-clever," Eve admonished, frustrated at the direction the professor was taking their discussion. Was this man for real? she had to ask herself.

"At least it's a logical negative," the professor continued, regardless of how uncomfortable Eve was feeling

at the depth of their conversation. "I like to deal with
neutral facts, figures, and information."

"I prefer to deal with feelings, hunches, and intuitions
without any need to justify them," Eve tossed back.

"Not even within a relationship?" the professor
pressed.

Eve gasped at the complexity of the question. Where
on earth did that spring from? Surely the professor
could not be wondering if she was dating someone. It
had never occurred to her whether he was married or
single, and certainly not whether he had any interest in
her, though the assistant commissioner had alerted her
differently. But she felt certain he was fishing, nonetheless, and decided to put him straight on that score.

"I believe asking too many questions in a relationship
can lead to emotional suicide," she answered calmly,
trying to dispel any emotion from her voice. Seeing the
disapproval in the professor's eyes, she added, "Obviously that's something you disagree with."

"You're judging me."

Eve was surprised to hear the defensive ring in his
tone. What exactly was the professor afraid of? She was
perplexed. "No, I'm not judging you," she returned.

"Negative judgments force a person to make an emotional rather than an intellectual decision," he explained, glancing across at her.

"And you're . . . not decisive?" she asked.

"I never said that," Theophilus said warily, appearing
nervous at the turn of the conversation which he was
notably aware he had instigated. "I've already made my
mind up in that area. I believe a person should always
question and be decisive about their feelings."

Eve felt like laughing to the brink of hysteria. It was
for that precise reason that Tyrone had walked out on
her. He had said she was too analytical about their relationship, about the nuances that obviously frustrated

him in the bedroom, and about the way she measured their attachment level as though it had been a yard of cloth. Perhaps if she had been less fussy, he would have stayed. But he had also accused her of being too much of a perfectionist and he found it hard to relate to her rank of self-importance.

"I don't think you've reached an awareness point," Eve proclaimed, disguising well the sorrow in her eyes.

"Aware of what?" Theophilus was intrigued.

"Love," Eve said flatly. "The idea of falling in love with somebody."

"That's a theory that doesn't work," the professor scoffed, his deduction surprising Eve further. "It's been tried and tested the world over and proven futile."

"So your evaluation is not to take the risk?" Eve demanded. When he did not answer, she asked, "Isn't the ease of testing an option to love somebody an important part of its value?"

"Not if there's no fallback position," the professor answered demurely. "The idea of a relationship cannot be demonstrated instantly. This is a weak position to find oneself in. There's no immediate answer as to how it's going to turn out and if things don't go according to plan, what are we left with? Exposure to vulnerability, nonacceptance of failure. The equation that persistence and determination do not always pay off."

Eve was flabbergasted by his dissection of the subject. "Does that mean you're not giving yourself a choice?"

Again she noticed the defenses whipped into his tone. "I didn't quite mean it like that," he said, sighing.

"Then what about the benefits from the learning experience?" Eve asked, her contentious instinct now thoroughly rattled and demanding that she settle their discussion.

"There are none," Theophilus concluded flatly. "Except defeat."

"I don't believe that," Eve gasped in disagreement. "Even in this un-ideal world, there are a lot of winners."

"You're quite good at picking values out of disasters," Theophilus admired, a faint smile forming on his face. "But when it comes to evaluating options, I prefer to look at the negatives to narrow the field. You're sensitive to nuances and trends, which is why you make composite judgments. I suspect that's why you're a fashion designer. You have a sense of how the world should be and dress it up to your tastes."

He pulled the car to a halt outside his home, an old white-painted stone cottage set by an ancient quay at the mouth of the River Almond. Theophilus cut the engine. Looking at Eve, he sized her up carefully, attempting to make her understand how he viewed the wakes of life. "I also have a sense of how the world should be, and it's not about war between countries or between the sexes. You see, concepts have to make sense to someone. And even so, there's always an alternative view."

Eve was utterly bewildered. Unable to speak, she simply followed the professor as he left the car, knowing in her mind that she would be swamped with further depths of his knowledge before her visit with him was through. It was a fete she hardly dared contemplate. It scared her. She chose to change the subject.

"Is it always so foggy?" she asked as she tried to reformulate her mind to expel some of the weight his perceptions had left on her. There was nothing safer than talking about the weather. She could just glimpse a wooded riverside footpath that led down past a two-oared boat to a weir and to what looked like a ruined mill. A picture-postcard image emerged in her mind as she neared the cottage.

"Scot's mist," Theophilus corrected. "It comes down from the highlands. Mind the step." He effortlessly carried her suitcase across the threshold and into the cottage. The lights were on and a roaring log fire greeted them both.

Eve hesitated at the doorway before stepping inside. There was an unmistakable intimacy about the room she walked into, about her standing awkwardly at the door staring at the face she had first seen in a photograph and whose chocolate-brown eyes were now inviting her into his home. She was understandably nervous at her pretense for being there, yet the guilt Eve felt at actually standing within such close proximity to the professor was oddly as powerful as her need to be near him.

"You have a nice cottage, professor," she said calmly, absorbing the calm orange colors on the wall where a tapestry hung, lending an air of historical integrity to the period touches, which did not displace the sitting room's original heritage, but rather enhanced its rich timber design. *Prestigious,* she thought, taking stock of the room's interior.

Eve could spot an antique when she saw one, even though she was a bit rusty at pinning down the century, and in this room she saw plenty. If her years in designing had taught her anything, particularly in view of the many homes she had visited to fit or refit her clients who bracketed in the middle upper class, it was that the furniture in the professor's home was more than eloquent and worth a tidy sum.

Under her feet was decorative carpeting laid on hardwood floor. Facing her was a Sheraton-period mahogany bowfront sideboard delicately graced with a Collas fine lyre clock on top. There was also a figured George III inlaid cylinder bureau, which he probably used for writing, situated next to a hand-carved bookshelf housing all manner of books. A pair of marquetry and carved gilt-wood pedestals of tulipwood and goncalo alves were straddled at either side of the room covered with pots dressed with fresh pink roses. But the focal point of the room was the rich brown leather sofas huddled around two octagonal tables veneered in ivory, which, she considered, dated back to the seventeenth century.

If she had discerned anything about the professor so far, it was that he liked his antiques, could amply afford them, and probably purchased for investment or for collateral purposes, which was the practice of quite a number of her clients. A polite smile formed across her face as she sought to tighten the belt around her white mackintosh, fearful of venturing any further.

"It was once the home to an oyster fisherman," Theophilus told her, placing Eve's suitcase on the floor, noting how awe-struck she seemed. "Of course, I've added my own touch to it."

He could see that she had willed herself to stand firmly in one place, close to the door, guarding herself against him. The professor knew it was because of their philosophical discussion in the car that she was feeling so uneasy. He had not meant to come across so stiff and stuffy. A man of his position was not prone to accepting matters on their surface level, but would delve into the deepest meaning of any given situation, despite whether his opinions may upset others.

His own mother had often accused him of taking life too seriously, desperately keeping their conversations to the minimum to avoid being immersed in something that went beyond her normal thinking capacity. Theophilus decided that if he was to make recompense and allow Eve to enjoy their next two days, he would have to bridge the gap between them and try not to take himself too seriously. By the same token, he had no wish to let down his own guard entirely. Eve Hamilton was at his home for a reason and he was not completely convinced that she was just interested in fund-raising for his foundation. He would need to tread carefully.

"We've started on a bad foot," he smiled easily, observing her immediate acceptance of this. "Let's start again. Call me Theo."

"You can call me Eve," she replied in return.

"So you're Adam's temptress," Theo's smile widened.

"Don't worry," Eve warned him with an innocent chuckle, praying that she could carry this off so that he would never know the real reason for her unexpected entry into his life. "There are no snakes in my garden."

Genuine or fraud? Theophilus suddenly wondered as he appreciated the way her face lit up. He told himself that it might be interesting to discover exactly what little game this young woman was playing. He reached for her suitcase and led the way, the suspicion planted in the recesses of his mind. Obvious scepticism kept him guessing whether she was working for Dr. Keltz, though she had given him no real reason to think so.

He thought back to having accused her at his seminar and wished he had not been so hasty. She had not questioned him about it thus far, but Theo made a firm resolution, nonetheless, that while Eve Hamilton was with him he would tap her brain. Just enough to amount some semblance of the truth to keep his fears at bay.

Three

Still dressed in her nightgown, Eve leaned over to the window and opened it. She poked her head out and breathed the morning air deeply. The tangy, unpolluted smell met her nostrils immediately, reminding her that she was not in London. Her fingers touched the leaves of the ivy that covered the outside wall and had wound its way around her bedroom window. They were wet from the Scot's mist from the night before, but the day was now clear, and, in the far distance, she could see the quay and the brink of the River Almond.

It was a remote village, she realized now while getting dressed. Cramond lay in its own shallow valley in the rolling countryside of the Lothians some thirty minutes west of Edinburgh. It was situated between two strips of beach, home to thirty yachts and a host of swans. This much she knew. She was sure there was more to be discovered about the place, particularly once she was to visit the professor's laboratory.

"How did you sleep?" Theo asked when Eve finally arrived downstairs, fully dressed in a strapped peach-colored flowered dress which suited the day well.

The morning sky was clear, and the sun was already bright for 10:30, making her feel alive and suddenly looking forward to the day ahead. Her vibrant appearance did not go unnoticed by the professor. He liked the way she had swept up her brown hair, pinning it away from her face so that her chestnut-brown complexion became her most arresting feature. She also wore only the thinnest veil of make-up and a clear gloss rather than lipstick on her lips. It made Eve look even younger than he had first surmised. Theo marveled why no other woman had found the secret to getting away with such youth. Her feet were bare beneath her cream-colored, leather sandals and the only jewelry she wore was by way of a gold-plated watch. He liked her simplicity. For a fashion designer, this was a woman not easily fussed.

"You have a cozy bed . . . guest room," Eve answered, noting that Theo had fresh morning stubble on his jawline and was dressed quite casually in faded jeans and a white, short-sleeved T-shirt, his feet bare against the carpeting, causing the raw frayed edges of his jeans to rub at his heels.

"I'm glad you slept well," he said politely, gesturing that she follow him toward the kitchen.

"Do you live here alone?" Eve asked, curious.

"No," Theo intoned lightly. "I have a housekeeper, but she is in Cornwall at her granddaughter's this weekend. She'll be back on Monday." They entered the kitchen.

"Coffee?" he added as he watched Eve take a seat at the stained-pine table.

"Actually, do you have any fresh orange juice?" she asked, clasping her fingers nervously against her dress.

The sunlight that poured in through the open kitchen window bounced candidly against the professor's skin as he reached into the refrigerator and extracted a bottle of citrus juice. He was not to know how healthy and athletic it made him appear to Eve. She felt, rather than heard, the small silent gasp at the back of her throat when he turned and faced her, God's heavenly rays allowing his smile to appear whiter and more notable than she realized before.

"Freshly squeezed?" he prompted, showing her the label on the bottle.

All Eve could do was nod her acceptance. She felt certain the assistant commissioner must have made a mistake. No one who looked this good in the morning could possibly be dangerous. The man was fine. Fit. Nice eyes. And what a smile.

"Eggs?" she said absently.

Theo placed a glass on the table and stood over Eve while he poured the orange juice. "Boiled, fried, poached, or scrambled?"

Eve was more than aware of his presence. She felt the frisson of it run down her spine, causing her to shift uncomfortably to reposition herself on the hard wooden bench where she was seated. The last time she was seated on a bench, it was at dawn and she was talking to Assistant Commissioner Humphrey Brown. Now she was in close quarters with the very subject of that conversation, quickly committing to memory the amount of hair on his arms. There was a lot of it, too. Smooth, fine, and silky. And his hands were big with chubby fingers. Clean, scrubbed nails, bony knuckles with speckles of hair above them.

"Scrambled. No, fried." She could not decide, such were the flurry of her thoughts.

He capped the bottle, aware that his towering over Eve was having some effect on her. Theo was used to it. His good looks, his charm, his personality had never left him short of women. One smile and they were often hooked. In another life he probably would have used all that potential to his advantage. Not that he had not done so in the past, but it had never been an extracurricular activity of his to play games with women. He was a man more designed to doing his work and keeping women within a certain distance; close enough to be contacted but distant enough not to bug his nerves.

"Cheesy egg dip," he told Eve suddenly. She faced him, bemused as he knew she would be. "It's bread dipped in egg and then fried with a layer of cheese in between," he explained watching her absorb the information. "It's a little invention I made up for Trey when he wouldn't eat his breakfast. It's his favorite, especially if I add tomatoes."

Eve stared for a blank second, wondering whether she had missed something. Her eyes narrowed as Theophilus returned to the refrigerator, her brain on the brink, waiting for him to add further information. When he did not, she decided to ask, "Who's Trey?"

Theo extracted the eggs and turned to face Eve. "Trey's my son," he said flatly.

A son! Eve's mind spun. This was data not specified in the assistant commissioner's dossier.

Born to Afro-Brazilian parents. As a child, excelled at his local state schools, followed by a scholarship to *Departmento de Botânica* at the *Universidade de São Paulo,* the very best his country could offer in his field. After graduating, became a research assistant at Iguassu Falls the year his godfather became ambassador, then research associate at his former university three years later. Attended the University of Oxford in England on a Ph.D. research degree at the Department of Plant Sciences and Forestry, proving his international understanding in his specialized area of molecular plant pathology and microbial ecology. Graduated and became a tutorial fellow specializing in fungi ecosystems and the design of novel defense strategies in plants. Four years later, established and affiliated the De Cordova Institute of Plant Genetics to his lecture classes at Oxford. At this achievement, was elected a professorship at the University of Oxford. No mention of a wife or kids.

"How . . . how old is Trey?" she asked, quickly intent on processing whether the professor was in a relationship. Was he married? Engaged? Was the mother still on the scene? Hell, just exactly when did this handsome man sire a child?

"Trey's nine," Theo explained, reaching for a frying pan, which he placed on an Aga gas range. "He's an intelligent boy. He boards at a school in England and visits me during the holidays and on some weekends. I'm expecting him tomorrow, in fact, so maybe you'll get to meet him before you leave."

Incredible, Eve breathed. How on earth did Humphrey Brown's specialist operations miss this most important detail? As she watched Theo make breakfast, she found herself beginning to reassess her entire profile about him. Theophilus de Cordova—a daddy. That meant he had loved somebody once and had committed to that relationship. Maybe he had been married and was now divorced. Maybe he was a widower. She had seen no sign of a woman about the place. He was not wearing a wedding ring. Eve was more than curious.

"I . . . had no idea," she began, wondering how she could tailor the conversation to extract all the information she needed. "Who does he look like?"

"His mother," Theo relented, cracking two eggs into a bowl.

Eve felt her heart drop. She could not explain why. Perhaps it was the idea that some woman had once taken the professor's heart and then gave him a child that looked nothing like him. Or, more to the point, perhaps it was because his son looked just like the woman he had once loved and would always be a reminder that his heart had been . . . broken? It was an area worth exploring, if only to get all the answers. She began to tread carefully.

"Does your son . . . Trey . . . still see his mother?"

"That depends," Theo began. "You see—" A sudden

knock at the kitchen door aborted the professor's attempt to explain.

Eve grimaced murderously beneath her breath as he threw the egg shells into the garbage and went over to the door. On answering it, a tall brown man coated in white overalls burst in. "We have a problem at the lab," he whispered quite exasperated before his gaze suspiciously fell on Eve.

"I'm sorry," Theo recognized his delay in making introductions. "Eve, this is my first assistant, Dr. Ira Keplan. He's a student medical researcher from Algiers on a temporary contract. He's been with me nearly a year and assists in some of my experiments."

"Nice to meet you," Eve nodded from the table, aware he held the exact status title as had her brother.

He returned his attention to Ira. "What is it?"

Dr. Keplan whispered the complication into the professor's ear. Eve tried to distract her attention elsewhere by looking around her, absorbing the flowered curtains, the shelves of homemade jam, chutney, and pickles purchased from the local village store. Her gaze swept the clean kitchen surfaces with the bare essentials of a toaster, kettle, and fruit bowl atop, but her subconscious was finely tuned into listening what the doctor had to say. All she could make out was that an experiment had gone wrong. She became more curious as to what the professor was working on. Perhaps it was the very thing responsible for Paul's death.

"I have to go to the lab," Theo finally told her after a brief two minutes talking with Dr. Keplan. "Maybe breakfast can wait until I get back?"

"Perhaps I can join you," Eve suggested eagerly, raising herself up from the table to ascertain the point. "It'll only take me a minute to get my cardigan."

Dr. Keplan looked alarmed. "That will not be necessary," he panicked, his accent thick and his voice strong willed. "The professor will be gone ten minutes."

Theo turned and faced Eve. "He's right." He reached for a pair of sandals situated close to the door. Slipping into them, he cast Eve a final glance. "You go ahead with breakfast. I'll be as fast as I can."

Within seconds he was out the door with the doctor hurrying at top speed behind him. Eve was perplexed. Exactly what was going on? A clock on the wall behind her suddenly cuckooed. She jumped before realizing it was sounding the stroke of eleven o'clock. Eve felt reluctant to retake her seat. She looked at the Aga, contemplated making the cheesy egg dip without the professor, then decided it was his invention and only he was the man to do the job.

Suddenly a thought occurred to her. She could snoop around. She had almost ten minutes to case the place for evidence. But evidence of what? Eve strode diligently into the main room and took a good look around. Nothing appeared any different from the night before, except the fire was not lit and the lights were out.

She immediately went over to the bureau. It was locked. She tried the bookcase. There were all manner of books lining the shelves: dictionaries, encyclopedias, a concise atlas, computer technology manuals, a Bible, and a good health guide. There were two drawers at the bottom, and she pulled them open. Inside the first one were sheets of paper, all handwritten notes. *Bingo,* Eve thought. But when she began to scan each sheet in turn, she realized they were answers to crosswords, one-liner anagrams, puzzle solvers, and conundrums the professor had obviously taken from newspapers or quiz books. Frustrated that she had not found anything important, she replaced them next to a pack of playing cards and looked inside the other drawer. Eve was riveted.

The items were more personal. A collection of house-

hold bills, two pairs of sunglasses, a checkbook and a
Visa card. There was also a small, burgundy address book
and the professor's imitation crocodile skin wallet. Eve
went straight for the wallet. The first thing she saw was
the photograph of a woman tucked inside one of the
sleeves. It was not the picture of a plain woman, but
someone quite attractive, a little older than herself. Her
skin was golden brown, her eyes dark and mysterious,
her hair short, brown, and professionally cut. It was an
angelic, cherry-shaped face. She had a nice smile, too.
Eve wondered suddenly whether she was glaring at
Trey's mother.

She stared for a few seconds, her heart pounding
loudly, then flicked through the rest of the wallet. It
contained two hundred pounds in bills, several more
credit cards, a key, and a folded piece of white paper.
Eve opened it up and read the two words. DOCTOR KELTZ.
Beneath the name was a phone number. She extracted
the paper and placed it inside her bra. No sooner had
she folded the wallet and was about to replace it, than
Eve heard a sound behind her. The wallet still inside
her hand, she turned to find the professor standing at
the doorway.

Eve froze. She felt the rush of blood burn her face
the moment she caught the professor's eyes. He was hor-
rified. For a moment she was convinced the room had
spun and then she dropped the wallet to the floor. It
made a deathly thud the instant it hit the carpet beneath
her feet. Eve felt like those very feet had weakened as
she bent to the floor and felt the left strap of her dress
snap. At that point, she wanted to die and be buried on
the spot. What on earth was she going to say?

"Do you mind telling me what you're doing and why
you're looking through my drawer," Theo pounced,
obliterating the distance between them in one fell
swoop. He was on the floor next to Eve within seconds,

reaching for his wallet before she could muster the courage to pick it up.

"I . . . I was looking for a safety pin," Eve wavered frantically, her voice trembling with guilt that she had been caught red-handed. "It's . . . it's the strap on my dress," she dithered to explain, feeling great conscience-stricken tears at the back of her eyes threatening to overload. "It's broken off and . . . and I didn't have time to change." She stood and faced the professor, the evidence all too revealing.

He saw her heaving cleavage clearly enough. Eve's dress had indeed dropped on one side giving him ample view of her chest. She was breathing so fast, that her breasts advanced and retreated from him with such alluring intensity, he felt his manhood rise at the sudden exposure. She wore a lacy pink bra, the expensive kind, which paled beneath the color of her dress. He could see the line that separated her cleavage and found himself longing to trace his fingers down it. Instead, the professor allowed his eyes to do the work. All the way down and up again until they met with Eve's frantic gaze.

She was shaking. He saw the fear in her. Her eyes signified more than the fact that he had caught her snooping in his drawer. She looked vulnerable, yet clandestine. He wondered what she was hiding. But he saw nothing in her hands. And the dress she was wearing revealed that she had only her underwear beneath. *Maybe she is just looking for a safety pin, after all,* he thought. The strap was indeed broken. He could hardly imagine that in the time he was gone she would destroy her dress purposefully to look among his things. But then again, he could not rule anything out. Yet Eve seemed so innocent, he could hardly bring himself to shout at her.

"I have a pin," he declared quietly. Theo turned and replaced his wallet in the drawer then reached into a trinket box on the bookcase from where he retrieved the small item. "Here, let me," he urged, reaching for the strap which lay dormant against Eve's shoulder.

She shivered as the professor's fingers gently brushed her skin, sending shockwaves like an electric current throughout her body. Eve saw the flicker in Theo's eyes and realized at once that he had sensed the awakening in her. A man of his worldly knowledge with women could hardly have missed the effect he was causing. She desperately wanted to still herself, forget that this man was slowly pinning the broken strap to her dress. But Eve was losing any hold on her sensibilities.

Theophilus de Cordova had her hooked the instant he fastened the pin and returned his gaze to her eyes. He inveigled her with one deep stare, right into her pupils. Eve's anxiety rose to peak proportion, uncertain whether she was really dazed or imagining that she was. The room had disappeared, all sense of time had stopped and her heart had stopped beating. She was suspended, then it was like she was falling.

Only the chocolate-brown eyes that faced her kept her upright, holding her spellbound to his will, moving ever so much closer to her that their darkness filled her entire view. They danced as if they held secrets he would be more than willing to share with her. Then they disappeared when her eyes closed—dreamy and sated—and she felt herself fall into strong arms, the strong pressure of a warm kiss being planted against her lips.

Theo knew exactly what to do next. There was no decision to make. The moment he saw that he had captivated Eve Hamilton to the brink of surrender, his primitive ego rose to the bait. He kissed like a man. Not softly, tentatively, or even speculatively. Theophilus de Cordova kissed Eve with intention. Frank, honest, and arguing no bones about it.

His mouth glided over hers with blatant deliberation, aiming directly for her pulsing lips, sweeping them into his own. And when he had achieved that, he softened the pressure slightly, causing Eve to tremble against him. When he felt her limbs, lax against his own, he added the pressure, this time unable to fight the meaning behind why he was kissing Eve with such ambition. The essence of it went far beyond what he had intended. To Theo's chagrin, he was aware that there was some significance of feeling attached to the way his lips drifted purposely over hers.

And Eve was aware of it, too. She had wanted to find some route to escape the way the professor had looked at her, but the moment she felt the conscious taking of her lips, there was no retreat. No man had ever kissed her with such furor. Eve was unsure what to make of it, whether the professor was playing with her affections or simply inciting them. Whatever he was doing, he had succeeded. She could find no avenue to withdraw from the sensuous haven he had plunged her into.

Her lips obeyed his thrusting command. They collaborated with every expressive movement he made. And with the kiss came a whole new wealth of emotions. Eve felt more than frightened of the consequences. Appalled at herself, she abruptly pulled away. Her mind told her that Theo had caught her red-handed and then he had kissed her. Surely this was not possible. Confused, she blinked, knowing she was not the kind of woman who could submit to someone responsible for her brother's death.

"I'm sorry," she stuttered, pulling herself away to a safe distance from the professor. Eve nervously folded her arms beneath her breasts and tried to compose herself. "I feel responsible. I . . . didn't mean to—"

"It's my fault," Theo interrupted, apologetic. "I overreacted. Your dress—"

"It's okay now," she assured, acutely embarrassed. She was still shaking, such was the turbulence hidden beneath that very dress, but Eve prayed it was not so revealing to the professor, because she was feeling a touch more than out of her depth. She should never have agreed to deal with this man. He obviously was more than she had bargained for.

"Breakfast?" he prompted suddenly.

Eve tried to smile. She had forgotten all about her stomach. "Yes," she nodded. Anything to distract her from what they had just done.

Theo tried to compose himself, too, but he had no idea what he was doing. He felt inadequate and there was no explanation for it. It was unlike him. But with Eve, he could not quite decide whether she would make an old man feel very happy or a young man feel very old. There was something about her he could not quite fathom, and that unnerved him even more because he did not like being in the company of a woman he could not read. *Call it suspicion of the opposite sex,* he thought. *Hell, call it distrust.* Distrust. He rolled that one word comfortably around in his mind. He needed to know more about this woman. He needed to ask more questions.

"After breakfast, I'll show you around the lab and tell you more about the work we do up here," he invited. "Then maybe you can tell me more about yourself over dinner tonight."

Eve nodded. She was back on track, but she was also silently aware that she was facing a man who had an unconscious fear of her.

The day had warmed by the time Eve and the professor left the cottage and headed toward the quay she had seen from her bedroom window. They had eaten nervously while facing each other across the kitchen table, but Eve felt that she had handled herself well by eating the entire cheesy egg dip and complimenting the professor profusely for the invention. She had certainly tasted nothing like it. Now as they walked down the rocky slope toward the quay, the professor began to explain a little about the village of Cramond, giving Eve some impression as to why he chose the place to set up his laboratory.

"The Romans built a harbor and fort here once," he began, "on the order of Emperor Antoninus Pius. It's the perfect hideaway for me to do my work."

"Not somewhere I'd associate with finding a black man," Eve spoke truly, beginning to feel at ease again.

"You'd be surprised," the professor continued. "There are quite a number of black people living in Scotland, even in its history. In fact," he pressed on, now in his element. "Frederick Douglass, an agent for the Massachusetts Antislavery Society visited here in 1845 as part of the organized abolitionist movement. The Jamaican Marcus Garvey visited in 1914 on his way to England." He carefully negotiated a few rocks and stones beneath his feet. "Even the great African-American inventor Elijah McCoy was educated right here. He studied machinery and engineering and was a great inspiration to me. During his lifetime, he acquired fifty-seven patents, and his lubricator for steam engines was what began the slogan, 'the real McCoy.' "

"So black inventors and scientists made an impression on you?" Eve asked, curious.

"Absolutely," Theo smiled, happy that she should challenge him with this. "The patent office provides concrete proof of their existence. During slavery, black people were great pioneers. I want to do great things, too, and Cramond is just the place to offer me the tranquility I need to work."

Eve saw an old mill, closest to the quay where iron was once imported and finished products exported. "It's lovely here," she enthused, looking about her, spotting an old weir much further down the river, and an old forge. The professor explained that the mill was now a private house. He also told her that the river was used to power no less than five mills, originally for corn and cloth.

"By 1752, they were manufacturing iron nails, spades, hoops, cart axles, and so on," he continued, leading the way ahead.

Eve realized that he was taking her down toward the forge. She imagined that it was once a ruined building, silent testimony to noisier, dirtier days, but now it seemed completely renovated and was certainly in use.

"Your lab," she surmised as they approached the building.

"Fairafar Mill," the professor announced. "That's its original name. I decided to keep it, sort of a traditional touch."

They entered through the wooden doors, and Eve immediately noted the security on her entrance. It was not the usual chain and bolt any layperson would associate with a village building, but rather a selection of two surveillance cameras, a motion detector, and a guard seated at a desk, pouring coffee.

"Geoff, I'd like you to meet Eve Hamilton," the professor introduced.

Eve smiled as a visitors book was thrust toward her by the security guard. "Please sign your name." He indicated the spot.

Eve did as ordered and replaced the fountain pen by the book. She noted immediately there had been two other recent visitors over the last few days, a Dr. Ken Marsden of Viotac International, and a person who simply signed himself as Dr. Kingsley. She made a mental note to commit the names to memory as further information to pass over to the assistant commissioner for cross-checking.

"Welcome to the De Cordova Institute of Plant Genetics," Theophilus prompted with a smile. "Follow me."

Eve did as instructed and they entered through a wooden door and into a large area which seemed to be the nerve center of the professor's work. She could see plenty of glass boxes built into the wall on one side of the room. The boxes contained plant life of various species. To the end of the room was Dr. Keplan, the man who had entered the kitchen earlier to report his findings.

He viewed Eve with suspicion as she approached with Theo, but he continued to pour a green-colored liquid into several test tubes positioned in a rack. A window above them brought in the sunlight, which bounced against a steel cold-storage incubator that Eve assumed to be holding something very important because a technician wearing white overalls, whom she had not seen before, was playing with a thermostat positioned at the side.

"The work I do here is not related to the foundation," Theo began to explain as he stationed himself near a glass box on a table where what looked to Eve like maize was growing. "What I do is do research on genetically modified food and crops."

Eve stared at the technology around her.

Theo indicated the glass box on the table. "Famine is a world problem, particularly in Africa. The soil is harder to work with, rain is scarce, and people need to be fed. I can't solve the entire problem, but I can find ways to help."

"With plant genetics research," Eve acknowledged, aware the professor was only giving her as much information as he felt she needed to know.

"That's right," he agreed. "My company used to do contract research and some consulting for clients who provided pest controls to farmers. Then I began to affiliate with the universities, with student research work and lectures. By reputation, I was commissioned to look at ways to produce food crops. I'm in the process of writing a report for the Henry Doubleday Research Association of my recent tests."

"This is all very interesting," Eve exclaimed, failing to understand the true purpose of why the professor should have his research laboratory so carefully guarded. "So what's the big secret?" Eve put her hand to her mouth. But it was too late. The question was out.

"Secret?" he harangued.

Eve's body quickened. "I mean," she coughed, clearing the constriction in her throat. "Did you arrive at a solution?"

Theo reared back on his heels, his eyes narrowing suspiciously. "My report is going to suggest to the association that mass production of genetically modified fodder maize is an acceptable solution as long as the risks are assessed."

"Risks?" Eve was hooked.

"From a prevailing wind for instance." The professor folded his arms beneath his chest, looking Eve directly in the eyes. "Would production affect neighboring crops like organic growths? And would there be any legal ramifications?"

Eve leaned back against the wall, feeling the intensity of the professor's stare; feeling the sharp edges of the boxes behind her—which were housing the very plant life he was researching—digging directly into her spine as he gazed into her eyes. She could have sworn she had gone dizzy, but she had not. It was Eve's brain spinning wildly with wonder as to why the professor should be goading her with a deep, penetrative glare.

Was he thinking that she was part of a small core of environmental fanatics? Or did he, in fact, have prior knowledge that she was snooping around for the assistant commissioner of the Metropolitan Police? Was his work so illegal that it had cost her brother his life? Whatever the answers, Eve truly knew now, more than ever, that Theophilus de Cordova had something to hide.

She ruefully swallowed the spit at the back of her throat and tried to show the professor an innocent expression. "I'm sure you're right about the scientific cautions that need to be adhered to."

"That's the conclusion I'm going to pass to the association when they hold their next meeting," Theo proclaimed astutely. "Then I can concentrate on the work for Green Light."

Eve was certainly intrigued as she watched Theo resume showing her around the rest of his laboratory. There was very little else to see except the face of his technician when they had walked passed the cold storage incubator. Instinct told Eve that there was something top secret about it, but she knew not what it was or why the professor had nodded discreetly at his two members of staff before they departed Fairafar Mill.

On their return walk toward the cottage, Theo told her that he had to go back to the lab to conduct some further experiments and hoped she could occupy herself in his absence. It was not what Eve expected. She wondered if he was thinking that he had told her more than he had intended. His sudden silence as they strolled along made her quite uneasy to that fact.

"Your work is very important to you, isn't it?" she said finally.

"As much as yours is to you, I expect," he said. There was a heightened note of concern in his tone, which Eve noted immediately.

"Have I said or done something wrong?" she probed carefully, as they took to the grassy slope.

She wondered whether he was thinking about when they had kissed. The experience had never left her mind, not even while she was touring his lab. Eve could tell it annoyed the professor. He had probably not intended her to pull away like she did. She imagined it was not the custom for a woman to do so once encased in his arms, feeling his desirable mouth pressed to her own. But she was not any woman. Her motive was not to get under his skin, but to bring him to justice. For a man of his perception, she knew Professor De Cordova realized something was wrong.

"Why are you here?" he suddenly questioned.

"You . . . you invited me," Eve gulped, her fears confirmed.

"So I did," Theo relented, stopping abruptly in his tracks that Eve had taken two steps ahead before realizing he was a tag behind.

She turned and faced the professor, her awareness amplified by the brooding expression mirrored across his face. "I'm very impressed by your work," she broached lamely, her nerves now on edge at the reminder he had caught her snooping around. She needed to bridge the gap between them and fast. "When Lola Henriques told me about your foundation, I became quite interested in collaborating on a fund-raiser."

He seemed to accept this for the few brief seconds it took Eve to swallow the anticipation in her throat. Then came the crunch question. "Just tell me one thing." He caught Eve off guard. "Did anyone send you here?"

Eve gasped.

"I'm sorry I had to ask you that," Theo added forlornly. He took two steps toward her and touched her arm. "It's just that last year . . ." He paused for amendment. "I don't like being lied to."

Eve tried to smile, but felt weakened by the churning of emotions inside her. Everything around her sounded so quiet, she could only hear the water trickling against the river bed and a few birds in the sky. Yet her inner being was making all kinds of noises, warning sounds that this man was suspicious. That he may choose to kiss her again because he was so unpredictable. Because she was so attracted to him. Because they both wanted to reexperience how wonderful it had been to have smooched the first time.

She took a step back for self-preservation. There was the truth, but there was also Paul's smiling face in front of her mind's eye. She felt the tears threaten as they had done before. She could not give in. Not now. Not ever.

"No," she told him finally. "I'm here on my own volition."

Four

There was only one glitch: she had lied. Eve's ambivalence concerning this one flaw in her disposition had nothing to do with vanity. She was beyond that type of self-analysis. On the positive side, she was on a mission, but what she had not expected was the compromising of the good attributes in her character to succeed with it.

In the fashion world, she was renowned for her flair, her amulet, her integrity to design simple, yet practical, day wear. The Hamilton touch was familiar to the select stores of London as it was to the metropolis of Europe, and though she was still young in the business, like a proper fashion designer, Eve showed two collections a year at London Fashion Week. Hers was a profession that demanded blatant honesty, and courage to dictate changes in trend. It was a trait she did not discredit and certainly not within her personal life.

Her female instinct was to come clean, but as Eve dressed herself for dinner that evening, the whole idea of honesty smacked of disaster. Theo would never understand. He had spent most of the day at his laboratory allowing her to be left free to wander around the village and along the River Almond where the clean Scottish air renewed the life in her cheeks, drained by the London smog.

The solitude did not leave her feeling guilty until she

had remembered their kiss. The thought of it caused heady feelings anew to run riot within her as she strode along past the Cramond Parish Church, viewing the whitewashed houses in her wake, which were situated on a slope leading down to the river. Theo's kiss had remained like a taste on her lips, a credible, tingling, sensational flavor of mint mouthwash and salty saliva which left her moody and slightly nervy.

Even while she found herself standing in pleasant grounds off Cramond Road South, taking in the ambience of Lauriston Castle, she was unable to enjoy the view of the country mansion. The slim moment of intimacy with the professor had left her with the reprehensible notion that she had done something wrong. By the time she found herself walking along the promenade, watching the flow of the river into the Firth of Forth, Eve was chagrined to find herself placing a call to Humphrey Brown on her mobile. She was relieved that his encouraging tone had declared his satisfaction with her findings so far.

"You're doing great," he had enthused on his side of the mouthpiece, unaware of the inner conflict Eve was battling. "Any idea what's in this cold storage incubator?"

"No," she admitted. "But it's in an old forge, and it has some buttons at the side."

"Coded digital sequence lock," Humphrey revealed. "He's really looking after what he's got in there. Let me know if you find anything else."

Instant guilt now set Eve's teeth on edge as she caught a reflection of herself in the mirror which hung on the back of her guest bedroom door. She was not wearing anything extravagant—she kept her name for the narcissism of her clients—but wore a pair of white cotton trousers with a multicolored georgette blouse, admittedly borrowed from her latest collection. Her hair was pulled away from her face and tied into a simple top-knot, and she had slipped into the sandals she had worn earlier in the day.

As if on cue, Theo's eyes widened when she joined him at the table in the kitchen. He had covered it with a clean cloth and laid out the necessary cutlery, plates, and glasses. A salad was prepared with all the raw vegetable pieces cut to precision, and an open bottle of red wine took center stage, inviting her in. The delicious smell of a cheese pasta filled the air and Eve smiled as she seated herself, unsure whether she had the gall to begin another interrogation.

Nonetheless, she was all geared up and full of expectations. If only, Eve wished, the professor did not look so immaculately attired in his navy-blue, tailored trousers and white shirt—its neck open to reveal the waft of dark hair present on his chest—her task would be made much easier.

"I'm sorry I had to leave you on your own today," he apologized, tossing a corkscrew around in his hand. He shot her a penetrating glance, then lost his concentration as his gaze roved over her compulsively, absorbing every beautiful asset. Theo was visibly shaken by Eve's appearance, the evidence of his fancy betrayed in the smoldering glaze of his eyes. "Were you able to occupy yourself?"

"Yes," Eve nodded, detecting his appreciation of her. "I made a few calls into London, then went for a stroll around the village. It's very quiet."

"Indeed," Theo agreed, his admiration of her rounded face, well placed cheekbones and doe-shaped eyes broadening the smile on his lips. "Another reason why I decided to buy this cottage. I can spend most of my summers here. My city home is in London."

"In London?" Eve added the information to memory while wrestling to control the flutters in her stomach.

"Mayfair," Theo continued, reluctantly making his way toward the oven, knowing it deprived him any frontal view of Eve. "But I prefer my laboratory to be here in Scotland, out of the way of prying eyes."

"So you *are* working on something top secret?" Eve proclaimed lightheartedly to camouflage the intent of the question.

Theo turned from the open oven and looked at her, his smile narrowing suddenly. "We were going to talk about you, remember?"

Eve stared at him, the flutters now jumping in alarm. She tried to decipher the change in his mood. *A man who makes decisions and sticks to them,* she mused. Secretive. Not given to idle talk. Did not crack jokes. Was not outrageous either, so he had told her. Someone who was perhaps intimidating to everyone except maybe his son.

"Sorry," she acknowledged, her face rueful. "Where do you want me to begin?"

"Tell me a little more about your work."

With a little frown on her face and recalling Theo's almost paranoia about her motives, Eve decided she would be as explanatory as possible in the hope that she could coax him to drop his guard. "I want to open a boutique one day," she began quietly. "But that requires a steep investment, which I don't have. At the moment I design from a small studio at the back of my house in Fulham."

"Sketching?" Theo inquired, removing a large dish from the oven.

"Designing," Eve corrected, raising her elbows to the table where she folded her hands together and diligently leaned her chin against them. Comfortable with talking about her work, she continued. "I'm fussy about fabric, to be precise, the quality of it. But once I've made up my mind on which one I'm going to use, my small team and I get down to work."

"Do you have a principle that each piece should be different?" Theo asked with a slight edge of impatience as he placed the hot dish on a cooling rack on the table.

Eve's nostrils were immediately treated to the pungent smell of cheese, pasta, and seasoned chicken, but her brain was more geared to the reminder of the conversation they had shared in his car the night before, where they had debated the essence of creativity. She had no wish to return to the subject.

"No matter how successful my business becomes," she relented politely, "my designs will always remain exclusive because they are individually made. I only sell to the most exclusive boutiques." What she did not tell him was that a number of them still owed her money in backdated invoices of payments long overdue.

"So there's a limit to your production capacity?" the professor instantly queried, seating himself next to Eve. He handed her the salad bowl, and she took it while disguising the scowl on her face.

"I've occasionally made to order where I do personal fittings for high-profile clients," she said. "Whoopi Goldberg wore an exclusive of mine at last year's Oscars because her regular designer let her down. I was given very little notice, but it was a challenge, and, as always, I managed to process the order on time."

Theo saw her agitation and recoiled. He had no wish to upset Eve that evening. The day in itself had not gone as he had expected. It had been his intention to show her around the village. While the tide was out, he even thought they could take the raised walkway across to Cramond Island where the acute isolation would have made it easier to tap her brain. But instead he had unexpected work to do at the laboratory and the unanticipated worry of wondering exactly how Eve would utilize her time.

He felt slightly sedated that she had taken in at least

some of the sights of the small village. There was much to see for an inquiring tourist, but she had chosen not to go very far. Perhaps she was not the venturing kind. Perhaps she was a quiet homebody like himself.

"C'mon, let's eat," he smiled. "I'm sure you must be starving."

Eve was not sure she was that hungry. She was more alert to the fact that the professor was feeling unnerved about something. It niggled her. That morning, she had been caught red-handed with his wallet, they had kissed, and then he had invited her to see his work in his laboratory. He had given too much away in such a short space of time. Why?

Eve imagined that the professor was not used to such rash behavior or leaping into idle indulgences with women. Because of his penchant for research, his experiences with women were probably based on a mutual interest in scientific subjects or were the natural result of a burgeoning friendship. And because he was the father of a young boy, his women were all most likely professionally minded, of the nonmaternal type, no doubt. His relationships were presumably accommodated for, at best, two to three months. There would be decent sex, a certain level of respect, but no emotional attachment.

Yet Eve knew that from the professor's standpoint, she was different. She could tell from the expression that frequently marred his face. He was thinking, pondering, working out what constituted the fabric of her character. Even now, his brooding chocolate-colored eyes were switching from the pasta to the spoon, to the salad bowl, before landing on the mysteries behind her façade.

Theo was as captivated as he had been the moment he had first seen Eve Hamilton. She was enough to make him want to analyze her with the same passion with which he researched his work. In fact, he had not been able to work that day. Eve had played on his mind the entire time he spent in his laboratory. The fact that he had caught her with his wallet did not formulate any real degree of suspicion in his mind. He knew that Eve was not a thief, and he was quite prepared to believe that she was indeed looking for something with which to hold up her dress. If he was smitten by her, he was even more the fool.

A hapless buffoon. But he could not help himself. Everything about her enthralled him, from the way she forked the salad onto her plate, to the scallop of pasta she applied, to the way she had kissed him. He wanted to compile every facet of information on Eve Hamilton, but for what reason, he had no idea.

"Were you born in England?" he asked, the thought of eating eluding him as he put his elbows to the table and clasped both hands together only to lean his chin against them, like Eve.

"Yes," she said, feeling a little nauseous as she stared at the food. She was not interested in talking about herself. The whole purpose of her visit to Cramond was to learn more about Theo. "What's Brazil like?"

Theo smiled. "It was beautiful when I was a child."

"And now?"

"It still is beautiful, but it's not the same." His gaze clouded slightly. "My country suffers from great poverty, racial differences, and high inflation. If you're a minority, it's hard to be the things you want to be. There's a lot of corruption. My parents remember the old days. Today, they are very demoralized. They do not want their grandchildren to know a heritage that is not thriving."

Eve's brows rose. "Grandchildren?"

"My son is one of seven that my parents have," he informed her casually, absorbing every part of Eve's rounded face. Her lovely doe-shaped eyes seemed to widen further in curiosity. "I have three sisters and a brother."

"They all live in Brazil?" Eve probed, charting Theo's assertive expression. She, too, began to confirm to memory the smallest detail about his assertively masculine features, his broad shoulders and sturdy build, the way he wrinkled his nose like a child which had a most endearing affect on her feminine instincts.

"No," Theo told her. "Nathan, he's the youngest, lives in Phoenix, Arizona, with an African-American lady he married three years ago. They have twin girls, Carolina and Georgia. Tamar is the oldest. She and her husband live in Puerto Rico with their young son Peter. Angelina is still in Brazil, in Rio. She's divorced with three children in their teens. And Rachel, the one born after me, is still free and single. No kids yet. Then there's myself and Trey."

"You were born—"

"Third," Theo finished, intrigued by Eve's level of interest. Most women would have switched off by now and have begun to delve into the food elaborately displayed on her plate, but he was in awe by Eve's fascination with him. He liked it. It spoke to every niche of his manhood. "We still see each other at Christmastime or Easter," he added. "We tend to all travel into Brazil around then as both my parents are now retired."

Eve's curiosity grew. "What are their names?"

"Augustus and Rosa." Theo smiled. "Mum cooks the best mariscada in Brazil. It's a traditional fish stew that I always look forward to when I go over. In fact," he chuckled. "Mum's quite warm. She likes most people. The acid test is Dad."

"He sounds like my mother," Eve recognized the ideal that everyone always had one stern parent. "Marlene," she added. "She did the controlling before my father died when I was very young. She's a retired schoolteacher now, and we've been fortunate to have a close friend my parents both knew to care for us like Dad would've done."

"Us?"

"My brother and I."

Theo missed the tense note in her remark. "What does he do?"

Eve panicked. This was not an area she wanted to get into, taking herself back to childhood and to the advent of Paul's death. Yet a favorite hobby of his sprung to mind and she found herself saying, "He used to collect stamps then got bored after he assembled three thousand in a scrap book."

"I'm a collector, too," Theo enthused, alert to the secretive way Eve held her lips. He mused over it for a few brief seconds then decided that it was probably nothing. "I like to save foreign coins from all over the world. My goal is to have at least one from every country."

"I don't think of you as having a hobby," Eve declared somewhat surprised, but more relieved that the subject had diverted without a hitch. "I mean, I like watching movie classics—*Gone With the Wind, Little Women, Brigadoon*—all the old stuff. But you always seem so serious."

Now Theo was hooked. "In what way?"

"The things you discuss, and your manner always being firm and forthright." She chuckled in recollection of something he had told her at their initial meeting. "You did say you don't crack jokes and are not given to outrageous behavior."

"Or deliver put-down one-liners," Theo remembered. "I was hot under the collar."

Eve's antenna closed in. "About Dr. Keltz?"

"It's a personal matter," he wavered, removing his elbows from the table to rest his wrists there instead. He clasped his hands together and immediately looked formal—but certainly not like someone who was about to enjoy dinner in the fine company of a woman. "I was still spitting fire from a letter I had received. It's . . . delicate. That's why I gave you my lawyer's card. I thought you were . . . never mind." He shook himself. "Do you plan to have kids?"

"Me?" Eve choked, suddenly knocked from being on tenterhooks in hope the professor was about to disclose something of use to her.

"You're a woman, aren't you?" he rebuffed.

Eve nodded. "Maybe." She thought again. "Yes, probably I will. I haven't given it much thought, but if I do, I'd like to be married. I don't fancy the idea of becoming a single mum."

"There's a lot of that around, isn't there?" Theo surmised forlornly. "My sister has lived the trend of a man not taking responsibility for his children."

"And women are being irresponsible by allowing a man to put them in that situation in the first place," Eve added, judgmentally.

"You can't generalize like that," Theo objected suddenly. He leaned his back in his chair as though the simple remark had touched an ugly chord within the matrix of his emotions. "Angelina was married and found herself divorced fifteen years down the line because her husband had cheated. As for Trey and his mother, I always—"

"I didn't mean . . . it was just a sweeping statement," Eve interrupted sullenly. "I didn't mean to be personal. I suppose . . . I'm a little highbrow on the subject." She paused to refocus the mood. "When you're born of a proverbial Caribbean mother like I am, raised on high moral values straight from the Bible, it's hard to go against all the hard work stamped into you."

"So you were a church goer?" Theo asked, recovering slightly from the depth of their discussion. He was being touchy, he knew, and Eve had handled it well. Something else he liked about her. "I guess I should've picked up on that."

"I think most of my generation born in England were," Eve explained, recalling her last visit nearly a year ago when Pastor Reeds presided over a memorial for Paul. "It was just something our parents did when they came to this country. I rarely go myself, maybe once in a blue moon," she added, thinking she really should make more of an effort, "but when I do, I'm reminded that even now, in the twenty-first century, you can't enter a black church in Britain without wearing a hat and decent clothes. The old culture still kicks hard."

Theo laughed. His mood was sedate once more. "You Carib girls like to hold your heads high," he acknowledged, respecting the sharp edge of her culture. "It's the same in Puerto Rico where my sister lives. Which part of the Caribbean were your parents from?"

"My father was from Jamaica," Eve confirmed, feeling more relaxed and decisive that she might actually eat something on her plate after all. "And my mother is Dominican. I've never been to either island, but I'd love to go one day."

"You've never seen your parents homeland?" Theo was shocked.

"I had other things to do," Eve answered lamely. "Like building my career, for instance. It's on my life's agenda though. I'd love to do some charity work to profile my name."

Theo moved forward in his chair. "Like?"

"The work I did in Malawi a few months ago," Eve revealed. "I helped to raise funds to build a school by using local workers to hand make some of my more expensive designs, which gave them an income. Then I sold the designs to a select few fair-trade-for-Africa boutiques across England, to keep the tag exclusive, on the provision that 10 percent of the sale go toward the trust responsible for the school's project."

Theo's brows rose in admiration. "That's a nice little idea." He smiled.

It melted Eve's bones. "I thought so," she applauded, the constricting band around her chest tightening suddenly. "When Jasmine, my personal assistant, suggested it as a way of attracting sponsors, I wasn't too sure. Then I saw the feasibility of it while planning some design ideas, then I tried it out. So far, it seems to be working, though it's still in its early days. I'm more interested in exploring other fund-raisers now that my name has become a marketing tool. It's alternative exposure. Tia Maria is sponsoring my show this coming week. It cuts both ways. I'm always open to new ideas, which is why I'm here."

Theo nodded his approval. "I remember Lola applauding your latest collection." He recalled while piling food onto his own plate.

"Yes. Spring's show was on African themes and my Fall predictions," Eve swallowed, realizing that her heart had begun to beat extraordinarily fast, a failing that often occurred when she was talking more intricately about her work. "I was inspired after an earlier visit to Malawi last year before my brother died. Lola's a friend of my personal assistant, and it was her second time, I think, attending one of my shows."

Theo's regard was direct and searching, his gaze boring a tunnel right into her soul. At last he picked up on the thread which tugged constantly at Eve's secretive lips. "I'm sorry about your brother."

Eve cringed. It was not her intention to tell him that. "I don't want to talk about it."

Theo nodded in understanding that a part of her must be still raw at the edges. "You were telling me about African themes?"

Eve's entire body stirred awesomely. "Colorful, sexier." She felt her throat go dry. "The crux was Kenyan, Sudanese, and Ethiopian culture. Mostly dresses, figure-hugging tops and skinny trousers."

"And sexy," Theo reminded. "Okay, I don't understand the whole slashing the top off a dress to symbolize the rape of a woman or whatever, but I do believe that fashion should be about making a woman feel sexy and cute."

Avoiding his gaze, Eve mumbled. "I'm working on next summer's line at the moment."

"It must be exciting to work so far ahead," Theo smiled, reaching for the bottle of red wine on the table. Doing the honors, he poured the contents into two glasses and handed one to Eve. "Lola's the obvious market type you cater to."

"I don't have a muse." Eve gulped, downing a large supply of the fruity red stuff. "I mostly design for myself or what I perceive the market demands. I'm just really happy that people appreciate my eye for style and continue to buy."

Theo downed a small sip from his own glass before casting Eve in a more professional light. "I'm very impressed with your achievements," he breathed on a serious note. "Especially for a woman who looks as—"

"Careful," Eve chuckled, the wine instantly warming her. *He may be lethal. He may steal your heart.*

"I was going to say 'as refined as you.'" Theo finished, searching her eyes, hoping to see a magical flicker in response.

"Thank you," Eve said, realizing her voice had adopted a purposeful, flirting tone. It had been a good while since she had found herself seated at a table enjoying the company of a man over a glass of wine. It was unfortunate, in her case, that Professor Theophilus de Cordova was under surveillance. Nonetheless, Eve told herself that she was allowed to relish at least one evening with her number-one subject. "I do my best," she added candidly.

"Tell me," Theo said, leaning into the gaiety of her mood while forking his way through his food. "Has your work compromised your personal life in any way?"

Eve laughed. The wine was really taking full effect, but Eve indulged her mood by sipping more from her wineglass. "There was a long-term partner once," she volunteered with a chuckle. "He eventually found me overbearing. His excuse was that I reasoned too much, but," Eve shook her finger in the air as though she was dismissing the point, "I think my career intimidated him."

"So?" Theo asked in curiosity.

"We ended our relationship," Eve finished, swallowing a large amount of wine. "Ssssh," she went on. "Mother doesn't know. She's very fond of Tyrone."

"Tyrone?"

"Tyrone Mosley," Eve revealed. "Captain of the West Indies Cricket Team."

"A pedigree relationship," Theo marveled, his eyes widening at the news. He had not expected this kind of competition.

"What I need is a man who doesn't have a problem saying those three little words," Eve reproved. She reached for the bottle of wine. "Have you any more of this stuff? It's delicious." She immediately added more to her glass. "*I love you* isn't a big deal to ask for, now is it?"

"That's an affirmation, not a request," Theo noted.

Eve chuckled. "That's just the sort of thing someone like you would say."

Theo's brows rose. "Do you have a low tolerance to this wine?" he objected, noticing its effect on Eve.

"Red wine does go to my head quicker than white,"

Eve declared, taking another large swallow. "Don't worry. I can handle it."

"Maybe you should lie down," Theo prompted, seeing how flustered Eve had become in such a short space of time.

"No!" Eve insisted. "I want to tell you about my fund-raiser. That's why I'm here, isn't it?"

"Shouldn't it be?" Theo contradicted, suddenly puzzled. He did not miss the question in Eve's tone.

Eve narrowed her brown eyes. Somewhere in the dizzy recesses of her mind, she realized that the professor was testing her. Or had she made a mistake somewhere? She could not decide. "This isn't truth or dare," she countered with another chuckle. "I may be a little giddy, but my brain is right where it should be. Now ask me about my fund-raiser. What do you want to know?"

She hiccuped, and Theo wanted to laugh. Eve was more than giddy; she was on her way to becoming quite drunk. It was obvious from her stance that she was not going to give in to that notion, though, without a fight. He would have to humor her, and what a prospect that was going to be. It excited him to know that she was so volatile, that she had the same weaknesses as anybody else.

"Tell me your big idea," he challenged, leaning back in his chair to contemplate her more fully. She had hardly touched her food, but that was little wonder. She had used the wine as sustenance instead. He could see the deeper bloom it had created beneath the chestnut-brown complexion of her skin. Rather than looking haggard by it, Eve appeared more robust and alluring: a vixen out to snare her prey.

"I do a charity show, like the one I'm doing next week, to raise funds on the provision that your foundation hosts the event and administers the donation," Eve announced, devouring more wine. "What's the name of your foundation anyway?"

"The Brasila Trust," Theo confirmed, his smile widening devilishly with the fantasy that he could easily have Eve Hamilton stretched out for dissection, only he was far too sensible to use her in that way. Instead, he kept an image in his mind's eye of a heavenly night that would doubtlessly dispell the hangover he knew Eve would suffer in the morning. Right now, she needed to lie down. Alone. This was a conversation that had to be finished another time. "Why don't we discuss this tomorrow afternoon," he suggested. "After my son arrives. We could go for an early dinner."

"Trey," Eve rasped. "He must be handsome like you, with impeccable manners."

The professor chuckled. "He holds his own."

"And does he know what you're up to?" Eve pressed, draining the last of the wine from the bottle into her glass. "Does he know who Dr. Keltz is?"

Theo sat up abruptly in his chair. "What did you say?"

"C'mon," Eve chided, bolting the remainder of the wine. "You accused me at your seminar, which I have to say was not very nice. And what did Dr. Da Costa mean by Project Phoebe? What are you hiding?"

Theo stared in solid amazement. Did she really remember all that? He schooled his eyes and tried to detect some failing in Eve's demeanor. Something that would give away a flaw, a drawback, an opening into her real purpose for being seated at his dinner table. He saw nothing that gave any leeway to what Eve Hamilton wanted. She was too tipsy for him to pull any sensible judgments from her, but Theo decided quickly that while she was in this inebriated state, he would glean Eve for whatever depth of information he could get.

"Eve," he prodded. He considered reaching for another bottle of red wine, but his conscience decided against it. "I want to ask you something serious."

"I've not touched my dinner," Eve apologized, staring ruefully at her full plate. "And you went to so much trouble, too."

"Forget dinner," Theo drawled, urging his chair closer to Eve.

"But I'm your guest," Eve protested tearfully, "and I've not touched a thing. I'm not normally this rude."

"It's all right," Theo assured. "We're having something again tomorrow before you leave."

"Am I leaving?" Eve railed, confused, the wine disrupting her thoughts. "But you haven't told me what's in the refrigerator in your lab."

Theo stalled, then stared at her. "Who wants to know?" Theo prodded suddenly, his tone harsh and abrupt.

"I do," Eve chuckled. "I don't like men who hide things from me."

"And I don't like women who lie," Theo reminded.

The glitch returned in full swing. Eve's sudden guilt made the room swim and she found herself standing unsteadily from her chair. "I'm going to be sick," she murmured on a queasy note. "I need the bathroom."

Theo was on his feet in an instant, holding her left arm to keep her on balance. "Did I say something wrong?"

Eve felt her composure slip, knowing that if she stayed any closer to the professor, she would surely buckle beneath his inquisitive stare. She could not risk putting everything at stake, nor put the assistant commissioner's case in jeopardy. And of course there had to be justice for Paul. "I'm going to be sick," she repeated.

"No, you're not," Theo breathed. "You want to hightail it out of here because I've clued in on something. What is it? It's Dr. Keltz, isn't it?"

"No!" Eve tried to break her arm free, but the room was still spinning. "I've told you before—"

"You haven't told me anything," the professor interrupted, shaking her. "Ever since I've met you, you've been snooping around, asking questions, hinting . . . I *need* to know."

"I don't know who he is," Eve's voice trembled, tears now stinging at the back of her eyes.

"He?" Theo released her arm immediately, bracing himself for the worst scenario. "Who's he?"

"Dr. Keltz," Eve wavered. "That's who we're talking about, isn't it?"

"What?" Theo's body shook with sudden relief. "Dr. Moira Keltz isn't a man. She's Trey's mother."

"More coffee?" Theo asked, pouring a second hot refill into the mug Eve was holding between her fingers. He retook his seat and added, "I'm sorry."

"No, I'm sorry," Eve murmured, having descended from her euphoria to a more calm state. "I asked too many questions."

"I just thought . . ." Theo paused. There was no sense in overanalyzing. Some things were better off explained than simply left to fester as he had done. "I haven't let go of the memories," he began with a heavy heart. "She . . . she abandoned Trey. He grew up never knowing her, and I never knew her at all, really." He paused, dismal. "She just wanted to conquer the world and everything around her like a man."

The pain was evident. It resonated like a loud church bell in every word Theo had spoken. Unconsciously, Eve's fingers reached out and held the strong brown hands opposite her, just as she had done when the assistant commissioner explained to her about the pressures of his job. But the strong, firm fingers which curled

gratefully around hers now created a seductive onslaught on her senses, which again placed Eve in a compromising position she could not ignore. Yet, dumb as
it may seem, a deep pathos of sentiment transported
between them. It shook her. Eve had never seen a man's
eyes look so . . . sincere.

"You need to confront your fears," she told Theo,
confused as to where such a sobering thought sprang
from.

"I know," he agreed. "I've been blaming everyone
around me for years and distancing myself from a lot of
people. Long-term, that's not good."

Eve flinched. In an innate feminine action, she gingerly pulled her hand away. She reminded herself that
the professor was a typical male who liked to deal with
neutral facts, figures, and information. He had told her
so himself. She, on the other hand, preferred feelings,
and her intuition told her that Theophilus de Cordova
had no concept of how to deal with those.

"Have you ever considered," she started, attempting
to choose her words carefully, "that you may be too tactical about how things should be?"

Theo raised a dark brow, already feeling the loss of
Eve's fingers rubbing gently against his own. His antenna was alert. "In what way?"

"That conversation we had yesterday in the car," she
reminded him. "You seemed to have a very plotted, almost strategical approach to conducting a relationship.
As a woman, I found it difficult to understand what it
was you were trying to say, and if your wife—"

"Moira and I were never married," Theo divulged
harshly. "We met, and we did not fall in love. You could
say we blundered. So, there you have it."

Eve leaned into her chair, amazed. It dawned on her
immediately—and she had heard the professor correctly—that he was admitting to failure. "You're beating

yourself up," she said, hardly believing that such a hand-some, ultraintelligent man could possess any such form of insecurity. It was a far stretch from the snapshot the assistant commissioner had given her, where a more as-sured roguish face had reflected into her mind. His vul-nerability smote her completely.

"You made a mistake, as we all do."

"Did you make a mistake when you fell in love?" Theo threw at her suddenly.

Tyrone! Eve blinked away the recollection of his name, but not of what they once had. A stormy relationship, that's what it was. Emotionally stressful and exhausting. Half the time, she did not know where she stood with Tyrone Mosley because his job had been so demanding. His travels and the celebrity of the sport made every-thing all the more difficult. At times, while designing in her studio, marginally cut off from the rest of the world, she would tirelessly pause to reach him by phone, only to be told by his manager or coach that Tyrone was busy.

How it had ever gone beyond eighteen months, she would never know. Even when Paul had been killed, and she had found it difficult to work, Tyrone was abroad somewhere, hitting a ball into the oblivion of a cheering crowd. In truth, he had never been there for her. Not physically or securely. And whatever pictures the glossy magazines had captured of them both were when his fleeting visits necessitated they be seen in public. Did she have any regrets? Had she indeed made a mistake? For the first time in Eve's life, she was suddenly con-fronted with the question.

"It was a learning experience," she said uncomfort-ably. "I've now accepted that I need to move on. Which reminds me. We haven't really discussed my fund-raiser."

"I've noticed that about you," Theo summarized smoothly, slowly taking another sip from his coffee mug.

"You're a rapid-switching thinker. You move from one mode to the next quite easily."

"I hate constant repetition," Eve breathed. "It's infuriating. You know, like the reminder of the conversation we had in your car."

Theo nodded. "You must find me intolerable," he sighed, suddenly feeling a touch unsure of who he was. "I've been quite harsh with you, accusing you wrongly."

"Well, a man doesn't go very far in life without having some raw edges," Eve nodded absently. "I suppose that's why Dr. Henri Da Costa is giving you problems, too."

"You remember a lot from one seminar," Theo said, realizing Eve had schooled a deliberate innocent expression to her face. "You should be invited more often."

"It's hard to forget a violent outburst," Eve declared plausibly. "It's only sound business practice that I check what's going on before committing my name to a fundraiser under your foundation. Why did he want you to tell us about Phoebe?"

The professor shifted uncomfortably in his chair. "Dr. Henri Da Costa is a French member of a rapid-response team of scientific vigilantes augmented from an ecological pressure group. They're against experiments of a pioneering nature. They have an elaborate network across Europe. We first met when we were both students at the University of Oxford. In his eyes, people like me are often accused of playing God. He believes I am abusing my knowledge."

"So why target you?" Eve inquired, keeping her tone professional while drinking more coffee from her mug.

Theo sighed. "Last year, my central laboratory in London was raided."

Piccadilly, Eve mused.

"I believe his group was responsible," Theo said. "Dr. Da Costa is under the impression that I have been conducting secret experiments."

"And have you?" Eve assayed, her nerves heightened.

"All my work is highly confidential," Theo answered.

"And Dr. Keltz?"

"Let's just say she has a sense of satisfying her competitive streak, which was probably something she wrestled with in her childhood," Theo confirmed, deciding not to refer to his current problems with his ex-lover. "Her mother was the famous African-American jazz singer, Kit Allen. A very ambitious black woman for her time. In fact, she's still remembered at the Edinburgh Jazz and Blues Festival held here in Scotland each year."

"I've heard of her," Eve said. "Didn't she live in France?"

"She moved there after the war because she couldn't handle singing in segregated clubs." Theo responded. "She married her German manager and became quite famous throughout Europe. Moira was born in France and lived a very privileged life. She's inherited her mother's love for attention."

"Quite a background," Eve said in awe.

"A far cry from my own," Theo admitted. "My father struggled financially for many years, even though he worked as the local doctor in São Paulo where I was born. In the early days, I had to hold down two jobs to pay university fees." Theo's eyes glazed over as he escaped into the past. "Moira was . . . headstrong. I liked that about her. She had an inner will not to collaborate with men, and my male ego rose to the challenge."

"What happened?" Eve was hooked, shaken by the depth of Theo's revelations, knowing that they had sidetracked once again.

"She got pregnant, unexpectedly, while we were both still at Oxford," he said. "Naturally, I thought we would get married. I was keen to do the right thing."

"And?"

"After Trey was born, she wanted out," he said flatly.

"I never knew a woman could be so cold. I became a single father when Trey was three years old. She went to work for a plant breeding company specializing in crop physiology. I began lecturing and investing in property, which paid off. If there had been no Trey, I probably would have gone back to Brazil."

"I'm sorry," Eve sighed sincerely. It was a hard story to swallow with cold coffee. Certainly nothing quite like what the assistant commissioner had prepared her for. Theo was beyond exemplary to take on the formidable responsibility of raising a child alone. Eve imagined how hard it must have been for him, not unlike what most women have to cope with. It left her in complete admiration of him. "What are you going to do?"

"Do?" Theo was bemused. "About what?"

"Dr. Da Costa?" Eve sensed that the professor was thrown by her sudden shift back to their initial subject. It was very insensitive of her, she knew, but she could not risk being swallowed into Theo's aura of foreboding.

He shook his head, a clear indicator of his disbelief. "I'm not using the foundation to front a secret project," he chortled firmly. "The Brasila Trust is strictly above-board and was set up to fund worthy causes, such as the money pledged to the South American Ecological Project. Green Light is part of their work to clean up Brazil. It has nothing to do with my experiments. That's a separate entity altogether. If you're considering attaching your name to what the foundation does, then I feel justifiably offended that you need clarification on my laboratory activities."

Eve was pinched by his sudden derision of her suspicions. "I . . . I was just confused about Phoebe," she wavered.

"Phoebe was a project I worked on that has nothing to do with the work of the Trust," Theo explained.

Eve reined back. She had pressed too hard. The professor was on the defensive. Yet, somehow, she did not feel convinced of everything he had told her. The expression on Theo's face seemed clear enough, but there was a mysterious component attached to everything he had said. She did not know him, certainly did not know if she could trust him. Did not know if he even *knew* Paul Hamilton.

Although he had referred to the raid at Piccadilly, which was consistent with what the assistant commissioner had told her, there had been no mention of an employee having died while in his employment. No reference to the coca base forensics found there. And certainly she was not told why the building had been registered in his godfather's name. Eve felt like she was in for a long haul waiting for the cracks to show. She was beginning to find it quite frustrating that they had not. Yet. Still, she had amassed enough to pass on to Humphrey Brown. No doubt, he would find meaning to it all.

"I think I'd better turn in," she announced, rising out of her chair, "before I risk offending you again."

"Of course." Theo rose to his feet, disappointed by Eve's impending departure. Despite their slight confrontation, he had never felt so relaxed, talking about himself or his work than with Eve Hamilton. It had felt so easy to off-load the pressures on his mind, and that was an intimacy he had never shared with anyone.

Theo was aware that it had a lot to do with the fact that she was not of his profession. Her scope of knowledge did not even come close and had gone a long way to sedate his nerves. What he liked most was Eve's aptitude for listening. She had endured his moaning and quipping remarks to the very end. It touched him. His distrust in her was beginning to disappear.

There were also the attributes he liked: gentle, tender, nurturing qualities which were reminiscent of his mother. He had sought such qualities all his life, but they had been lacking in his choice of female companions. Tomorrow evening Eve would be leaving. She was scheduled to be on the six o'clock train to London. He did not want their evening to end so abruptly.

"There's a lovely bistro in the village," he said, advancing a step forward so that he could register the faint smell of her perfume. "Maybe you'd like to enjoy a late lunch tomorrow. You're welcome to join Trey and me before you go."

Eve felt the warmth of him again, heard the softening in his tone, and stepped back. She could not risk Theo kissing her. "Yes. That would be nice."

It was a faint whisper as she turned away from him, but before Eve could hurry from the kitchen, Theophilus grasped her shoulders and turned her to face him. He had one shot, and he'd be damned if he did not take it.

"Before you go to your room, alone," he asked, "how did you feel when I kissed you today?"

The question came unexpectedly, but Eve already knew the answers: *Woozy. Lightheaded. Dynamic.* These were the words skittering around in all directions in her head. The professor was analyzing his position. That was to be her first lesson about the man. *I believe a person should always question and be decisive about their feelings* was the statement he had thrown at her.

Indeed, the kiss had been wonderful; smoother, more sensual, and more assured than any Tyrone had ever given her. Again, she was reminded how much that one kiss had played on her mind throughout the day. Even now, Eve's body trembled with yearning for Theo to retake her lips with such fervent demand.

But theirs was a situation she could not encourage, should not encourage if she were to successfully return with her findings to Humphrey Brown. Any thought of repeating the experience was already doomed the moment she thought of her brother Paul. There was only one answer Eve could give under the circumstances. She had to lie again.

"You left me cold," she remarked, shaking her head. She flinched the moment she noticed Theo had reared back, evidently stunned. Racking her brain for a much kinder and more plausible explanation, she added, "I haven't gotten over Tyrone. I hope you understand."

"Certainly." Theo pulled away as though his hand had been burned. "I'll see you in the morning."

"Of course," she said. His exaggerated movement left Eve pained by her deceit.

She immediately retreated to the personal space within her heart where she often went when she did not want to face her feelings. Oddly, the place felt hollow and empty, offering her no comfort at all. How could it when she was faced with the awful realization that the most unbearable consequence Theo could arrive at by her behavior was that she was as cold as Trey's mother?

There was nothing she could do without confessing. She told herself that in time he would forget her. But the question that lingered in Eve's mind as she returned to her bedroom was could she forget him?

Five

Her sleep had been troubled. And then Eve awoke to the sound of voices. She was alarmed when her watch read 11:58 A.M. Had she really spent an eon trying to vanquish her pining memories of last night? Eve knew that seeing Theo that morning would probably make her weak in the knees. It was not enough that she now had finally admitted to herself that there was a definite chemistry between them, but she was also plagued with the bleak admission that she was being deceitful.

She tried to dress quickly with that one thought still riddled on her mind. Perhaps it was just as well she was leaving today, Eve tried to convince herself while applying a thin veil of make-up to camouflage the ravages beneath her brown eyes. The visit had obviously revealed its fair share of surprises, even though she had been able to gather information that would prove useful to the assistant commissioner. But her stay in Cramond lacked the business authority she was revered for and that had shaped the shrewdness behind her profession.

It told Eve that Professor de Cordova probably never intended to take her fund-raiser seriously. He had not given her the opportunity to outline her idea, and, as Humphrey Brown had warned, it was likely that he saw her as a pretty face suitable only to satisfy his manly whims and nothing more. It was another tall order having to make that concession, along with the truth that she could never be as intellectually minded as his female conquests. Certainly not a rival to Trey's mother. Though that was not a failing in itself, for although Eve's attributes were already successfully proven in the work she enjoyed, she was still left feeling somewhat defeated by the notion the professor had not found her duly challenging.

Immersed with that same sense of dissatisfaction and yet somewhat empowered that she had accomplished more than what she had imagined possible, Eve applied the final layer of a two-coat mascara to her lashes, a touch of gloss to her lips, and enough powder to even the tones in her chestnut-brown complexion before she hurried downstairs.

The voices she had heard were coming from the television, but Eve did not see anyone in the room. She turned on her heels and was about to make haste into the kitchen when Theo materialized at the doorway, a cup of tea in his hand and a slightly impatient expression on his face.

"I'm sorry. I overslept," Eve apologized, feeling the sudden rush of hot blood into her cheeks when she realized her clothes were a slight touch ruffled.

By the same token, she had not expected the professor to be formally dressed. His pristine gray suit and pale blue shirt, a navy tie adding the finishing touch, gave him all the charisma and splendor any young woman would find irresistibly appealing. The sight of him standing before her, like the Nubian prince he was, filled Eve with such anticipation it was akin to being caught red-handed again. She found his imposing figure overwhelmingly magnetic, as was his gentle smile and deep chocolate-brown eyes which embraced her in silent invitation.

"I was wondering whether to raise you from the dead." He chuckled, watching as Eve nervously fixed the top button of the white blouse she was wearing. "But seeing as it's Sunday—"

"You should've made an earnest attempt," she interrupted, her ears overly sensitive to the hoarseness in Theo's tone. It spoke volumes to Eve that he was contemplating his approval of how she looked, too. "It's never been my practice to stay in bed," she added with a more controlled voice.

"There's always a first," Theo reasoned smoothly. "Have you met Trey?"

Trey! Eve turned and suddenly realized a boy was sprawled across the decorative carpeting on the floor, actively engaged on a Sony PlayStation. She had not realized someone else was in the room, though it had not occurred to her to wonder why the television was on. Trey had his back to them both, his attention fully trained on the game he was playing.

"He's very preoccupied." Eve said the first thing which sprang to mind, amazed that the boy had not been distracted by the mention of his name. Her mother would have frowned on such rudeness. As a young girl, she had been raised to respect her elders and certainly to offer a courteous greeting whenever visitors arrived at the house. It seemed hardly credible that Professor de Cordova's son was not in possession of good manners.

"It's his favorite game," Theo explained, looking at his watch. "Something he understands."

"Obviously," Eve agreed, tucking the bottom end of her blouse into the tailored cut of the black trousers she was wearing.

She drew the strings at the waistband until the pants hugged at her tummyline so she would not appear so ruffled. Theo caught the swift motion but kept his expression fixed. If his last wish was to listen without fault to his thought processes at that precise moment, he would be obeying the rampaging command of his hormones. Wild as they were for any sane man watching a woman hasten to finish dressing herself, Theo repressed the urge of his fanciful daydream to have Eve just as easily remove her clothes again.

It was the awful reminder of her rejection that ultimately closed off his emotions. That she was nervous and edgy at seeing him, which still manifested itself in the way she purposefully played with the strings she had just tied at the waistband of her trousers, did not make him feel any more relaxed. He was edgy, too. It was just as well she was leaving on the early-evening train, he tried to convince himself. It would be less of an embarrassment for them both, especially now that his son had arrived.

"Trey can be . . . a little difficult," he began, venturing into the sitting room where he placed his cup of tea on one of the nearby ivory tables. "But he's a good boy."

Eve remained rooted by the doorway, more due to the fact that she also realized she was barefoot and had left her sandals upstairs. "When did he arrive?" She threw a glance across the room at Trey. He seemed totally oblivious to her being there, enveloped as he was in his own little world.

"I picked him up at the station just after nine. You were still in bed."

She flushed, finally looping the tie string at her waist into a bow. "Last night was well past my bedtime," Eve said absently, returning her gaze to Theo. He had seated himself on one of the brown leather sofas, taking the end nearest to Trey, his legs slightly ajar with his elbows resting comfortably against them. Feeling a little alienated by the doorway, Eve decided to join him. "He's very quiet," she said. *Too quiet.*

Her last memories of nine-year-old boys were that they were rough, big headed, nosy, and possessed rampant adolescent behavior often despised by parents and teachers alike. Yet Theo's son had ignored her. He had not turned once in curiosity of who she was, just simply accepting that she was an acquaintance of his father's and was no business of his.

Eve took this impolite conduct as brazen and ill-bred. In her view, it was definitely a lack of correct parental guidance. Suddenly, all her fondest musings of the professor being beyond exemplary to have raised a child by himself diminished into obscurity. He may well be good at his profession, but when it came to the real practicalities of teaching manners to his own child, Professor de Cordova was a nonstarter.

"Did he travel alone?" she asked.

"His private carer brings him on the train, and I collect him at the station," Theo explained, seeing the inquisition in Eve's face.

"Private carer?"

Theo stalled, aware of her cognizance. "There's something I didn't tell you about my son." His alert tone roused Eve's full attention. "Trey has impaired hearing."

The news smacked Eve right in the face. "What?"

"That's why I never returned to Brazil," he added. "He boards at a special school in England." Theo continued. "He gets to use some of the best facilities not available in my country to aid his learning." He paused. "It's also the reason why Moira abandoned him."

"I . . . I'm sorry," Eve exclaimed, punishing herself with a discreet pinch of her wrist as she threw another glance at Trey. It was more a case of telling herself that she was indeed awake, but Eve was also goading herself that she should never have been so judgmental. "Does he know I'm here?"

"Probably not," Theo said, his tone holding a hint of impatience. "Sometimes it helps to tap him gently on his right shoulder, then he doesn't get too alarmed."

She did not know what to say. "Does he—"

"Talk? Yes, quite well," Theo interrupted. "He wears hearing aids. It's often when he's distracted, as he is now, that it sometimes becomes difficult."

Eve inhaled deeply. She found herself suddenly feeling nervous at being introduced to the boy. The entire situation was going way beyond anything Humphrey Brown could have guessed. It suddenly occurred to her that there had to be some kind of mistake. Maybe the wrong files had gotten mixed up somewhere. Maybe she was probing the wrong man. All Eve knew was that the information that was slowly unfolding about Professor Theophilus de Cordova, her number-one suspect in the murder of her brother, was not fitting the picture of a suspected menace who needed to be investigated by the Met.

To her chagrin, Eve was besieged with an awful stab of conscience and a desire to tell Theo the truth. If she came clean, undoubtedly the whole matter could be sorted out in no time at all. The professor would state his innocence, she could admit that she was wrong and then maybe . . . maybe. Eve girded herself. What was she thinking? Theirs was a relationship not destined for a beginning, let alone an end. Her world was far removed from the professor's. She liked the city and the speed of the rat race. He liked the peace and tranquility of the country. And, of course, there was his son.

"This must have been very hard for you," she said, her mind still spinning in a quandary of confusion.

"I've learned to live with it," Theo said uncomfortably, looking at his watch. "You must want something to eat."

"I can make it." Eve stood up, feeling the same level of discomfort. Perhaps it was the shock of it all. But she knew the truth. Her attraction toward the professor had deepened.

Their eyes locked briefly, and Eve was in for yet another surprise. The swift current of electricity that passed between them was as tangible as it was frightening. She saw the telling of it in Theo, too, as he abruptly stood.

"I know this is going to be an imposition," he ventured suddenly, his voice coarse and laden. "It's just that . . ." He paused. "I have to meet some people on business. It's very short notice and I was wondering, can you . . . can you look after Trey?"

Eve was moved. This was a responsibility she had not anticipated. She was also aware that Theo was offering her an acute level of trust, probably not given to just anyone when it came to his son. She looked at him and suddenly there was an understanding between them that she felt inept to explain.

"When will you be back?" she asked, nodding in acceptance.

"Two hours, tops." Theo smiled his relief. He looked at his watch. "Then we can all go for something to eat in the village before you catch your train."

"I'd like that," Eve returned the smile, her heart warming at this newly acquired level of friendship between them. Dinner, she knew, would be her last opportunity to spend some time with the professor before her departure to London. Oddly, she felt saddened that she may never see him again.

Theo immediately picked up a briefcase from the floor near the door, his impatience amplified as he walked toward Trey. He tapped the boy gently on his right shoulder and received an immediate response. Trey turned and looked up at his father then across at Eve who threw him a warm smile. Theo explained about his emergency meeting. Then he was gone.

To Eve's surprise, Trey's curiosity did not extend beyond what his father had told him. Instead, he re-launched into his game and she found herself staring at the TV screen, the loud animation having no appeal to her. Finally, after a few minutes, her hands clenched together, Eve reseated herself close to Trey and decided she would attempt to talk with him. Tapping him gently on his right shoulder, her tone moderately pitched, Eve introduced herself.

"Your father has told me a lot about you," she yelled above the sound of the TV, realizing his attention remained on the game. Eve persevered. "How's school?"

"Okay," Trey rebuffed finally. "It keeps me out of the way."

Eve reared back in her seat. She had not realized his voice would sound disorganized. Though it was easy to understand him, it required concentration on her part. "You can spend some time with your father now," she began with a hint at gaiety. "I'm sure—"

"He'll just want me out of the way," Trey repeated, struggling to formulate his sentence, his outburst causing Eve's eyes to widen. "He's always working, and Mother only visits when I'm in school."

"You see your mother?" Eve asked, confused by what the professor had told her. She decided she had heard Theo incorrectly.

Trey nodded. "But no one has time for me now."

His words were hard enough, but they were untainted with emotion. Eve realized that he was not pained. It was more a case that he had given up. And he had spoken all this without even turning to look at her. In fact, Trey continued to play his game, actively engaging the buttons on his console as though his outcry and the game itself were both intricately entwined.

Eve worried. A boy of his age should not be burdened with such problems. Clearly he was lonely. Understandably he was hurt. She imagined he probably lived his days making great efforts to control his feelings. In a flash of disappointment, Eve's judgmental regards about the professor's parenting of his son began to resurface along with her own feminine instincts which reached out to Trey.

"I have time," she offered gently.

It was as though magic words had been spoken. In an instant, the PlayStation was switched off, and Trey was rising to his feet, a huge smile spread across his face. For the first time, Eve had a full view of him. She was immediately smitten with a reflection of a chubby boyish face, brown complexion, and black curly hair. It was uncanny for Eve to feel like she had met this boy before, even more spooky that she impulsively found herself warming to his childish nature.

"Can we go on the boat?" he asked slowly, waving his hands in excitement.

"Are we allowed?" Eve wavered, unsure.

"It's my boat," Trey gushed. "It's moored just outside the house."

That would be the one she saw on her arrival, Eve mused, considering the prospect of drowning. She did not know how to swim, but that was something she could not tell Trey when he was looking forward to them going out on the river. His little face lit up with such joy, she could hardly deny him what he wanted. Without knowing she had told herself so, Eve decided she would always be a friend to this boy.

"I'll just get my sandals," she said in acceptance. And when she saw the smile in his eyes, Eve smiled, too.

"I suppose this is your favorite sport." Eve said loudly as she watched Trey take full charge of the boat. He was a good navigator, rowing it steadily along the side of the river away from the yachts that dominated the Almond. He held on to one oar and she the other, diligently obeying his instruction on how she should steer in the direction he was leading.

"I love sailing the best," Trey enthused, glancing down the river as they glided along. "Theophilus first took me out on the river when I was eight. It was wonderful."

"Why do you call your father by his name?" Eve asked, confused.

"We agreed," Trey explained slowly. "It helps me with my . . . pronunciation."

"I see," She paused. "So your father likes the river, too?"

"Yeah, we used to have a small yacht," Trey giggled. "We called her Phoebe."

"Phoebe!" Eve crooned, surprised.

"Yeah, but she had wood rot," Trey said, disappointed. "She was an old boat, and we had to sell her for scrap last year. But Theophilus says he's going to buy a new yacht when he finishes the big one."

Eve's brows rose in curiosity. Perhaps she had not understood him correctly. "The big one?"

"His top-secret project," Trey explained, glancing across the River Almond in admiration. "Look, there's the bridge," he pointed out to Eve.

She looked across the Firth of Forth, but Eve's mind was elsewhere. Finally, she had stumbled onto something, and she wanted to know more. "So, what's the big one about?" she queried, her voice raised as she offered Trey a friendly smile.

"It's a formula." He volunteered the information as only a child could, his eyes widening with the incredulity of it. "He made me christen it, so I called it Phoebe, after the old yacht. Theophilus told me that it's top secret, but I know he likes people to talk about his work, really."

"That's a very original name," Eve said. "Have you told anyone else about this?"

"Well . . ." Trey yawned, his face becoming shifty as though deciding on something. ". . . my pet hamster, I think. I'm allowed to keep her at school and take her home during the holidays. Would you like to see her when we get back?"

"Of course," Eve smiled. "What's the formula for?"

"Look, there's Cramond Island," Trey chimed, distracted. "You can get stuck out there when the tide comes in if you're not careful."

"You didn't answer my question," Eve interrupted, her tone marginally polite.

"What question?" Trey asked bemused.

Eve raised her voice, recalling Trey's hearing impediment. "The formula. What's it for?"

Trey giggled. "I forgot."

"You don't remember?" She hid her disappointment well.

"I've forgotten what it does," Trey went on, "but Theophilus has it written down somewhere in his bedroom."

Eve sat erect in the boat, almost dropping her oar in the process. "You've seen it?" she coughed, her voice raised even louder.

"He showed me," Trey crooned. "It's in a yellow folder. He's a genius, but I want to be a footballer like Pelé. He was the best."

"Are you good at football?" Eve asked loudly, her mind spinning an abundance of deceptive thoughts. She had to get her hands on that folder. She needed to know whether the information contained inside had anything to do with her brother's death.

"I like to score," Trey assured, measuring his speech carefully. "My project at school was about football. I wrote about Pelé because he's from my daddy's country, but my friend Alan, he wrote about Arthur Wharton, the first professional black footballer in England. He's dead now."

"Born in 1865," Eve said absently, now anxious to return to the cottage.

Trey's eyes widened in surprise. "How did you know?"

"I'm a woman," Eve chuckled, recalling a history teacher at Sabbath school forcing the information into her. "We know everything." She looked at the sky and detected the blue clouds rising. "I think we should get back now."

Trey followed her gaze. "Yeah," he agreed. "Theophilus will be home soon."

The moment they docked the boat, Eve stepped out and headed quickly toward the cottage. She had already premeditated what she was going to do: nose around in Professor de Cordova's bedroom. There were no scruples as to whether she was doing the right thing, nor did Eve care. Her vision was one-track and full of determination. It was a case of discovering the truth to satisfy all her doubts. At that point, nothing else mattered. Certainly not any pangs of conscience.

Trey ran ahead of her initially, but before they reached the cottage he slowed down, a dead giveaway he was tired. Eve had noticed him yawning on the boat. She was already aware he was looking sleepy from his journey. It occurred to her she should perhaps give him something to eat, which would present some delay as she had very little time to search the professor's room before he would be arriving home.

She was lucky. The moment they entered the cottage, Trey excused himself to lie down. "Can you look at my hamster later?" he asked.

"Of course," she agreed. "I'll just make myself a cup of tea."

When she heard his bedroom door close, Eve was up the stairs and across the landing, prying open the door to Theo's bedroom. She entered quickly and quietly closed it behind her. Darting her eyes around, she realized the room was empty. A mahogany four-poster bed, nicely made and draped with exceptional handmade bed coverings, leapt out at her as the main focus of the room. To one side was a mahogany chest of drawers, pants presser, and shoe rack. On the window side of the room was a large mahogany wardrobe and a small table with a laptop computer on it.

Eve wondered where to look first. There was a door by the side of the bed that was slightly ajar, appearing as though it could be a closet. Eve pondered the possibility of whether the professor kept his secret papers in there. But when she inched her head to one side and glimpsed a wash basin, she realized it was where the en suite bathroom was located adjoining the room.

She heaved a huge sigh, visibly not detecting any papers or folders anywhere. It was possible the professor had moved them elsewhere since showing the formula to Trey. Eve felt frantic at the mere possibility. How was she going to unearth the truth if she could not present the correct evidence to the assistant commissioner for checking at the Met?

She walked across to the window and caught the view from the back of the house. It looked across the valley, green with trees and fields. Birds, grouped together, flew across the darkened clouds as though answering to the dictates of nature. It occurred to her it might rain, and when she glanced at her watch, Eve realized she had less than three hours in Cramond before her train journey back to London.

She sighed again and turned to the task of searching

the professor's bedroom. But the moment Eve put her hands to her hips in readiness to begin the guileful chore, she was knocked dumb when the door to the en suite bathroom shot wide open, and Theo, standing tall and majestic like an ebony god, emerged and stared blankly at her.

He wore a blue towel around his waist, and his hairy chest and muscular body were wet, an indication that he had just stepped from the shower. Eve was aghast. She absorbed Theo's beguiled expression with nervous embarrassment. It was obvious from the way his face began to change to one of sheer amazement that he **had not expected to find her there**.

The dawning that she was actually in his bedroom came like a hammer blow to Eve's conscious senses. *What am I doing?* her mind screamed, astounded. It was one thing registering the professor's reaction, quite another to be questioning her own. And Eve was chagrined, for her body had begun to make its own adjustment to Theo's untimely presence.

Her wayward, primitive instincts were tangibly aware that the towel was the only impediment that concealed his naked flesh. That same subconscious also took the rare opportunity to assimilate his athletically structured physique: his rounded shoulders, medium-sized biceps, sturdy arms, and lean torso, tapered amiably to an equally trim waistline.

Her downward line of vision was broken the moment Theo shyly and protectively tightened the towel around himself. He was not fooled by Eve's dumbfounded exhibition. Beneath those sultry doe-eyes he had first admired at his seminar, he detected her sheer, unadulterated fascination with him.

"What are you doing in here?" he asked, his tone light and seemingly assuaged.

"I . . . I thought I heard something," Eve stuttered,

raising her hand to her throat where she nervously stroked and scratched at her neck. *What's going on?* her mind questioned.

"You've closed the door," Theo observed, walking boldly toward the foot of his bed where he leaned against the bottom post, folding his arms in wonder. "Why?"

Eve swallowed and briefly closed her eyes, thinking she could dispel the frisson of excitement that rushed through her body. Her heart was racing like a wild thing, and there was a throbbing sensation between her legs that made her feel like they had weakened suddenly. She tried to move them. They refused to budge, remaining rooted as though set in cement. Amazed at herself, more so by the fiery emotions cascading inside her, Eve choked out the only plausible lie she could muster.

"I didn't want to frighten Trey. He's gone to lie down."

"Is he all right?" Theo asked, his brows risen in concern.

"He's fine," Eve gushed, clasping her hands together, now recognizing that she was suffering from carnal sexual frustration. It was beginning to stifle her. "We went on the river in the rowboat. It was . . . wonderful." She paused to school her thoughts. "When . . . when did you get back?"

"About a half hour ago," Theo said softly, glancing at his watch. "I'd better get dressed and check on Trey. We're still on for dinner?"

Eve nodded, too overawed to speak. But at least her feet had regained motion. She was able to advance toward the door, deciding that she needed to repack her small suitcase and change her own clothing. She did not expect Theo to restrain her, yet no sooner had she passed the bottom post of his bed, than he took hold of her arm and gently tugged her toward him.

"Eve, wait."

His voice was soft and soothing, tainted heavily with raw emotion. Eve's gaze shifted to his face. For an instant she saw the snapshot of the man in the photo the assistant commissioner had given her. The image she had seen back then had been condemned guilty. Now, that same façade seemed innocent, humane, and most definitely sexy.

"If you'd like to attach your name to the Trust, then that's fine with me," he told her simply. "I'd be more than happy to have you on our team."

Eve willed herself to stand firm, conjuring a seductive smile to her face. It occurred to her that if she could coerce the professor to lie down, maybe offer him a massage, she could question him into revealing where he had stashed the formula.

"Why don't I give you a back rub—my way of accepting your offer to join the team," she suggested on impulse. And then her hand was at his waistline, gently pulling Theo toward his bed.

He seemed stunned by her performance and wavered a little, but this in no way dissuaded Eve from what she was doing. Standing in front of him, amazed at her blatant candor, she moved in closer until she felt the telling sign of his arousal press gently against her; the serpent provoked in the name of lust. It was a temptation too strong and too powerful for Eve. She was too weak to resist the yearning of her body for Theo to kiss her again.

"I've got magic fingers," she coaxed, raising her head to meet his gaze. Her heart quivered at how deeply he bore his dark eyes into her own, his head incredibly close. She thought that he might kiss her then, but Theo instead stroked her neck with the back of his hand, shaking his head as though in disbelief.

A silence enveloped them as her fingers crept up his arm to his shoulder. The silence stretched and twanged as she gently urged him to lie down on the mattress. On his back, he looked up at her bemused, his chocolate-brown gaze deepening with intrigue. Like a spider, Eve crawled over his knees, bracing her legs apart to straddle him until her bum rested neatly against his thighs.

"You have a lovely, strong chest," she complimented, working her fingers gently against the circles of black hair until they tickled her fingertips. "I suppose working so hard at the lab gives you very little time to relax."

She circled his nipples, delighting in the tremor she felt beneath the power of her hands. He made no comment and Eve took that as a clear sign that she was beginning to sedate him. Egged on, she used the balls of her palm to knead a gentle rhythm against the hardened muscles of his shoulders, exploring every dent and curve. "I'll do your back in a minute," she breathed, fighting the strongest of compulsions to kiss his clean flesh.

She skimmed a finger over his navel. It was soft. Well nestled. Cool. For a brief moment, Eve almost lost the thread of her intention. "I was wondering about your work," she began, keeping her hands busy. She saw his own hands squeeze the sheets ever so subtly and marveled at how well she was doing. "As the latest recruit to your foundation, does that allow me to know more about what you're working on?"

She spread her fingers for a repeat examination, but was grabbed immediately by her arm so that she tumbled onto the bed. In an instant, Theo took control and moved over her, gently pinning her down. Eve laughed and smiled up at him, thinking she still held all the aces. "I didn't expect that."

"I didn't expect to find you in my room, under me either," Theo returned huskily, suspicion mirrored in his eyes. "You're an oddball."

"Really?" she giggled, only because she wanted to deflect the longing to kiss him again.

His body was hard, like the manhood between his legs, and he looked restless and eager and fresh, the way a man might look when he was buffed, ready for a night of wild sex. Just what kind of lover Professor de Cordova would be presented itself as a fantasy in Eve's mind. Her pulse raced a little faster at the thought. He would be attentive, cheeky, a little on the exotic side. He would discover places Tyrone failed to behold. He would locate all her touch zones and take her into temporary madness—but not yet. She needed to know more about his formula. Whether it was responsible for her brother's death.

"In what way am I odd?" she murmured, running a hand along his neatly cornrow-braided head of hair. Their lips were only a breath apart.

"You're not angry that I didn't find time to listen to your ideas?" Theo began, his nostrils invigorated with the scent of her perfume. She looked a tempting picture of beauty to him with a flawless complexion that was an endless deception to her age. He found it difficult to swallow and felt his heart thud hard against his ribcage. Desire ate a hole in his groin. But he winced at the reminder that Eve did not feel the same way. He could not face another rejection by trying to kiss her again and so pulled his mouth a fraction away when she spoke.

"I'm not angry," Eve told him sweetly, deliberately softening her tone. She fluttered her eyelids in an attempt to hold him in her seductive lair, feeling his response with the tremor of his body against her own.

But Theo was not fooled. "Things have been hectic at the lab lately," he said, repressing his most primitive urges. Her persuasive nature had not won him over. "I hope you can forgive me."

Eve nodded, thoroughly dazed as he rolled over and glanced at his watch.

"I'll meet you downstairs."

"Yes . . . of course," she mustered, swallowing hard. Eve was taken aback by his sudden formality. By his supreme level of control. She watched in disbelief as Theo rose to his feet and walked away from her.

"Eve," he paused at reaching the en suite bathroom door. "I know what you told me last night, but if you ever wake up one morning and find that your heart wants to head north for a break from London, you'll always be welcome here."

It was polite courtesy. At least that's how Eve read it as Theo reentered the bathroom. Undignified, perhaps, but hardly tragic. Yet Eve was bitterly disappointed. She headed for the door, the wealth of ragged emotions scattered within her running riot. On the other side of the door, she was trembling. She had gone into that room to search it thoroughly and left searching for her own sanity. The professor had not tried to kiss her, but what did she expect? It was no less than what she had done turning him down the night before. He was respecting her wishes even though it now went against her growing desires.

So you're Adam's temptress? he had said with a characteristic hubris on her arrival to Scotland. Eve scoffed at the very notion. Right now, she felt as though she could not even tempt a fish to drink water. She could easily down a glass with cubed ice to cool the furnace the professor had lit inside her. Disillusioned, Eve turned and headed for the staircase, deciding to do just that. The burning cinders that were the residue of her arousal were an obvious distraction from changing her clothes for dinner, and she needed thinking time.

She hurried downstairs in a flurry and paused to compose herself. Then she saw it. The professor's open briefcase. It was on one of the ivory-veneered tables staring right at her. Eve's mouth fell agape when the yellow folder Trey had told her about met her gaze in an instant. Her mind went blank. Her fiery emotions were stunned. The wet ducts she knew were hidden at the back of her eyes brought on by her humiliation in Theo's bedroom held their place. The only conscious thought which trailed across Eve's mind was her mission for being in Cramond. Suddenly, the supreme image of what might have been, what life might have held, what the professor could have meant to her was sacrificed on a whim.

Eve did not question her actions. She did not even question her conscience. She did the only thing the assistant commissioner would have demanded of her and that was to be in possession of evidence which would prove Professor Theophilus de Cordova's involvement in her brother's death.

As Eve returned to her room, she did not realize she had been seen. Dr. Keplan, who was returning to the cottage, watched her every movement from the kitchen window and decided he would not disturb her.

Six

"I hope you're satisfied," Eve almost spat at the assistant commissioner when she handed over the yellow folder. "When I think what I had to go through for this . . ."

"Quite an achievement for two days," Humphrey applauded, ripping open the folder, which revealed a single sheet of paper with several complicated mathematical equations typed into various columns. He stroked his mustache. "With this I can nail that bastard who killed your brother. You should be congratulating yourself. We may get justice after all."

Eve was unconvinced and stared at the birds which hovered around in the cloudy sky above St. James's Park. Only yesterday, she had been in Cramond taking in the view of the island of Inchcolm, land of Macbeth, from the small bistro window where Theo had taken her and Trey to eat. The quintessential coastline view was fashioned in her head not in an appreciative manner of the river, where fishing for salmon or sea trout was the favorite pastime, but as a reminder that she had done something dreadfully wrong.

She had not enjoyed the generous helping of lamb, carrots, and potatoes, nor the red wine the professor had selected for their farewell drink. Instead, her mind had been filled with guilt, though she had camouflaged it quite well by schooling her features to one of cordial courtesy. By the time Theo had taken her to Waverley Station and beckoned her a safe journey home after their eyes had locked briefly in whimsical longing, she was nauseous with shame and wanted to confess to all her sins with as much repentance as was deemed fit for someone in her circumstances.

The train ride left her riddled with just as much remorse, so that by the time she called Humphrey Brown, she was more than relieved to finally divulge to someone what she had done. Of course, his reaction was not what she had expected. Even now, as Eve watched the assistant commissioner refasten his briefcase to safely secure the yellow folder she had given him, his voice was filled with the same jubilation she had heard through the telephone on her arrival home.

"Don't worry about a thing." He heartily patted her right knee, considering to himself that Eve looked a little peaky with her thin veil of make-up and her hair tied up away from her face. Dressed in a pair of faded denim jeans, a white V-necked jersey, and a houndstooth jacket, she appeared more unsettled than when he had last seen her. "I can take it from here."

"That's it?" Eve was alarmed. "I should just forget about what I've done?"

Humphrey raised his dark brows, confused. "Of course."

"I *stole* a top secret formula," Eve reminded him.

"You were doing me a favor," Humphrey Brown insisted. "For God's sake, I'm like an uncle to you. You *do* trust me?"

"Professor de Cordova trusted me," Eve quavered, twisting her fingers together in earnest. Theo's smiling face suddenly mirrored in front of her mind's eye and Eve heard herself gasp. "If he finds out what I've—"

"We'll get to him first," the assistant commissioner interrupted, standing. "I'm on my way to the Met now.

You go home and calm down. I'll call you the moment we make headway."

He kissed her on both cheeks and within seconds was gone. Eve remained seated on the bench and watched him hurry through the park toward the exit gate. Only when he disappeared through it did she get to her feet and dismally returned home.

Her watch read 3:00 P.M. when Eve turned the key in the lock. Her home was hidden within a row of houses on a long, thin street in Fulham, where a tiny blue door took her along a small cobbled courtyard to what looked like an industrial building. It was Eve's studio at the back basement of her house.

Jasmine Halpern, her personal assistant, was already finalizing the details for the charity fashion show that weekend. Eve did not feel up to the task of sorting her schedule with her usual burst of energy and enthusiasm. Rather she was filled with the awful foreboding that the assistant commissioner was chasing the wrong man.

"You said you would only be gone an hour," Jasmine bellowed as Eve slowly made her way into the room. "Leon's been wanting to talk to you. He said if you don't call him by 3:30, he's pulling out."

Eve shrugged and seated herself in a nearby chair, glancing at the boxes littered across the expanse of the floor, her collection chaotically strewn all over, ready for packaging. Jasmine, who was so absolutely right for her—a woman who liked to get things done promptly and dressed immaculately in a tailored green linen suit, her auburn relaxed hair shining as pristine as her Italian leather sandals, and with a clerical efficiency that was still as sharp as the day Eve hired her—was naturally a little agitated.

She stared blankly at her employer when she heard the silent retort, "Tell Leon to go to hell," drop from Eve's lips.

Jasmine registered the comment with acute alarm. "Eve!" She walked the length of the room and leaned against the long wooden refectory table often used by Charlotte McBrien, Eve's chief pattern cutter. "What's wrong with you?" Jasmine pressed, annoyed. "We can't jerk men like Leon Cavalli around. One bad word from him and you can kiss everything you've worked for good-bye."

"I'm sorry." Eve shook her head, placing her handbag on the table. "I'm just a little tired that's all. Where is everybody?"

"Joseph's gone to get himself a sandwich," Jasmine explained, her hazel gaze narrowing with serious intent.

She folded her arms against her chest, realizing she had not seen Eve so irrational since doing her show in February. She looked drained, her doe-shaped, dark brown eyes sullen in the sadness of her face. Unusually, she was not wearing mascara, and her make-up had been badly applied: just a touch of foundation powder to her complexion with no blusher, eye shadow, or gloss to her lips. She could see Eve was stressed and tried to be sympathetic. "He's been helping me hold the fort since you popped out, but he's really your finance administrator Eve. He's been trying to chase the thousands of pounds owed to you in invoices that date back for months."

"Any luck?"

"If he could get on with his work, he would fare better," Jasmine pointed out. "He's only been here a month and can't believe the state of your books."

"I hear you," Eve said absently, knowing full well she had neglected her business affairs since Paul had died. "I hope he doesn't tell me I've overbudgeted for this charity show, or I'm going to be pig sick."

"Charlotte's coming in tomorrow with the girls to press and pack your collection," Jasmine went on looking at the number of boxes around her. "And I've sent out all the press releases and guest invitations." Seeing Eve's disillusioned face, she added, "I thought those two days in Scotland would have done the trick."

"Excuse me?" Eve raised her head and glanced at Jasmine, bewildered.

"In helping you to forget Tyrone," she explained.

"Tyrone!" Eve exerted an hysterical giggle when she realized he was the least of her problems. In fact, she had not given her ex-fiancé a moment's thought since her arrival into London. "You wouldn't believe what's on my mind."

"Let me make you some coffee," Jasmine offered, already striding her way over to the beverage table. "You probably didn't get enough sleep, coming home so late last night."

Eve nodded, though she knew Jasmine was far off the mark. How could she tell anyone that she had gone up to Scotland on an unofficial covert operation and had ultimately stolen a secret formula from a foreign professor who happened to be the most handsome man she had ever met?

She removed her houndstooth jacket and placed it on her knees before burying her head in her hands. Eve tried to think. The only thing which sprung to mind was the objectivity of male models. Lord knows she had used enough of them, but Professor Theophilus de Cordova had that unique blend of sensual maturity marked into the faint lines on his face which she found so appealing; he rivaled any male Adonis she had ever worked with. Even now it was hard to reconcile that he was, in fact, a professor.

And when he had kissed her. . . . Eve's body stirred at the heady reminder. Every fiber in her body was alive. *Woozy, light-headed, dynamic*, were not words enough to describe what he had made her feel. It was temptation enough for any woman in her right mind to want to make love to him. She imagined it would be toe-curling sex. Oh, the bliss of it. If only she had not been so stupid as to steal his formula.

There was no way she could ever return to Cramond should she wake up one morning and her heart feel the urge to go north as he had suggested to her. No way for the opportunity to arise where she could take a bite into that Adam's apple she so desired.

"Eve!" She looked up to find Jasmine holding the handset of the telephone. "It's Marlene."

"Who?"

"Your mother."

She shook her head and whispered. "Tell her I'm not in."

"She knows you're here," Jasmine warned. "She's heard about Tyrone."

Eve closed her eyes and sighed heavily, picturing her mother's heavyset profile stampeding across the floor, her plump, brown face, alert velvet-colored eyes, and full, pink lips set in the permanency of a scowl. She did not have the headspace for this. Her brain cells could only deal with one thing at a time, and at that precise moment, she preferred to wallow in sympathy thinking how she could offer some form of apology to the professor for what she had done.

Eve knew it would only be a matter of time before he realized that his written formula was missing. That, within minutes, he would put two and two together and arrive at the correct conclusion that she has taken it from his briefcase. She felt shaken thinking about it. She took the telephone handset and dispelled that thought for a moment while Jasmine returned to making coffee.

"Mother!"

"Don't 'Mother' me," a voice quipped at the other end. "Is it true?"

Eve feigned ignorance. "Is what true?"

"No feisty with me," her mother broke into Caribbean lingo, uncustomary for a retired English teacher. "Tyrone left you?"

"Yes, Mother. I was jilted at merciless speed the instant I asked him whether he loved me."

"But kiss me neck back," Marlene said. "You ask him that de question?"

"Why shouldn't I have asked him?" Eve relented. "I needed to know."

"You should never ask a man that," her mother chastised. "When him know, he will tell you."

"**Well considering that he's never told me, Mother,** I think that should be answer enough."

"Now listen to me," Marlene started in a tone Eve recognized to be on the brink of dishing out an order that required obeying. "I want you to call Tyrone and tell him how you sorry."

"Me, sorry?" Eve feigned sarcasm.

"Just a little misunderstanding," Marlene continued. "Me sure him will come round, for him such a nice man. You can't be too fussy with a man like him."

Eve sighed again, imagining her mother now seated in the back-supporting chair she had bought for her sixtieth birthday. "Mother," she began. "I gave his ring back. It's over."

"But Lord in a heaven," Marlene choked. "You mean to say you a go pass by that nice, upstanding man because him no tell you him love you?"

"That's right, Mother," Eve concluded. "Until I hear those three little words, no man gets my heart."

She heard her mother whimper. Eve did not expect her to understand. Marlene was from another generation, which gave men more importance than they deserved because of their earning power. A woman's reliance then was not the same as it was now. Now their freedom allowed them the opportunity to search for true love. So Eve told herself. At least while of that belief, she was steadfast and firm.

"Me frighten for you," Marlene said finally. "Me fear you will never find a man."

Eve cast her eyes heavenward. She did not need to hear this now, not while Theo was still in the forefront of her mind. "I have to go mother," she restrained from letting out another sardonic remark. "I'll call you after I do my show."

She handed the phone back to Jasmine. "I believe I handled that very well," she said quietly. "Now all I need to do is deal with Leon Cavalli."

"Shall I call him now?" Jasmine asked, handing over a hot cup of coffee.

"Yeah," Eve nodded. "I may as well get it over with." She sipped her coffee and waited.

Only for a few seconds did Eve's mind stray to Theo in curiosity of what he might be doing at that precise moment. *Calling the police, no doubt,* she thought. It suddenly occurred to her that she could be arrested. Then what would she say? That she was working in collaboration with Assistant Commissioner Humphrey Brown of the Met. That the professor was suspected of being responsible for her brother's murder. That the charges of theft would have to be related to a vital clue linked to a possible homicide. It all seemed so surreal. She sipped more coffee then stared blankly at Jasmine.

"I have Leon on the line."

Eve nodded and took the receiver. Folding one knee over the other, she smiled sweetly. "Leon! How are you?"

"You've got a nerve," he objected murderously. Eve winced at his tone. "You disappear for two days without a word, without so much as leaving me your mobile number. No one at your office knew how to contact you. Do you think my time isn't worth money?"

"Leon, I'm sorry," Eve attempted an apology, his murderous expression of dark brows knitted together beneath his brown, shaved head flashing before her very eyes. "I took a couple of days off to go up to Scotland for—"

"Lucky for some," Leon interrupted. "Well, while you were, no doubt, putting your feet up over a whisky and dry, I've been designing your pavilion. You do remember you're part of *Style Paradise* this weekend at Miss Shola Onyeocha and her partner's chateau in aid of the Nelson Mandela Children's Fund?"

"Of course, I remember," Eve said, quite peeved, visualizing he was probably at that precise moment pacing the floor in his black boots and skin-tight leather pants, spitting smoke from a cigarette.

"For a designer who should be running around panicking, you're taking all this remarkably calmly," Leon objected. "I have had to make one thousand and one decisions without your approval. Without even knowing anything about your collection, except the brief your assistant, whatshername, Jasmine gave me."

Eve was convinced she could feel a headache coming on. "I'm sure I'll be more than happy with your work," she told Leon. "Especially from someone who's worked with the likes of Giorgio Armani, Donatella Versace, and Stella McCartney. I've learned to delegate without complaint."

"As your show designer, I expected better cooperation," he sadly rebuffed. "It may not be as high key as the *Frock 'n' Roll* festival last year, but *Style Paradise* will give your collection world coverage." He paused, and Eve felt the frisson of his anxiety run down the telephone line. "When are you planning to arrive in Paris?" his voice suddenly demanded.

"Friday," Eve flinched without thinking how she was going to make the trip to the small village she had never heard of seventy-five miles west of Paris.

"That's a novelty," Leon derided. "I'll have one day of your company to finalize everything. When will the models be arriving for a rehearsal?"

"What?"

"Hello!" Leon derided. "Are we on the same planet?"

Obnoxious little prick, Eve ranted quietly to herself. "Leon, let me call you tomorrow morning with all the details," Eve promised. "Right now, I need . . ." *A large brandy,* sprung to mind. ". . . to make some calls."

"You can't afford to mess up," Leon warned suddenly. "Some of the best in fashion's upcoming designers are going to be at this event with pavilions. There's going to be a champagne reception, followed by dinner, a fireworks display, and a charity auction."

"I know," Eve insisted.

"And I heard today the Sean John collection is definitely going to be showing," Leon added with enthusiasm. "So you're up against a lead contender on what the African-Americans have on offer."

"I get the picture," Eve sighed exasperated.

"Just so that we're clear," Leon advised. "Call me tomorrow."

The phone clicked off and Eve stared at Jasmine in disbelief. Leon Cavalli was a hard act to follow, but that was precisely what she had hired him for. To do the job properly. "Just tell me we have the models sorted," she breathed, desperate to hear something in the affirmative.

"You checked them last week, before you went to Scotland," Jasmine reminded. "Have you forgotten?"

Obviously, Eve blinked, recalling the occasion from the deepest recesses of her mind. Her trip to Scotland had apparently thrown her in more ways than she cared to realize. "Afrique Model Agency. Right."

"You really are tired," Jasmine decided. "I suppose it's all that business with your brother."

"What?"

"Scotland. The memories," Jasmine said in sympathy. "I suppose that's why you went up there. It'd be nearly a year now since he—"

"I know," Eve nodded.

"Why don't you go and lie down," Jasmine offered. "I'll clue Joseph in and lock up. We'll see you in the morning."

That was the best idea Eve had heard all day. "Thanks."

She downed what was left of the coffee, picked up her handbag and jacket, threw Jasmine a grateful smile, and then left her studio through the stable-style door which took her to the ground floor of the three-story house she called home. Essentially an enormous kitchen and dining room, the centerpiece of which was a floor-to-ceiling glass-fronted cabinet full of dolls dressed in the most elaborate of her designs, it was the one place Eve felt she could really relax.

The second floor was street level where a Victorian bathroom and a huge lounge painted white and covered with colorful wall hangings of rural Africa were located. She had designed it with gigantic white sofas which took up most of the bleached beech wooden floor space and had draped the large windows in white to reflect light into the room. The top floor contained her bedroom and a spare room, both dominated by wrought-iron beds, gauzy white linen, and potted green plants, though using her bed right now did not appeal to Eve in the slightest. She was feeling out of sorts with herself and needed something soothing like a hot bath.

Eve sighed and placed her jacket and handbag on the

kitchen table and turned to make her way toward the stairway which led directly to her bathroom. No sooner had she done so with a sobering heart and feeling blissfully unhappy, than the stable door behind her shot open and Eve was struck dumb when Professor de Cordova barged in. A flustered Jasmine followed quickly behind, quite startled.

"I'm sorry," Jasmine breathed, her voice weakened in awe of the man. "I couldn't stop him."

Eve stared, immobilized. "Theo!" she gasped. "What do you want?"

He took large pantherlike strides toward her, his chocolate-brown eyes ensnaring her like a wild animal. "My formula," came the harsh reply. "And I want it now."

Eve panicked and looked at Jasmine. Her personal assistant was obviously affected by Theo's magnetic presence. She was rooted to the spot, simply staring at him. "I can deal with this," she assured her assistant quickly.

Jasmine remained unsure, eyeing Theo speculatively as though studying a pop idol. "If you prefer that I stay—"

"No!" Eve returned her gaze to Theo. "I need to explain something in private."

"This had better be good," Theo bellowed, as Jasmine nodded while throwing the professor one last wistful look before reluctantly leaving the kitchen. He was standing directly opposite Eve now and she felt that her knees were about to weaken when her mind balked at the word 'handsome.'

Everything about the professor leant a certain latent *power* to his demeanor, from his cornrow braided hair, his chin, rough with a night's coarse growth of beard, to the ruffled ivory-colored pants and white shirt he was wearing beneath a suede brown jacket. His roguish appearance had its own primitive appeal, but Eve could tell from the look in Theo's eyes that he was not about to swim neck deep in the attraction he could plainly see she had toward him.

"How did you find me?"

"Lola was more than accommodating," Theo thundered.

"Theo—"

"You were about to tell me what happened to my formula," he bluntly interrupted.

Eve wavered. "How did you get here so—"

"Quickly?" Theo finished, his tone harsh and menacing. "Plane and a rented car." He paused. "Well?"

Eve nervously gazed at him and saw his loathing for her. Her heart was immediately jolted with immense guilt as she spoke. "I don't have your formula," she told him, embarrassed.

"Then who in the hell does?"

Eve came clean, her eyes glazed with tears. "His name is Humphrey Brown. He's the assistant commissioner for the Metropolitan Police."

"Wait a minute," Theo gasped, thrown by her admission, both hands resting arrogantly against his hips. "Are you telling me you're a cop?"

"No!" Eve reared back, her voice quivering. "I was doing him a favor. He's like an uncle to me."

"You've got one hell of a nerve," Theo blazed, lunging straight for her arm. He caught it in a viselike grip and held on tightly. "After meeting you like I did, after—"

"Say it." Eve dared to meet his fiery gaze. "After you kissed me."

Theo eyes bore directly into her stare. "You used me in Scotland."

"I didn't plan to get involved with you," Eve declared, seeing the hurt behind his gaze. "It wasn't meant to happen."

"A regular she-devil, are you?" Theo accused. "I was easy game?"

"It wasn't like that."

"How was it Eve?" Theo asked harshly, his grip digging into her skin. "How was it that you were invited into my home, given full hospitality, met my son, and then walked away with my life's work?"

The tears threatened. "I didn't expect to care about you."

Theo blinked. "That's rich," he sneered. "Well here's a good one for you. My work at the lab, it's not on genetically modified crops. What I do there is at the cutting edge of biological warfare."

Eve stared. She was stunned. *Biological warfare.* In a small place like Cramond? "So Dr. Da Costa was right," she mouthed, thinking aloud as the pieces she could not quite fathom fell into place.

"It's top secret work," Theo continued, "But you have a strange way of showing how much you care, considering you may have just caused a situation here. I can't imagine that'll bother you too much, either, so spare me any crocodile tears."

"I don't know what you mean," Eve defended tearfully. "Humphrey Brown told me that—"

"That I'm working as a specialist consultant for the United Nations Drug Control Program," Theo revealed arrogantly. "That I had experimented on a fungus spore and created a formula that could effectively wipe out every drug crop grown around the world."

Eve's mind went blank, such was her shock in discovering the truth. "I thought—"

"You didn't think," Theo hotly accused. His grip tightened. "Next week I'm expected to deliver my pathological research in front of a seminar. What do I tell them?"

"The real truth," Eve spat out, attempting now to free herself from his hold. "You killed my brother."

Theo let her go immediately, his eyes narrowing with incredible disbelief. "What are you talking about?"

"My brother, Paul, worked for you," Eve told him sternly. "Last year, he was murdered. You didn't come to his memorial service, and now I believe that this top secret formula you were working on was responsible for his death."

Theo stepped back, raising both hands in a display of innocence. "Whoa!" He shook his head as though the blow hit hard. "I'm sorry for your loss, but I don't know where you're coming from. I've never heard of Paul Hamilton."

"You must have heard of him," Eve raged in allegation. "He worked for you. You were the last person to see him alive."

"No one of that name has ever worked for me," Theo yelled back, his Brazilian accent now pronounced in his anger. "Who told you that?"

"The assistant commissioner."

"Humphrey Brown," Theo acknowledged, his tone tinged with worry. He folded his arms beneath his chest and spoke harsh and sternly. "I'd like a word with this *uncle* of yours 'cause I sure as hell would like to get my formula back. Preferably before he does something stupid with it."

"He's investigating you on a possible homicide," Eve said, shocked by what Theo was telling her. "I can't imagine him wanting to use it for anything other than to force a conviction."

"You don't get it, do you?" Theo blazed. "Whoever killed your brother is the person *he* was working for. If that wasn't me, then who else could it have been?"

"I don't know," Eve screamed.

"No, you don't know much do you?" Theo roared

furiously. "Well until you figure out that this dear father figure . . . family friend . . . uncle of yours has been lying to you, I'm going after my formula. What's his number?"

"I'm not telling you," Eve defended, enraged. She had known Humphrey Brown a long time—her entire life, in fact. In her mind he could never betray her. But there was so much confusion, so many things left unexplained that Eve hardly knew what to think anymore. She needed answers, and she needed them from someone she could trust. "I'll call Humphrey Brown."

"You do that," Theo conceded, annoyed beyond his normal endurance. "Have him suggest a time and place, then tell him I'll cooperate."

"You'll find you're very wrong about him," Eve declared, reaching into her handbag for her mobile phone. "He's a fair man."

Theo eyed Eve in disappointment that his fears had been confirmed. He had hoped she was not working for an outsider, had prayed for his suspicions about her not to be proven. Now Theo found himself faced with the awful predicament that he must ditch this woman and fast. If only his heart would agree.

"For your sake, I hope you're right," he conceded, sighing with deep dissatisfaction that she could have fooled him and let him down. "Because as long as he has my formula, your assistant commissioner is living on the sharp edge of life, not the blunt one."

Seven

"I don't see why I need to come along," Eve complained as she glanced through the car window at the flotsam of traffic. "Humphrey has agreed to meet you, as I said he would."

"Let's just call it a little insurance policy," Theo derided, steering the rented car at full speed along the M25 freeway that circled London. "I am surprised, though, that it didn't take me much coaxing to get you here," he added with derision. "You accused me of killing your brother, remember? I would've thought you'd be thinking you're next on my list."

"If you must know," Eve said, turning her head sideways from where she was seated in the passenger seat to take a good look at Theo. He was wearing Foster Grant shades so she could not see his eyes, but it was evident he was still simmering with his anger. "There was something about you which made me think that the assistant commissioner must have made a mistake."

"Didn't stop you from taking something you knew was forbidden," Theo vented his fury.

"I was only trying to help Humphrey Brown," Eve tried to explain in vain. "When he showed me your picture, I knew—"

"My picture!" Theo's heavy foot slammed on the accelerator, pumping the car to go faster. "You *knew* what I looked like before you met me?"

Eve's body shook at the inadvertent slip of information. "I wanted to find out who killed my brother," she yelped. "It wasn't personal. And if what you're saying is true, Humphrey Brown will have no choice other than to eliminate you from his inquiries."

"A woman's relative stupidity is probably her greatest resource," Theo chided, swerving his way through traffic. "I suppose your naiveté is what's gotten you this far."

Eve felt the tears sting in her eyes. "I'm trying to undo the mess I've caused," she said. "And I'm sure Humphrey Brown will apologize, too. He was only trying to find out who killed Paul and bring them to justice."

"Just how did your brother die?" Theo demanded, intrigued.

"A car bomb," Eve whimpered, dipping her head. "In Edinburgh. Humphrey Brown organized his memorial. He was a rock when my mother and I needed him, and he was very cut up about how my brother died. They were very close."

Theo paused to correlate the information while negotiating traffic. When he finally spoke, his voice had mellowed slightly. "There's an old saying in my country," he said flatly. "If you find out how a victim lived, you'll find out how he died."

"Are you saying my brother was . . . doing something he oughtn't?" Eve asked, her voice cracked with emotion.

"I'm sorry about your brother," the professor began, "but—"

"Don't say that," Eve jabbed, her nerves agitated. "You don't have the right."

"I have every right," Theo returned, equally discomfited. "You try to place my neck in a noose, then expect me to roll over like a hyena? You pay a lot of lip service to how good your brother was, but did it ever occur to you that he may have been responsible for what happened to him?"

"Stop the car," Eve railed. "I want to get out."

"We're on the freeway," Theo harangued.

"I don't have to listen to this," Eve bellowed tearfully. "You're just trying to make me feel worse than I do already because I handed your formula over to the Met."

Theo pulled the car into the fast lane, his frustration brewing to a boil as he gunned the engine, pushing the speed to eighty mph, which just about registered the level of his choler toward Eve. "Where do you get off?" he came right back at her. "I'm the one suffering the sins of your brother and the hapless one you've committed against me. And right now, I don't know what I'm walking into. A double-cross or—"

"You're thinking I'm setting you up?" Eve breathed in amazement. Couldn't this man see that she was doing the best she could to repair the situation? She had thought about telling him how sorry she was, but now she decided he could go to hell. "You're something else."

Theo shot her a considering look and immediately slowed the car on seeing the hurt in her face. Eve did not just look mortified by what he had insinuated about her brother, but seemed wounded by his further accusation. There was, of course, every reason in his heart for him to level such complaints. He had found her in possession of his wallet, then she had been in his bedroom appearing nervous. Looking for something, he now realized. Naturally, he had to remind himself that it was on his invitation that she had visited his home in Scotland, but that was by the by. It did not give her reason to steal his formula. And it certainly did not give her any leverage to tickle his fascination for her either. He was vexed.

From the moment they had met, he had had his suspicions. They may have been wrong at first and he would have kept up his vigilance in trying to discover what lay behind her interest in collaborating a fund-raiser with his foundation had he not found Eve so damned attractive. Even now, with her hair pulled away from her face, her brown eyes teary, she looked like that adorable, innocent woman who had first confronted him at the seminar he'd held in Oxford.

Little did he know then that their meeting was all part of her elaborate, calculating scheme contrived to infiltrate his laboratory. She may not have gotten away with his real achievement, he told himself secretly, but the very fact she had successfully laid her hands on something just as important rattled him to the core. He was vexed.

He liked Eve. Correction. Theo was loath to admit he adored her, and with that admission, he felt the pain. He still found it hard to believe a woman of her years could possess such youthful features, a shapely body, and a successful, creative mind. Equally, he would not have expected a woman of her caliber to be orchestrating a deceitful act against him. So what if her motives were to find her brother's murderer. So what if she had told him their kiss had left her cold. To him, it had been an intensely fiery experience, it still lingered in his mind long after the event.

There would be no repeat performance now that she had revealed her true colors. He would have to be a crazy man to want to go back there. So why did the very thought of not being with her make him feel like he had reached the end of the world? Was it because he never wanted a woman more than he wanted Eve Hamilton right now? Even after everything she had done? Theo's mind was in conflict with the dictates of his body.

His very fiber was drawn toward her, his nostrils could not help but pick up her scent, and, if he was truly honest, when he had first stormed into her kitchen to confront her for what she had done, his first instinct had been to hug her, such was his joy at seeing her again.

More the fool he was, he chastised himself, the ache of her deceit deepening further. If he was going to survive this, he would have to keep his head. That meant putting the image of Eve with her tempting eyes, full, pink lips, wonderful chestnut-brown complexion, and the memory of their kiss firmly at the back of his mind.

"Why are we not meeting this assistant commissioner at his office headquarters?" he challenged, his unease now amplified by his distrust for Eve. More so by the notion that she had not even offered him an apology. "Don't I get to make a formal statement?"

"You haven't been charged with anything," Eve returned despondently. "I'm sure there'll be a good explanation."

"You really *do* trust this uncle of yours," Theo recognized with an acute measure of compassion, his Brazilian accent softening slightly. "I'm not accustomed to meeting a member of the nation's protective forces in a public park. Either I've lost my senses, or I should be calling my attorney."

"You said I was your insurance policy," Eve derided with a hint at irony. "I should be back in my studio trying to finalize a thousand and one things for a show I'm doing on Saturday."

"And I should be back in my laboratory in Scotland finalizing my research for my seminar on Monday at the International Antidrugs Summit," Theo announced scathingly.

A summit! Eve rubbed an unsteady finger against her right brow. Just what kind of adventure had she gotten herself into? "Look . . ." She paused. "If I can take time out to try and make amends for what I've done and Humphrey Brown can, too," she implored him in earnest, forcing a slight smile, "then I'm sure you can understand why we're being discreet. No one is trying to abuse either your reputation or mine."

"Considering you're already an unscrupulous, scurvy, little mercenary," Theo attacked. "With a devil-made-me-do-it smile, which isn't going to work on me."

"You'll get your formula back with an apology," Eve yelled. "I made a mistake and I was wrong. I'm sorry."

There. She had said it. It was a long time coming, but Eve finally knew that if she were to release the built up anguish that had plagued her over the last few days—the last few months—she would logically be admitting to herself that Professor de Cordova could not possibly be responsible for killing Paul. Of course, she had always known this in her heart. She just had a harder time telling herself so. Now that she had verbalized the truth, Eve felt she could relinquish some of the grief.

"I was wondering when you were going to get around to that," Theo addressed, momentarily facing her head on. "What are you anyway? Creole?"

Eve repressed a weak chuckle at the suggestion. "Hey! Less of that." She paused. They shared a moment's silence in reflection of having greeted each other with nothing but resentment and anger. "How's Trey?" Eve finally asked, deciding she would make the first move to bridge the gap between them.

"He's fine," Theo answered. "Missing me of course, but that cannot be helped."

She winced. "He's with your housekeeper?"

"She wasn't too pleased," Theo returned just as quickly.

Eve leaned against the padding of the passenger seat, dejected and unnerved. "You'll be back in Scotland with Trey by nightfall," she assured. "I won't cause you any more trouble."

The professor eyed her despairingly. He had not

wanted to shout and he certainly did not want to be parted from Eve so soon. He only wished he could calm himself, but his feelings were mixed with all manner of emotions. Uppermost in his mind was the letdown he felt by her misuse of his trust, made worse by the fact that it had come from a woman he was immensely attracted to and whom he had hoped in his heart would see again. Equally so, he had to remind himself that she did not feel the same way about him, causing his innards to churn in a potent cocktail of anger and frustration.

It made him edgy. "Let's hope you're right," he acknowledged, steering the car off the freeway toward central London. Could he forgive her when he got his formula back? He would have to wait and see.

The car was parked three blocks away. Professor de Cordova and Eve Hamilton were on foot, making their way through the gates of St. James's Park where they had agreed to meet Assistant Commissioner Humphrey Brown. They were on time, five o'clock on the button. Eve led the way toward the bench where she had kept her prior meetings with the assistant commissioner.

"I'll do the talking," Theo prompted, walking steadily beside her, his hand holding casually onto her right elbow, his eyes still hidden beneath his dark shades. "And no heroics."

"Get a grip," Eve scoffed, throwing him a derisive look. "This is England, not *Miami Vice.*"

"Just show me the place," Theo said sternly. He glanced around the park seeing nothing extraordinary. It was a lovely day for the end of May. Puffy white clouds in the sky, the sun peeking out every now and then. Few people sparsely situated around the park walking their dogs. There was no need to worry that he might be hoodwinked without a moment's notice.

"There he is." Eve pointed to a park bench directly ahead where she could see Humphrey Brown seated alone waiting for them. She waved to prompt his attention, but he appeared not to have noticed her. "He's reading a newspaper," she told Theo as they inched closer.

The professor looked over his shoulder. Meeting the assistant commissioner in such a wide open space did not feel right, but he could not see anything suspicious to alert his attention. He eyed Humphrey Brown as they came closer. The man looked normal enough, though his head was buried in a copy of the *Nubian Chronicle*. A gray-brown face, mustache, piercing brown eyes which stared coldly ahead, Theo girded himself to face the assistant commissioner head on.

"Humphrey Brown?" he started, straightening his shoulders expectant of a direct, militarylike response. "I'm Professor de Cordova. We need to talk."

"We came as soon as we could," Eve added, immediately seating herself next to the assistant commissioner. When he continued to stare silently ahead, she frowned. "You don't look yourself."

"Eve!" Theo slowly removed his Foster Grants and arched his brows, his eyes narrowing suddenly.

"Maybe we should . . ." She touched his arm, and slowly, bonelessly, Humphrey Brown slumped to the ground, leaving a smear of blood on the back of the bench. Eve froze. She did not scream, her mouth agape in total shock.

She had never seen a dead person before. The jolt of seeing the assistant commissioner hunched on the ground, his walnut-brown complexion gray as mud, his eyes wide open and yellow, left her paralyzed. He was holding a white piece of paper in his hand, and her only movement was to point at it, her mouth still agape.

Theo reached down and immediately pried it out

from between Humphrey's fingers then took a hold of Eve by the arm. "Come on," he ordered, putting every effort into dragging Eve to her feet. He placed the paper and his shades into his breast pocket. "We need to get out of here, now."

Lost of all manner of speech, Eve simply nodded. A glance over her shoulder as Theo rushed her away from the scene left her with the image of two people rushing toward the dead body. One of them looked over at her, almost in recognition and then there was the sound of a loud scream.

"Shit," Theo bristled, as he saw two foreign men at the park gate, dressed in plain gray suits hustling toward them.

Eve's mind was in a daze. Her vocal cords were numbed. She hadn't a clue what was going on.

"This way." Thinking fast, Theo shoved her in the opposite direction which led down a pathway filled with trees and shrubbery. He had no idea where the path led, only hurried along it with Eve in pursuit behind. "You're going to have to keep up," he yelled, reaching for her hand in an attempt to pull her along.

The image of Humphrey Brown was still fresh in Eve's mind as she grabbed Theo's fingers. A shiver skimmed along her skin when she imagined the sound of a gunshot being fired. "I'll keep up," she murmured, finding her voice.

The path took them directly to a perimeter fence. They jumped over and landed on the street. Cars zoomed by in a flurry of rush-hour noise. Eve had to blink at the sudden reminder she had been thrust into reality.

Theo spun on the spot, adrenalin pumping through his veins. "Damn. The car's on the other side of the park," he breathed, furious. "We need a cab."

They ran along the sidewalk, side by side, scanning

the road as they went along hoping to flag down an available taxi. If there was a matrix to their escape, Eve could not see it. The professor meandered down streets, zigzagged his way through human traffic, even had her jumping over fences until her breath was haggard from the effort of keeping pace.

They were watched by onlookers with surprise, some sidling expectantly out of their way as though collaborating their effort to get away. And all the time, Theo kept looking over his shoulder, checking to make sure she was still with him, one eye trained on the way ahead with no plan as to where they were going. Eve had no idea where the two men were, her only thought trusting in Theo. When he finally dragged her down the stairs toward an Underground station, she had to grip the rails to slow her descent lest she fall due to the strong pressure of his pull.

"Don't stop now," Theo warned. His gaze looked over her head and for the first time, Eve saw panic in those deep, chocolate-brown eyes she had come to know so well. "They're behind you."

Eve did not dare look, deciding instead to take Theo's word for it. Holding his hand, she followed his fast tread as he calculated his way through the mass of people, noting that he was keeping his head down so that his towering frame would not attract attention. Every now and then, his eyes would stray sideways to divert his way from where the two men were located.

"We haven't got tickets to use the trains," Eve told him as they approached the turnstiles. She was perspiring heavily. The weather had become quite humid, making her feel sticky and uncomfortable.

"Do you think I don't know that?" Theo muttered, working his way around the crowd. He could see a guard talking with a young mother holding her baby. She had a stroller and luggage and needed to use the gate for admittance to the trains. "Follow me." They were greeted by the crying baby. "Let us help you with that," Theo told the mother, immediately handing Eve both luggage bags and himself gripping the stroller. "We're going down to the platform."

The mother nodded gratefully and Theo led the way ahead, offering the guard a polite nod with his head to distract him from asking to see their tickets. The ploy worked. Theo tossed his head back to find the two men standing in frustration at the turnstiles, their hands frantically digging into their pockets for loose change. He had not lost them. Theo figured they had five minutes before the hunt would begin again.

"Where are they?" Eve asked as the escalator took them downward.

"Buying tickets," Theo returned, feeling a sudden sting in his right shoulder. "We're going to have to get on a train as quick as we can. Can you handle it?"

Eve nodded. It was all she could do after seeing a murder and running for her life. On reaching the platform, they set the mother and her baby to rights then ran the length of it to the far end. There were a lot of people of different nationalities and cultures, chattering in a variety of languages while waiting for the train. Theo glanced over his shoulder and squeezed Eve's hand tightly. She knew it was a signal that they had been followed.

It was all timing now, she knew, as a mild wind brushed against her face. The train was coming. She could hear the rattle of the floor beneath her and the clinking sound the tracks made. Theo pulled her along suddenly and Eve turned to find the two men fighting their way through the crowd. The train's arrival made it all the more difficult for them. People were getting on and off the cars, and Theo had ducked his head so they could not mark his location.

He pulled her into a car, keeping his head down. Sandwiched in a cluster of Muslim women, dressed in their black *abaayas* and wearing cheap dark veils over their faces, they were hidden from view of the open doors. Eve's heart lurched in trepidation. It was now ultimately down to luck. The waiting seemed to last eons, to the point that Eve squeezed Theo's chubby fingers by way of deflecting her feelings to one of solidarity. Then she heard the doors closing and felt the movement beneath her feet as the train slowly pulled out of the Underground station. She looked up to find Theo grinning and offering a half salute to the two men.

A quick glance through the window across from where she was hidden among the haven of Islamic women and she could see them standing frustrated on the platform. *We are safe,* Eve thought. *Safe at last.*

"Where are we going?" she asked, feeling exhausted and sick. She observed the satisfied look mirrored across Theo's face. He had pressed his back against the wall of the car where he leaned the bulk of his weight, tired and sapped of strength.

"My flat in Mayfair," he told her with relief, pulling her by the wrist from among the women so that she was within inches of his chest. The strong scent of his sweat and the power which emanated from him tickled her nerve endings, but Eve was not swayed by the potency of her attraction toward Theo this time.

"Don't touch me," she wavered, pulling her wrist away, her body now shaking with emotion. She could feel the rising pool of sorrow in the pit of her stomach which made her all the more reluctant to obey her instinctive pull. "This is your fault."

"*My* fault?"

"Yes, your fault."

"Oh, please!" Theo cast his eyes heavenward, grimacing as he felt a sudden spasm of pain run down his arm. "We got away."

Eve's lips trembled. "Humphrey Brown did not."

She turned her face from him and looked through the car window, grateful that Theo chose not to comment, but instead left her to privately wallow in her anguish. She was back in that hollow place she knew so well, the place which did not weep at Paul's memorial, nor get upset when Tyrone had walked out. Eve told herself she would not fill the empty space now with tears. But as the Underground train sped along the darkened tunnels, the bleak and gloom hemming her in, Eve realized the world's troubles were beginning to build. Then the first tear fell.

Eight

"You knew this was going to happen, didn't you?" Eve accused as Theo turned the key in the lock and watched her storm into his apartment. "That's what you meant when you said Humphrey Brown was living on the sharp edge."

"I didn't expect him to wind up dead," Theo said, wondering how he was going to knock the grief out of her. She had cried all the way into Mayfair, thumped against his chest on two occasion while they had switched trains, and just when he thought she had spent her tears, here she was starting the waterworks again. "I'll get you a brandy."

"Make it a large one," Eve wept as she angrily threw her bag into the nearest chair on her approach into a large sitting room.

Theo made his way directly toward a period chiffonier, wincing briefly as pain shot across his right shoulder as he quickly turned over two glasses situated on a silver tray and reached for a decorative glass decanter. Twisting the top, which required little effort, he added generous proportions to both glasses and carried them toward Eve. She almost snatched one from him and downed the strong stuff in one fell swoop, her actions making it evident to Theo she was more upset than he had first realized. "Maybe you should sit down."

"You sit down," Eve sobbed, holding his gaze and

wondering why Theo was grimacing. "I want to know exactly what's going on. I want to know . . . why . . . why . . . he's dead."

The tears fell in large drops down her crestfallen cheeks. She was in mourning and equally as terrified. Theo stood patiently watching her, feeling helpless. Then following his natural instincts, he took Eve into his arms and held her close. In the quiet haven, snuggled against his chest, he claimed her shaking body and thought less about the pain in his right shoulder as he allowed her to bawl.

Eve was not aware she was embraced against this formidable man whom she had been told was the enemy. Her only thought was to cling to something alive. Breathing. Warm and safe. She tried to formulate in her head step by step what had happened, but her grief made it impossible to think. The only vision which sprung to mind was Humphrey Brown's sprawled body on the ground. And with that awful picture came more stored tears. Some were for her father. She cried for her brother. She even cried for being abandoned by Tyrone. It all emptied in heavy sobs from deep within her soul.

"What am I going to tell my mother?" she wept, her eyes tightly closed, her cheek pressed hard against the suede jacket Theo was wearing.

"Don't tell her anything," Theo urged, running his left hand across her shoulders in comfort. "You're still in delayed shock."

"But he sounded . . . he sounded okay on the phone," Eve remarked, uneasily. "What happened?"

Theo sighed. In his mind, there was only one thing that could have happened. The assistant commissioner was on the brink of selling his formula. What occurred was either someone covering their tracks or punishing the colporteur. "There's been a backhander on the deal," he told Eve as gently as he could. "I think this *uncle* of yours was doing something illegal."

Eve raised her head, alarmed, her tear-stained face swollen. "What are you talking about?"

"You really should sit down," Theo advised, feeling weakened and knowing he should be seated himself. He took the empty glass from her shaky fingers and inclined his head toward a French walnut sofa, styled with a carved frame and cabriole legs. "Let me get you another brandy."

Eve reluctantly took his advice. Shedding her hounds-tooth jacket, she angrily threw herself onto the sofa, pushing her jacket to one side in frustration. She took a quick glance across the room through her tears, seeing in front of her a rosewood coffee table designed with ormolu mounts, a Queen Anne walnut longcase clock in the room's corner, two cabriole leg chairs carved with cabochons at the knees and a rosewood chiffonier housing books in the cabinet below with decorative decanters filled with all manner of liquor on the open shelf above. Then her eyes fell on Theo pouring more brandy.

The expanse of the room was made more beautiful by deep-pile beige carpeting beneath her feet and the large windows facing her, which would ordinarily let in plenty of daylight, though vertical blinds were now shielding the early evening glow.

Theo returned to stand over her, handing over the half-filled glass. Eve reached for it, immediately taking a sip. The first glass had knocked the shock out of her, and she suspected this one would now soothe her anxiety. But what it would not do was erase the fact that Assistant Commissioner Humphrey Brown was dead.

"Who were those two men?" she demanded hotly, her nerves still jiggered.

Theo joined her on the sofa, seating himself close. "I

don't know. Dealers probably." He took a shot of his brandy and closed his eyes to feel its effect numbing the pain in his right shoulder.

"Dealers!" Eve threw him a sidelong look.

"Eve," Theo began, leaning back into the sofa, his eyes still closed as though there were a weight on his shoulders that needed to be absolved. He opened them again and held her gaze. "Either your uncle couldn't be bribed, or he couldn't be trusted."

The slap came clean and swift. Eve had not expected to release her frustration in such a precise manner. She had tried to find meaning to the danger they had just faced and was no closer to the truth about Theo's involvement in the whole mystery surrounding her brother's murder than when she had first met him. Now two murderous, shadowy adversaries had pumped her adrenalin, which carried her through the streets of London on the brink of a frenzy until her body protested against the agony of her situation. She was at her wit's end to think it could all have been the assistant commissioner's fault.

"I just want to know one thing," she demanded, her voice high on a crackle. "What is Phoebe and who's prepared to kill us for it?"

She is not as innocent as she looks, the professor thought, rubbing the sting Eve's handprint had left on his left cheek. In looking at her, he could plainly see how unnerved she had become. She had lied and schemed against him to find her brother's killer and now was suffering the consequences. She deserved to be told the truth, he decided. Whether she could stomach it all was another matter.

"All right," he nodded in agreement, moving weakly forward to place his brandy glass on the nearby coffee table. "I think it's time we both came clean. Seeing as

I don't like being lied to, and you were the one who was staking me out, I think you should go first."

Eve's eyes blazed as her brandy glass joined Theo's on the coffee table with a bang. "Fine," she snapped, taking her mind back to her first meeting with the assistant commissioner. "You were our number one suspect," she began. "My brother died last year in a car bomb explosion. The only thing we knew was that he was working for you. There was an inquest, but it didn't show anything, so after we held a memorial for Paul, Humphrey Brown decided to do his own investigation."

"Solo or with the Met?" Theo asked, bemused.

"He told me it was with the Metropolitan Police," Eve continued, rubbing the tears from her eyes. "They responded to a break-in at a building in Piccadilly last year that was registered in your godfather's name. They found traces of coca base and linked you to working on a new drug with the Cali Cartel."

"Me?" Theo was evidently alarmed.

"He gave me a dossier," Eve went on, unaware that Theo was beginning to look tired. "You're very well educated in plant pathology. Humphrey wanted to find out whether you were involved. He asked me to find out. I knew Lola and thought up a fund-raiser premise to attend your seminar. You weren't what I expected. I didn't want to do it."

"But you did," Theo reminded.

Eve nodded, large self-condemnatory tears rolling down her cheeks. "When you invited me to Scotland, I was only going to nose around," she explained. "Then Trey told me you'd invented a formula—he called it the big one—he samed you named it Phoebe. I was convinced it had something to do with Paul's death. I saw your open briefcase and—"

"Took it," Theo finished, blinking twice to refocus his gaze. He ran his left hand along his braided head, digesting the information as calmly as he could. She had been honest, he had to give her that. Her actions were a little silly, but she was motivated by her quest for justice. "So what changed your mind?"

"You did," Eve reminded, wiping her wet cheeks with the back of her hand. "Your generous nature, your son, your home. The way you kissed me," she added.

That last one tugged at Theo's heartstrings. "I thought—"

"I lied," Eve admitted, placing her face into the palm of her hands, sighing heavily as she now avoided looking at the professor. She was rankled with guilt. "I've been so stupid."

Instinctively, Theo's hand went to the top of her right shoulder where he rubbed her gently. "You made a mistake," he said, his voice sounding sleepy, though moderately toned. "But it would've been far easier if you'd just asked me."

"I couldn't," Eve quavered, keeping her head down. "Humphrey Brown said I should be careful with you because you were the last person to see Paul alive. I believed him after I saw the way Dr. Da Costa behaved at your seminar and the way you accused me of working with Dr. Keltz."

"I explained about her," Theo implored, tapping Eve's shoulder in the hope that he might coax her to raise her head from between her hands and look at him.

"I know," Eve conceded, feeling worse at revealing the awful truth behind her behavior. "A part of me believed you until I visited your laboratory. I didn't expect to see such a high level of security. I became so confused. Then your unexpected meeting on my last day in Cramond . . ." Eve raised her head and dared to meet Theo's brooding gaze, her brown eyes still glazed with tears; she was unaware of how much he was perspiring.

"I told you I don't like men who hide things from me. So I think it's time you filled in the blanks."

Theo realized she deserved an explanation, seeing as they were both caught up in this. Okay, she had made him realize that there had been something between them when he had kissed her. It was the faintest of come-ons, but it woke him up like nothing else could have done. He had not believed her earlier remark when she revealed how much she cared for him, neither could he quite stomach her story that she had not meant to coerce him. He could see there was something quite genuine which allowed him to muse over the pros and cons of dealing with Ms. Hamilton.

Right now, she was vulnerable. Her face was masked with the same innocence he had first seen when she had attended his seminar. He could still remember what it was like when she was beneath him on his bed, her mouth a teasing inch away from his. The pleasant, breathless sensation was as exhilarating then as it felt to him now that he began to reminisce how it would feel to kiss those interesting, pink lips once more.

Not as long as they had the problem of recovering his formula hanging over their heads. He would keep matters on a practical level and ignore the rampaging demands of his body, which was beginning to awaken with the scent of her perfume and the way the impact of her shaking limbs had left its imprint on his muscular frame while she had cried.

"I'll tell you about Phoebe," he informed her quietly, carefully removing his suede jacket to make himself more comfortable. He winced again, this time more heavily when an acute pain shot through his right shoulder. It was such that Theo was forced to lean against the sofa before he began his side of the story. "You remember that I told you I'm working for the United Nations Drug Control Program?"

Eve nodded.

"That I had experimented with a fungus spore and created a formula that could effectively wipe out every drug crop around the world?"

She nodded again.

"It works," he drawled slowly. "My tests were originally done in London on the coca plant. It behaved similarly to a discovery called Foxy, a mysterious fungus found in Hawaii. The fungus proved to be self-propagating and deadly. It attacked from the root and killed internally, but there are two problems. It may be difficult to contain." He sighed and blinked to refocus. "I later developed a method of spraying the fungus and tried it on opium poppies. The results were quite effective. The other problem is, the UNDCP seems reluctant to accept that mass production fungus spores against drug crops may carry risks."

"Risks?" Eve was hooked.

"Mutation," He told her, feeling another sharp pain. "Is it safe? Could it spread uncontrollably? Could it hurt animals or human beings?" The professor readjusted his right arm to assuage the pain and closed his eyes briefly, forcing himself to think. "The formula you stole detailed my genetic modifications to the fungus to develop a more aggressive strain. It would leave no residue and would taint the soil to prevent further drug crop growth."

Eve's heart dropped at the enormity of what Theo was telling her.

"But there have been no proper field tests with this new strain," he continued, his mind becoming hazy. "The two men I had a meeting with in Cramond were . . . Dr. Kingsley and Dr. Marsden." He blinked. "They work for a company called Viotac, which has interests in Afghanistan under the new coalition goverment. Viotac was consulted to advise on how to destroy narcotic crops propagated during the Taliban rule. Both doctors were involved in sensitive discussions on my behalf to get consent to conduct a field test in that country, which has now been approved. The purpose of our meeting was to discuss . . . green warfare and how we were going to target plants committed to die." Theo paused. He blinked again. "I've only lodged a patent application for the weaker fungus which I don't believe has yet been published."

"But the formula I took was—"

"For the deadlier strain," Theo finished, sighing heavily. The pain was becoming unbearable.

Eve's mind went into a tailspin. The possible result of her actions suddenly began to weigh heavily on her brain. What a fool she had been. "I had no idea," her voice trembled with emotion. "I thought the assistant commissioner—"

"Was telling you the truth," Theo interrupted, grimacing more readily. "The truth is there are many crop-growing countries that unleash chemicals on our children without consent. It's a high stakes game and . . . you can go to any rehab clinic to check the results." He paused again, running his left index finger across his sweaty forehead. "Whoever the assistant commissioner was working with is into counter terrorism. All they need is to find someone who can interpret my formula, and they're in business."

"What do you mean?" Eve could hardly bear to ask.

"War," Theo concluded.

"Oh, my god!" Eve suddenly saw the consequences of what she had done. "Humphrey Brown was selling the formula to a drug baron?"

"Who'll probably use it destroy rival crops," Theo explained ruefully, readjusting his arm again. "Humans, animals, and healthy crops may suffer. I need to get that formula back before one of several men I could name puts it into premature production."

Eve's heart stopped, and a cold shiver ran along her spine. "How . . . how did anyone find out about what you were doing?"

Theo was at a loss, his head becoming a daze. "I don't know how your assistant commissioner found out," he admitted forlornly, feeling weaker by the moment. "I was wondering whether he had been tipped off by Dr. Da Costa. He and his group initially bombarded me with e-mails after . . . reading the paper I published on the Internet." He blinked. "I approved pioneering experimentations on food crops which was why they raided my lab in Piccadilly last year. I was hoping my purchase of the building in London via my godfather, the ambassador of Brazil, would deflect the real intent of my experiments there. That's why . . . Fairafar Mill in Cramond is so secure."

Eve's eyes filled with tears again. "I'm sorry I hit you," she ventured, overawed at everything she had been told. "How can I help? Is there anything I can do?"

"You can go . . . into the kitchen and get me the first aid kit," Theo bridled suddenly, unable to take the pain in his right shoulder any longer. He gritted his teeth and panted heavily. "I need . . . a dressing."

"For what?" Eve asked, confused.

Theo adjusted his arm for a third time, and that was when Eve saw the blood. It had soaked into every measure of fabric on the underside of the white shirt he was wearing, dripping down his arm to his wrist. Alarmed, she jumped off of the sofa. "Theo?" She saw the perspiration on his forehead and realized he was beginning to look dazed. "I'll be right back. I'll get some swabs."

Frantic, Eve hurried across the room and through the first door she could see. It took her directly into an elaborately designed bedroom. She panicked and left, hurry-

ing toward another door close by. It led straight to a
bathroom. She squealed with disbelief and tried a more
obscure door across the large sitting room. That opened
up and revealed a closet. It was only when she ran along
a small corridor and thrust open the double glass doors
did she find herself in a large modern-day kitchen.

It was a while before Eve found the first aid kit. She
also had the initiative to fill and switch on a kettle, deciding she would need plenty of hot water. While doing
so, she did not hesitate to call out to Theo from the
kitchen, letting him know she was still there. With the
hot water in a bowl and plenty of cotton swabs, Eve hurried back to the sitting room and placed everything on
the coffee table.

"Theo?" She stared at him, finding him half dazed
and semiconscious. Eve sat next to him and took hold
of his shirt. From the wrist she ripped the sleeve in half.
He was breathing heavily as she tore all the way up until
she saw the wound on his right shoulder. Blood oozed.
"What happened?" she asked, overwrought at what she
saw.

"Bones of my bones, flesh of my flesh," he confided
deliriously. "I want to make love to you." His temperature was extremely high and he had a fever.

"Theo?" Eve's voice crackled with concern, ignoring
his quotation from the Bible. She quickly dabbed his
forehead with a bunch of wet swabs.

"Do you . . . sweat when you . . . make love?" His
voice was failing in his delirium.

"Theo?" She shook him gently to rouse his attention.

"I'm going to make you scream," he confessed.

"Theophilus?" Eve sounded out his name much
firmer and precise.

"Bullet," he whispered on a frail note, becoming conscious for a fleeting moment. "You have to . . . dig it
out and . . . kiss me so that I . . . feel your tongue."

A bolt of fear and something akin to desire flooded the full length of Eve's body. She could not recall when or where . . . then she remembered that when they had jumped the perimeter fence that took them out of St. James's Park she had heard what sounded like gunfire. She thought she had imagined it, but now Eve realized one of the two men had fired a bullet which was lodged in Theo's shoulder. She froze at the realization that it was up to her to remove it. It was either that or call an ambulance and risk being asked awkward questions.

"I can't do it," she breathed on a high note. A quick glance at Theo, and Eve was made aware he was no longer with her. His tawny complexion had paled significantly, his breathing had become shallow, and blood still pumped from his shoulder.

"Love me," he murmured on the brink of hysteria.

Ignoring his confessions, Eve opened the first aid kit. A gasp left her lips as she looked at all the equipment—bandages, tweezers, antiseptic potions. She heaved a sickly breath, considering the worst. All she knew was she had to stop the blood. Anything else was second-guessing. She closed her eyes and, this time, crossed her fingers behind her back and prayed.

Theo awoke to find his shoulder wrapped in gauze and the pain a distant blur of memory. He jerked his arm and refocused his gaze to find himself lying on his back in bed. He surveyed the room. It was his bedroom in his Mayfair apartment. Closing his eyes briefly, he breathed a sigh of relief. Opening them again, he found Eve sitting at the edge of his bed, a shallow smile playing across her lips.

"How's the patient?"

In reflex, Theo moved his arm. His shoulder felt stiff,

without doubt already healing. "Feeling like he's had better days."

Eve's eyes filled and she nodded.

"Our lady's tears," he told her, reaching out with his free hand to touch her cheek, brushing a single tear away. Eve looked at him bemused. "Your perfume," Theo added. "Very old-fashioned phrase for lilies."

They measured each other in silence, then she held out her hand. He looked at the bullet and felt a tremor run through his limbs. Eve had made a good job of his shoulder though he could not recall a thing. His last memory was of her running to the kitchen in search of the first aid kit. He could not remember her returning or how he had reached his bed.

"You did this?" His tone crackled with emotion, the scene of his shoulder pumping blood rushing to his mind. It was all clear to him now. The pain. Where the gunshot had come from. Returning to his Mayfair apartment with Eve. He tried to sit up.

"Don't move," Eve gently forced him to stay lying down. "You'll only weaken your shoulder."

Theo thought quickly. On his reckoning, it was probably early evening. That meant they were safe, for now. Only a few people knew where he lived. He moved his arm again. It must have been a wrench for her, digging out the bullet, cleaning him up to prevent infection and bandaging his shoulder. He marveled at her stamina to do so and avoid their early detection by being questioned by the police.

It would only be a matter of time before the assistant commissioner's murder would be broadcast on the news. That's when the countdown would begin. They would have to fight the clock in order to find the culprits before they themselves were accused of the crime. In which direction he should be searching, he had no idea. Perhaps it would be easier if he returned to Scotland to make preparations for the International Antidrugs Summit and leave the matter in the hands of the UNDCP.

"I have to go back to the lab," he told her calmly.

"Not tonight, you're not," Eve cautioned. "I think you should rest. I've just had a hot bath after the scare you put me through."

Theo smiled weakly and looked at her. She had slipped back into her clothes, though she was out of her boots and socks, and he could see her hair was slightly wet. He could also see how tired she was. Eve's bright chestnut-brown complexion had paled and the doe-shaped eyes he admired on first meeting her were now sullen with exhaustion.

"I'm sorry. I'm being selfish, aren't I?"

Eve nodded. "Just what I would expect from a man." Her smile broadened very subtly. "I think you can thank me later when this is all over with a big bunch of flowers."

Not that she could see the day considering the hectic few hours they had both been through. She had been sorely tested and felt the full measure of it as her gaze traveled along the gauze she carefully wrapped around Theo's shoulders. It had not been easy. There was a point when she had feared Theo may die. Her handiwork, by all accounts, surprised her. She had imagined Theo's fragile skin to be a delicate inch of fabric which required the most expert repair and stitching.

His delirium helped her along, mainly because he was totally unaware of the pain. Now that she had removed the bullet and saw the color return to his tawny cheeks, she felt a little less uneasy about the peril they were in, though she was nonetheless still on edge.

Theo welcomed her smile and found himself responding in kind. "You did great." He moved his arm to prove the point. "You've got yourself one satisfied patient."

"A very talkative one," Eve relented.

Theo carefully sat up and leaned his back against the headboard, his eyes widening in amazement. "I talked?"

"Deliriously," Eve corrected. "I was privy to all your most intimate secrets."

Now he was intrigued. It surpassed his present anxiety about what they had both been through. "What did I say?"

"Just that you want to make love to me," Eve disclosed with a chuckle.

Theo closed his eyes, acutely embarrassed. "I said that?"

"And more."

"More?"

Eve nodded. "There was the question of whether I sweat."

Theo laughed and prized the bullet out of Eve's hand. "I think this little thing has caused enough trouble for one day." He tossed it to the other side of the room and reached directly for her wrist. "But it's done me one small favor." To her chagrin, he tugged her into his arms, his confidence boosted that their kiss had meant something after all. Staring deeply into Eve's eyes, he saw them widen in anticipation and his heart lurched in longing. "It's made me admit to something I wouldn't ordinarily tell you." He paused. "I do want to make love to you."

Eve could not answer. She was too overwhelmed and a little awestruck that Theo should be feeling this way after everything she had done. On returning his gaze, she was reminded how she had told herself she would never give in to his charms. Now those very chocolate-brown eyes which had first greeted her from a snapshot had her caught. Hook, line, and sinker.

Nine

"Do you really want to consider an unscrupulous, scurvy little mercenary like me?" Eve whispered as she tried to pull away from Theo, fighting the swift current of heat which ran from her groin to her heart. But Theo merely drew her closer, kissing her forehead with warm lips.

"And the devil-made-me-do-it smile?" He shook his head in mild self-derision. There was a lot more to Eve Hamilton than met the eye. Theo had known it from when he earlier had considered that she was hiding something from him. Now the sensation that she was hiding her feelings felt strong in him, vying with the intense surge of sexual energy which had him hard as a rock.

How long had it been since a woman made him feel this way? Years? Over a decade, in fact. He thought of Dr. Moira Keltz, and he was surprised the memory of her ceased to hold any power to hurt. Eve had miraculously healed his pain there. No other woman had been able to do that. From the moment he had tasted her, he wanted more.

"You could have worn one of my shirts after your bath," he suggested, sliding a hand down her arm.

"That would have been imposing," Eve said shyly.

His eyes danced. "Kiss me," he coaxed on a hoarse note. Theo's desire was growing stronger by the second and he pulled Eve's wrist so hard, she could not help but tumble to within inches of his lips.

"No." She was a little wary, and understandably so, after the revelations of their earlier conversation.

Theo immediately caught her chin in his left hand and held it there. "Why fight it when you know you really want it," he taunted, his gaze boring deep.

Strangely, in view of the circumstances, Eve did not feel panicked or distressed. Rather her heart melted. She was filled with the self-knowledge that she wanted to feel Theo inside her. Feel his arms about her, his caresses, his sweet taking of her. Because he had been on the brink of death, she wanted it more. When he raised his head in expectation, she could not deny herself. She lowered her lips and allowed him to taste her. It was not a quick assault. His mouth moved slowly and tenderly over her own. Eve felt herself relax into his hard, rigid frame, sighing lightly as she curled her toes.

Theo's breathing was erratic, sending little flutters throughout her body. Her senses were drugged as he expertly coaxed her mouth to open wider, allowing him to delve in with his tongue. She groaned softly, drifting into a haven of wonderful delight, her body melting in liquid desire. Eve's eyes closed, and her breath became shallow as Theo tantalizingly explored the inner tissues of her mouth until she shivered in deep response.

Eve was lost in bewilderment of her feelings. She had not expected to come this far, not after her deceit and lies. Yet here she was, helplessly molded to the rigid hardness of Theo's frame, receiving his plundering tongue in sinful temptation. She was aroused. Her body was responding to his in a way it had never responded to a man's before. And she could not stop.

Melting deeper, she returned Theo's kiss with total abandonment, thrilling as her lips kissed him back, hard and then gentle, and then throughly coaxing until he gave her greater access to his inner mouth. She tickled his teeth, played with his tongue, sweetly licked at his bottom lip until his body shook with the impact of her teasing.

She paused briefly to glance at him. His eyes were closed. Peaceful. Relaxed. It was hard to believe what they had gone through earlier. Now, they were wrapped in their own little world, sharing their adoration, soothing the anguishes of the day. She kissed his eyelids. His forehead. Dropped a seductive brush across each cheek. Then Eve returned to Theo's lips and heard the delightful moan he exerted at receiving them again.

There was no need for her to feel guilty, not now. Theo needed her and she needed him. His expression of it was quite avid as his hand began to delve beneath her white V-necked jersey, smoothing his fingers over the softness of her skin, enjoying its velvety texture under his fingertips. Eve giggled as he tickled her side, and she raised her head to see that his eyes were now open, sparkling with approval at how he loved the sound of her laughter. His expression seemed so warm and affectionate, Eve's heart was flooded with a whirlwind of sensations that had her eager and longing for more.

She closed her eyes as his hand moved upward until they tugged at the satin and lace of her bra. Eve knew he would be able to sense the rapid beat of her heart, that he would want to delve further until he could feel all of her beneath his bold fingers.

"Take this off," he ordered her gently, tugging at her white jersey with his weak arm.

Eve felt her breasts throb with the expectation of experiencing his fingers against them. She was on her knees in an instant, obeying Theo's command. With jean-clad legs, she straddled his body and pulled her white jersey over her head. Before she could toss it to one side, Theo was already working his way from her navel to her breasts, making a slow trail with a single finger until he reached his destination.

His fingers immediately outlined the shape of her bra, slowly stroking against the sides of it until Eve eagerly, and without prompting, released the fastening at the back. Her full breasts tumbled out, one of them directly into Theo's cupped hand. He had kept it there, waiting, and instantly weighed it like a man who enjoyed the load before pleasing himself by squeezing the nipple.

Eve squealed, the sound totally alien to her. Her eyes watered at how good it was to have Theo's fingers twisting, shaping, and defining her, when hours before he was so weak with a bullet in his shoulder. The bra fell from her limp fingers to the sheets of his bed, and she gazed at him with lusty appreciation.

"You have soft fingers," she whispered and leaned forward to retake his lips.

Theo smiled deeply as he raised his head in acceptance, reveling in their endless kiss while he enjoyed the onslaught of touching Eve so intimately. He enjoyed the diversion she made to brush her lips against his dark brows, the playful lick across the bridge of his broad nose, the way her gentle savaging teeth bit the side of his neck ever so sweetly.

Eve was making him feel alive again. Wanted. Needed. Loved. "Undress me," he coaxed, surveying Eve through the slant of wickedly aroused eyes.

Theo was still dressed, his right shirtsleeve ripped and dangling from his arm, a little stained from his bullet injury. The one thing Eve had not been able to do was take his clothes off before walking Theo to his bed. Delirious, he had hung on to her and unsteadily made the short walk from the sitting room to his bedroom, his weight burdensome. But now Eve was faced with the glorious delight of removing Theo's clothing piece by piece, her pulse racing double-time at how exciting she found the prospect.

She leaned forward and let out another squeal of delight as Theo's hardness poked between her legs. Though dressed in jeans, Eve's eyes widened at the unexpected cheekiness he exulted. It was fun. Something she had gone without for far too long. When he poked her again, she was encouraged to take off his shirt quickly, careful not to upset his shoulder. Theo grimaced slightly as he raised his back allowing her to pull it from his arm.

Her gaze instantly landed on his hairy chest and arms, the sight of him touching every nerve ending in Eve's body. Theo looked so strong and fit for his forty-two years, his tawny skin evenly colored and generously adorned with plenty of dark, curly hair, that she was smitten by his muscular frame. He looked good enough to eat. She paused before raking her fingers through his hair, relishing the touch of silk at her fingertips.

Perfect. Absolutely perfect, Eve told herself. Leaning farther forward, she caressed her lips across his chest, delving her tongue into his navel before working her way up to his nipple. She kissed one and then the other, sensing Theo shiver beneath her. Eve felt empowered. She was on top. Only she could tempt her lover in this way. She trailed a line of kisses all the way over to Theo's bandaged shoulder and then brushed a gentle kiss against the clean gauze.

The gesture was so affectionate, Theo rolled over onto his left side and pulled Eve with him. She laughed at his power. He still had enough strength to take command. He pulled her against him, into his free arm and in one swift movement crushed her into his hardened body. Eve's lips opened immediately and met his searching mouth, his tongue flighty and erotic as it probed into all the secret places of her mouth.

He let her lips go and moved downward to her neck, gently nipping and nibbling the soft flesh, his nostrils invigorated by the sweet smell of lilies, the scent of Eve's perfume. He molded her even closer and continued the journey south to her breasts. Again, Theo reacquainted himself with every part of Eve until she was wriggling beneath his caresses. The surge of renewed feelings was such, he found himself gasping at how much he was enjoying himself. It made him bolder, more eager to discover everything about Eve, his fingers now attacking the belt of her jeans.

Eve helped him along his way, unclasping the buckle and zipper on Theo's ivory-colored pants while he attacked hers. His actions were made more clumsy for using his weaker hand. Eve felt the strain of squirming in anticipation beneath Theo's capable fingers, eagerly awaiting the opportunity to remove her jeans. The moment the buckle of her belt and zipper were free, she was out of them in an instant before pulling Theo's trousers clear from his legs.

Dressed in cotton briefs, herself in complementary satin-and-lace knickers, they gravitated to each other like magnets. The naked contact of her breasts against his hairy chest was carnal and erogenous. Neither Theo nor Eve had experienced such a wild, hedonistic reaction to the meeting of their bodies. The lewd sensation of Eve's voluptuous breasts pressed against him, where her hardened nipples rubbed gently up and down through his hair, was as erotic to Theo as it was to Eve.

The emotion was sealed and immortalized forever with another heartfelt kiss. This time the pressure was lazily slow and coaxing, each taking turn to push the pleasure level higher than what they envisioned possible. The unison had a symmetry of its own. Unspoken. Wordless. Only instinct led the way, and they blindly followed, making small shifts and movements to increase the flow of intensity.

Passion raged with fury the moment Theo tugged at the line of Eve's knickers. She took a jagged breath, her mouth dry as he delicately began to pull away the fabric over her hips, down her thighs and over her legs until they were entirely removed from her person. Eve did not hesitate to do the same with Theo's briefs, knowing he would find it hard to utilize his weak arm. When she finally removed them, their lips met again igniting a reaction that was pure bliss.

Theo did not hurry, despite Eve's reaction. His body still felt weakened by the trauma it had gone through, but not too feeble to explore the cavity of Eve's mouth and certainly not frail enough not to share in their love-making that night. He enjoyed the way her hands ran along the expanse of his chest, the way she nibbled at his lips, and the way she whimpered softly whenever his tongue tickled hers. The rapture that coursed its way along his limbs was too intense to wait any longer.

"I need you now," he whispered, panting heavily. She was sweating, and he liked it. He liked it a lot.

His voice was like raw silk on Eve's sensitized nerves and she moaned her response as though her very world was caught up in Theo's web of sin. She moved into the hardness of his muscled body and rubbed herself against his rigid flesh. The very movement made Theo feel as though he had become a wild animal. With an instinct as primitive as any wild beast in a jungle, he rolled Eve onto her back and gently smoothed his hand over her thighs, delighting when she began to part them to welcome him in.

He wanted to roar out to the world the power of his manhood, such was the urge within him to holler. Instead, he directed his hands toward the secret place of Eve's desire, telling himself he had every right to touch her there. He heard her moan helplessly, coaxing him to apply the rhythm his mouth had begun on her lips, smiling to himself as she withered beneath him.

All Eve could feel was the sweet ache at the pit of her stomach building into something explosive. It was frightening because she had never experienced it before. It was as though Theo had taken her to a new place of sensual discovery, a place she had never traveled with Tyrone. It was so alien, the newness of it served only to inflame a whirling kaleidoscope of desire she could hardly control.

Theo's expert hand was thrilling her, pushing her on so that she could not help but to widen her legs further to allow him deeper access to explore her thoroughly. His answer was to keep his hand working while he took the hard tip of her nipple into his mouth and gently squeezed it with his tongue. Eve gasped his name and closed her eyes tight, stalling the premature rush of pleasure by closing a firm hand around Theo's hardened flank.

It felt wet and wonderful and firm between her fingers, like a red hot poker devised for rummaging among the flaming cinders of a burning fire. Only she was that fire, burning more out of control with every passing moment. Her hand moved gently up and down, measuring the width and length of him like she would a strip of fabric, her head forming designs on how Theo would take her.

"Get the bag," he whispered against her lips. His eyes moved over her head and indicated a tiny multicolored tote bag hung loosely over the bed frame.

Eve did his bidding and reached for it, loosening the small ties to find it packed with condoms. "This is handy," she marveled at the way his organized mind worked. "How long have these been here?"

"I change them regularly," Theo chuckled, plucking

a single packet from inside the bag. He handed it to Eve and took the bag from her, allowing it to fall to the floor.

Eve knew he was incapable of putting it on and found her excitement rising to a peak by the sheer knowledge she would have to do the job for him. Carefully, she opened the packet and extracted the colored latex. Its coolness tingled her fingers as she tipped it over and reached for Theo's throbbing rod of pride. It went on easily. She rolled the end down to the bottom and squeezed the tip to make sure no air was trapped. Theo watched her every movement, the agonizing, bestial glint in his eyes snapping the last cord of restraint that was holding Eve intact.

"I need you now," she repeated Theo's order while circling her legs tight around his buttocks, staring deeply into his brooding eyes which had glazed over in blatant desire.

Theo needed no more urging. Seeing Eve, so beautiful and innocent waiting for him, sent hot blood rushing through his body. He could not resist the strong power of his pounding heart. Eagerly, he began to position himself, but his weaker arm was still in low-key pain and only his left arm was able to reach the small of Eve's back to move her closer. Realizing this, Eve did the work instead and marveled at the breathless gasp which escaped Theo's lips the moment he felt her inch him in.

Every part of him reacted. He was out of control. For a moment he felt blinded as the desire took over, propelling him to strike up a rhythm that pushed the pleasure further. His eyes closed and he felt the hot rush of Eve's breath against his cheeks. She was enraptured by the same feelings, too. Her body worked a magic that was born from time itself and that only the most sensual of females could achieve. She moved her hips and shook her fanny in a motion that made him howl.

Like a wild wolf he growled as Eve pumped his manhood. He told himself she knew exactly what she was doing, but when Theo dared to chart her expression, panting heavily as he ensnared the deep pigment of her eyes, he saw a bewilderment that made him realize this experience was something new to Eve, too.

Her eyes were glazed and teary. Eve had never known such exquisite desire. With an inane intuition unknown to her, she seemed to possess the knack of knowing when to make the necessary shifts and adjustments to maximize every measure of hot electric current which leapt between them. It was sheerly thrilling. Fully charged and powered, she kept the momentum until her body protested to release the pressure.

It was rising, strong and fast. Eve was aware that Theo felt its presence, too. His thrusting began a race with her own, pacing the way for the final peak of satisfaction. It made her aware of just how fit he was. Forty-two was not over-the-hill after all. In all respects, his body was more in tune with hers than any man's she had known in life. Her face flushed with fierce desire as he took her higher with the agility of someone much younger.

And when the final thrust came, she was propelled into the unknown. A nameless place she had never visited before. It was not like anything she had experienced. Whatever her past life had been about, Eve now knew she was only taken halfway there. She exerted a long sigh and slowed her rhythm, closing her eyes to savor the euphoria. Seconds later, she heard Theo sing out his final growl before his body fell against her own.

Eve slung her head back. She pressed it into the pillow, sated and happy, reflecting on a day filled with so much adventure it felt quite surreal. In that instant, she had a stunning perception. Like it or not, their fates were entwined. She could never be rid of Professor Theopilus de Cordova until they had walked the full length of their path. With that on her mind, she slipped into slumber.

Eve awoke to the smell of mint. She rubbed her eyes and refocused her gaze to find a cup of tea being handed to her. Theo was sat at the edge of the bed, dressed in a pair of faded jeans with the gauze removed from his shoulder and replaced with a single swab covered with two straps of Elastoplast. She could see it would allow him to move his arm more readily though she could not understand why he had removed it so soon.

"Wakey, wakey," he mouthed, forming a wry smile. "Time to get up."

"What time is it?" Eve questioned, sitting up immediately and taking the tea from him. His bare chest met her muzzy expression.

"Time we went back to Scotland," Theo pressed. "I have some work to wrap up at my laboratory before—"

"You're not expecting me to go back to Cramond with you?" she asked, taking a sip from the cup, finding the infusion of mint and sugar was rousing her.

"You can't very well stay here," Theo reasoned. "There are two bad guys out there on the hunt."

"They don't know me from Adam," Eve reminded.

"They do now," Theo proclaimed, holding up a fresh copy of the morning newspaper. "I took this from the letterbox next door. You seem to have made the morning news."

Eve's eyes widened as she saw the headline. AWARD-WINNING DESIGNER ON THE RUN "Oh, my god," she gasped, snatching the newspaper from Theo's hand. She read further along the commentary which briefly stated that she had been seen near the body of Assistant Commissioner Humphrey Brown who was found murdered in St. James's Park, located close to the London offices of His Royal Highness the Prince of Wales.

"I knew that woman in the park recognized me," she said sickly. "But I hate the way the media are trying to glamorize the disaster by making it seem royalty should be better protected."

Theo rubbed her legs through the sheets. "The reason I want to go back to the lab is to compile my paperwork before we talk to the police."

"Will they believe us?"

"If they don't, both our careers are on the line."

Eve panicked. "I have a charity show on Saturday. What is everyone going to think when they see this?"

She looked at the article again, wondering if the news had reached France. EVE HAMILTON IS WANTED BY POLICE TO FURTHER THEIR INQUIRIES. A helpline telephone number was provided along with a photograph of her that had appeared in the publicity material given out at her last show during London Fashion Week.

"Come on. Get dressed," Theo prompted, hurtling to his feet and walking across the room toward a suite of pine wardrobes.

The curtains were still closed, so Eve's only view was a dim picture of a room neatly ordered with two side tables at either side of the bed, a TV on a table in the far corner, and a glass coffee table with a collection of men's magazines on it. She placed her cup by the side table closest to her and slowly got up. Her nakedness came as a sudden surprise. Then came the memory of last night.

She looked across at Theo who was struggling to push his head through the opening of a burgundy T-shirt. Feeling self-conscious, Eve hurriedly reached for her knickers and bra on the floor and plunged herself into them. When Theo's head popped up, she was quickly getting into her pair of jeans.

"That was fast." He sounded out his surprise while tucking the T-shirt into his waistline.

"I've got a lot to sort out, too." Eve returned, finding her white V-neck jersey beside her boots. Pulling it over her head, she added, "I'd like to go home first to shower and change. I also have to make some phone calls and visit my studio to check on my staff."

"We haven't time for all that," Theo debated, fastening his belt and reaching into his wardrobe for a pair of socks. "I want us to be on a plane by lunchtime."

Eve looked at her watch. It read 9:33 A.M. She pictured Leon doing his nut, prancing around like a mad hyena at having been left in the dark about what she wanted since she agreed to hire him to design her pavilion. "I'll be letting too many people down." She paused. "I need to call my mother at least. And Jasmine, my personal assistant."

Theo thought for two seconds then answered. "Okay. Do it quickly."

Eve nodded and stood up, pushing her jersey into her jeans. Slipping into her socks and boots, she ran toward the door. Theo delayed her as she reached there, his chocolate-brown gaze deepening suddenly.

"Did you enjoy me last night?" he queried, a smile tugging at his lips.

"It was fine," Eve nodded, deciding to keep her voice equable and cool. What she wanted to say was that it had been fantastic, but men could often get on an ego trip and she could not imagine Theo to be any different.

His brows rose. "That's it?"

Eve was polite. "What else do you want me to say?"

Theo stepped back, appearing worried. "Nothing." He placed his hand on the doorknob and pulled the door open, allowing her to leave.

Eve briefly glanced at him as she left and considered that he had wanted to hear something more. Something different perhaps than what she had told him. It kept her guessing as she made her way toward the sitting room to locate her bag. She was reminded he was a man who felt that feelings, hunches, and intuitions within a relationship needed to be justified, and her brain was not in gear to be discussing the finer elements of last night.

If that was what he was looking for—that she should give him some reason as to why they made love—he would soon know she was not prepared to explain her actions. In her world, emotional bonding of any kind was something unexplainable and accepted by both people involved. It had taken her years to learn that.

Often, she had wondered why it took so long. Perhaps not ever knowing what her father was like and being propelled to succeed by her mother, who had pushed both her brother and her to their fullest potential, had hardened her in some way. Tears were futile. Hugging someone was once an action she had found so hard. Meeting Tyrone had softened her a little, but not even he could understand why she had been so analytical about what made their relationship tick.

On entering the sitting room, Eve realized she had been searching for the feelings as to why they had been together. She never found them. In simple terms, they were never in love. The chemistry had never been there between her and Tyrone. It was a confusion which made her question so many things before finally coming to terms with the fact that the deep, unquestionable bonding she longed for was not something you searched for, but something that instinctively happened.

It was an awareness that had stayed with her after Tyrone departed from her life. It was this that made the idea of falling in love escape most people because of their lack of self. Now she had reached that point, she hoped, rather than chosen to make any effort to be forceful with Theo. He would have to find that kind of awareness alone.

She reached for her handbag and removed a brush, loosening her hair. A quick brush to position her hair around her shoulders, and she recalled that Theo saw love as an impossible goal to reach. It was a risk factor not worth taking. No fallback position exposed vulnerability, and with that exposure came failure and all other manner of internal wrenching, which proved persistence did not always pay off. His objections were very precise and calculating in her head, and she now wondered whether he had an alternative view at all.

On finishing her hair, she immediately extracted her mobile phone and decided to divert her attention to the calls she needed to make. When this was all over she would quiz Theo, or so she thought. For now, there were more pressing matters at hand.

"Mum," she bellowed into the flip mouthpiece. "It's Eve. I'm all right."

"Well buck me toe on rock stone," Marlene shuddered. "I see the newspapers. Is it true? Humphrey is dead?"

"Yes," Eve admitted forlornly. "He asked to meet me, but when I got there—"

Eve heard her mother sniffling. "The police have been here," she said, her voice quavering but controlled. "They came last night. I gave them your office number."

That meant they had spoken with Jasmine, Eve thought. Whenever she left the house, she would always divert her office calls to her personal assistant. "Did they say anything?" she asked, curious.

"You were seen in St. James's Park," Marlene cried. "First your father, then Paul, now . . . I can't take anymore."

Eve heard the tears and felt her heart lurch with

mourning. She had cried, too, having kept everything bottled up inside for so long. Yesterday, she had realized she was human after all. Fragile and feminine and not the hard rock she had tried to be for her mother.

"Mum, I'll call the police as soon as I can," she assured. "Just . . . just remember Humphrey for the good man that he was." She said this because it occurred to her there may soon be a leak to what he had been really up to. "I'll call you when I can, okay?"

"Yes." Marlene accepted everything.

Eve clicked off the phone and sighed heavily. She needed another brandy, but not before she called Jasmine to find out how Leon and her other colleagues within the fashion establishment were taking the news.

"Jasmine, it's Eve," she began with her second call.

"Eve!" Jasmine's voice lowered to a whisper. "I'm surprised you got through. Your phone has been red-hot all morning."

"What's happened?" Eve grew alarmed. She had the sinking feeling that Tia Maria, the sponsor of her pavilion, was about to pull out.

"I thought *you* could tell *me*," Jasmine chortled. "Two police officers came here this morning expecting to find you. I pretended you were across town doing a private fitting with a customer and wouldn't be back until late afternoon."

"Thanks," Eve sighed with relief.

"What's going on?" Jasmine demanded. "Ten of your customers have telephoned already. We've been bombarded with personal visits by six of them demanding to know if their dresses will be finished on time, and Leon is doing his Zulu dance. The model agency is also feeling a little nervy at releasing their models for rehearsals until you personally reassure them."

"It's a long story," Eve began, noticing Theo had entered the sitting room with his brown suede jacket in hand. He was rummaging through the pockets in search of something while she continued her conversation on the phone. "I'll be back in the studio as soon as I can."

"You're in the newspapers," Jasmine voiced her objection strenuously. "And you made the breakfast news. The police are looking for you. They say you were at the scene of an incident and that two men were seen chasing you and some other fellow as you left St. James's Park. I read in the newspaper that an assistant commissioner was found murdered."

"Jasmine."

"As I also do your public relations," she reminded, "I need to know what's going on to release a statement."

"I can't tell you right now."

"This is more than my job's worth," Jasmine added the pressure. "I want to keep my head in this industry, too. It doesn't help having people thinking I work for someone . . . shady."

"I'm not shady," Eve objected, hurt. "It's just that—"

"I told the police you were with Professor Theophilus de Cordova," Jasmine went on, unperturbed. "Lola Henriques is a good friend of mine. We understand each other when it comes to trading information."

"Jasmine!"

"You were here with a handsome man, and I got curious." Eve heard the hint of jealousy in her tone. "I'm sorry, but I'm going to have to hand in my resignation if I don't get an answer by the end of today."

"You're resigning?" Eve was shocked that envy could stretch this far. "What about the show on Saturday?"

"Which reminds me," Jasmine continued. "Charlotte's pressed and packed your collection. A courier picked them up an hour ago. They're on their way to France. And Leon says he wants to hear from you or he's packing up."

"But I've paid him." Eve's blood was beginning to simmer. "The little toad rag."

"Your check bounced this morning," Jasmine said coldly. "Joseph said you haven't enough money in your business account to clear it at the bank if he submits it again. This is one you're going to have to deal with on your own."

"Where's Joseph?" Eve boomed.

"He's gone home," Jasmine rebutted. "Which is where I'm going. I'm shutting up the studio for the day. I've already told everyone to go home and I'm putting a notice on the door. You can call me at home later."

"Fine," Eve spat out her annoyance, hardly believing her own staff could be so fussed. *So much for loyalty,* she thought with derision as she ended the call. She turned to find Theo standing in front of her with a white piece of paper in his hand. "I'm in a crisis," she told him, agitated and tearful.

"You're in more than that," he answered, his voice harsh. "What's this?"

He handed over the paper. Eve recognized it. He had pulled it from Humphrey Brown's hand. Carefully reading it, her blood ran cold. It was the same piece of paper she had extracted from Theo's wallet in Cramond with Dr. Moira Keltz's name and phone number written on it. She hardly knew where to begin telling Theo how it came to be in the possession of a dead man.

"I . . . I can explain," she stuttered, feeling as though this had to be the worst day of her life. After the wonderful night she had spent in Theo's arms, she could not bear him to think badly of her now, especially when they had seemingly repaired the differences between them.

"I hope, for your sake, you can," Theo countered, his

voice holding steel. "Because the last time I looked, this was in my wallet. You took it, didn't you?"

"Theo . . ." she implored.

"Save it."

He rushed to the telephone and began dialing the number detailed on the piece of paper. It rang endlessly. Eve saw the panic in Theo's face as he sighed heavily, frowning while he waited. His brows touched each other as he threw her a tireless glance. He was at the point of hanging up when someone answered.

"Moira?" he barked. Eve fell silent as he questioned the whereabouts of Trey's mother. When he hung up, his face seemed to lack its usual color. "Get your jacket," he ordered, unable to look at her. "We're going to have to make a detour."

"What?"

"Don't you see, you stupid woman," he bellowed, plunging his arms into his jacket with such force, he grimaced at forgetting he had sustained an injury. "This assistant commissioner of yours must have been under the impression that Moira could interpret my formula. I need to get to her before those two thugs do."

Eve pressed her hand to her lips. "But . . . do you think they've seen it?" She thought of her own pressing engagements, of her own world falling apart at the seams. "Where are we going?"

"Birmingham."

Eve's mind spun. "Why are we—"

"Moira works there," Theo confirmed.

"But . . ." Eve protested. "I'm one of those people who like to sort out their immediate environment like work, friends, family. My own affairs. I have no interest in saving the world or other people for that matter."

"You're being selfish." Theo brushed down his jacket and picked up his keys. "C'mon."

He headed for the door in good conscience, uncaring of what crisis Eve herself was facing. As far as he was concerned, they were facing a bigger one and he was in no mood to deal.

Ten

"We're being followed," Theo remarked casually. They had left his Mayfair apartment and were making their way toward a bus stop when he noticed the two men lagging behind. It was the same two who had chased them from St. James's Park. That meant they were armed and dangerous. Theo took a hold of Eve's hand and squeezed it to allay her panic. "Stay calm," he told her, spotting a black cab. He hailed it immediately and watched it slow to pull in at the curb. "Come on."

Their adversaries were quick on the mark. Seeing that Eve and Theo were about to get away, they took chase. "You get in and I'll stall," Theo said as he opened the cab door.

But the two men were upon them before either one could get inside. Eve did not have time to think. She held tight to her handbag and aimed at the nearest man's face with all the strength she could muster. It knocked him off balance. Seeing his opportunity, Theo used his head and butted directly into the other man's stomach. It winded him, giving them both precious few seconds to get inside the cab. Eve was quick to slam the door.

"Fulham Palace Road. Hurry."

The taxi driver clicked on his meter and pulled out into the early-morning traffic without passing comment.

This was London. People fought for cabs all the time. Eve glanced through the window behind her, seeing both men making chase before realizing any attempt would be futile. "How did they find us?" she gasped, amazed.

"They've obviously been doing their homework," he said, surprised he had not considered it earlier.

Whoever they were, they knew enough about him. Not many people had knowledge of where his London home was located. He was grateful he had chosen a building that offered round-the-clock security, because it had prevented the men from storming his apartment. Their only option had been to wait outside and keep vigil until he chose to leave the building with Eve. It unnerved him.

"We don't have time to go to your studio," he bristled, glancing through the back window to check that they had not been followed.

"I need a change of clothes and breakfast," Eve protested, making new plans. "And a hot shower, if that isn't too much to ask."

"You're wasting time," he objected strenuously. "I need—"

"Some breakfast, too," Eve reasoned. "Besides, those two men don't know where I live. We'll be safe at my house."

For how long? Theo wondered as his arm felt stiff. He absently pushed at the injury and gave a little grunt of annoyance at the discomfort. If it was not for the bullet he took, he would have used his fist and knocked one or both men cold. As it was, he felt annoyed at his limitations, that he had only been able to wind him. If they chose to attack again, his adversaries would soon pick up on the fact that his sore shoulder would put them at an advantage.

Theo leaned into the backseat and submitted to Eve's

decision. Perhaps it would be best if he listened to her for now. His brain could not formulate a better scheme, and he was hungry. He closed his eyes, trying not to worry, and allowed the hum of the traffic to relax him a little. But the thought of Eve having taken Dr. Moira Keltz's phone number from his wallet popped into his mind like a ping-pong ball, forcing his eyes open in an instant.

Six months ago, he had received a letter from her attorney stipulating that she wanted full custody of Trey. Considering she had not seen their son in years, he was more than surprised at her interest in the boy now.

He never spoke of her to his son, and, curiously Trey never asked questions. That was another surprise, because he had expected Trey to have some curiosity about his mother. It was due to this lack of interest that he had chosen not to push the issue with his son. Of course, he knew there would be a time when he would sit the boy down and talk to him about her, but that time had not yet arrived.

Naturally, his response to Moira's attorney was not what she had expected. A personal letter followed which had enraged him beyond belief. She had threatened him with court action and further cited that his work was proving harmful to the normal functional development of their child's life. The accusation that Trey was neglected and suffered from low self-esteem and a narrow field of social skills was directly attributed to him not providing the boy with enough quality time, she alleged. *What did she know?* his head screamed at the reminder of her letter, still housed in the bureau at his cottage in Scotland. Moira would not recognize Trey from a lineup of boys, and he wanted to challenge her with that.

He shifted uncomfortably in his taxi seat and looked through the window, his anger toward Eve for stealing from his wallet growing with every passing moment. He may not be able to tolerate Moira, but he would never want to put her to any harm. If the fact that two bullies were chasing them was to tell him anything, it was that he had to find Dr. Moira Keltz before they located her and forced her to try and interpret his formula.

"You all right?" Eve asked, concerned.

She had been aware of Theo's grimace and his fidgeting with his arm. It was not quite rocket science to figure out that he was obviously still angry with her for extracting information from his wallet. It was wrong. She knew the moment she had taken it, but he had to understand that she just wanted an explanation for her brother's murder. Surely he could see that now?

His refusal to answer gave her every indication that he was still fueled with fury. It was understandable under the circumstances. They had just reached a level of trust after a wonderful night and then her actions had ruined it. How unlucky could a girl get? Hurt, she turned away from him and glanced through the window, watching the traffic go by.

Her feelings toward Theo had magnified after their night of lovemaking, and Eve knew it. To keep up the pretense of making her feel guilty was a cruel pill to swallow, because she thought they had reached a meeting of minds on the subject of Paul. Eve felt her heart drop by Theo's apparent coldness toward her now. What was he thinking? Did he now think that she was not worth the effort to even be spoken to after everything she had done? Undoubtedly so.

Her eyes closed as she forced back the tears. Why she was still by his side, Eve could not quite fathom. Like she had a choice. Right now, her whole world had fallen apart. She could not see a clear path to solving anything, except to make amends with Theo. But even that may be taken as an empty gesture and her heart sank to its lowest point. Theo was going to jilt her as soon as he saw his way through their demise. That much she knew. She kept her eyes on the traffic and chose not to say another word.

They hurried along the cobbled pathway and she saw the notice Jasmine had placed on the door. CLOSED UNTIL FURTHER NOTICE. *So much for loyalties,* Eve thought again on entering her design studio. Theo followed her in and she immediately locked the door behind her, leaving the notice in place. It was best that it remained there, she decided.

Her telephone was ringing. After the seventh ring, Eve realized that Jasmine had not diverted the calls. Her annoyance grew as she threw down her bag on the large refectory table and placed both hands on her hips.

"Aren't you going to answer that?" Theo said at last.

Eve turned and looked at him, surprised he was acknowledging her. "Talking to me now?" she chided.

"Only under duress."

Eve winced. "While you're in my house, the least you can do is be civil."

"Maybe you can direct me to your closets upstairs so I can have a good rummage through those," he retorted.

Theo was letting off steam, and Eve knew it. She threw him her set of keys which opened the door leading to the house. "Help yourself," she said, pointing the way ahead. "I don't have anything to hide."

She headed toward the telephone and yanked it out of its cradle, watching in agonizing dismay as the professor left the room through the white stable door. It would take him to the main house where he would probably seat himself in her lounge and calm down, she thought. The mere fact that he did not even want to stay in the same room with her was evidence that he was not going to settle easily.

"Yes," she barked into the telephone handset.

"So you're alive then?" Leon crooned.

"What do you want?" Eve snarled. He was the last person she wanted to talk to right now.

"I thought that would've been obvious," Leon returned, his tone milder than usual, making Eve aware he was on a fishing expedition. "I heard the news on the radio this morning. They've picked up a rented car in the name of some professor you were seen with last night. Care to tell me anything?"

"No," Eve relented. "My personal assistant will be releasing a statement. My collection is on its way, and I'll have the models to you by Friday for rehearsals."

"So you're not in trouble?"

"No, Leon," Eve said emphatically. "I'll also be reassuring my sponsor."

"My check—"

"You know I'm good for it," Eve interrupted, squealing in silence. "I'll see you on Friday."

Eve hung up the phone and winced at herself before deciding she needed to sort out a thousand and one other things. She seated herself at the table and banished Theo's grumpy expression from her mind while picking up the phone. *Damn Theophilus de Cordova,* her mind raged as she began dialing the first number.

Eve made fifteen phone calls, one after the other, and each one professionally pitched to ensure she was keeping everyone at bay, sedated, and happy. The models were arranged, Tia Maria consoled, clients addressed for prompt payment, her staff encouraged to come back to work and Jasmine was given an official statement and an apology. The last person she rung was her mum, just to be sure that she was fine.

By the time Eve replaced the phone in its cradle, she

felt a sense of regaining control. She looked at her watch. It read 11:57 A.M. Sighing in relief and feeling much better for reorganizing the dishevelment the last few days had caused, she picked up her handbag and headed for the house, knowing she had skipped breakfast and deciding it was time she made lunch.

Theo admired the room. It was painted white. He liked the rural paintings of Africa hinged to the walls. The room's appeal was made more inviting by the gigantic white sofas and the large windows, also draped in white. *She likes white.* He thought it was perhaps Eve's favorite color. The room did not smell of anything. No flowers, he thought. He, on the other hand, liked fresh arrangement of roses in his room everyday.

He wanted to sit down, but felt edgy. The last few days were still working on his nerves. He left the room and saw stairs leading upward. They took him to the top floor where he saw two rooms. The first was Eve's bedroom. He looked around. An iron bed. Not quite like his. Hers was more modern and draped in gauzy linen. *White, of course,* he told himself. It was an airy room. Bright. Seductive. A man could make love to Eve Hamilton in this room.

He pictured her naked chestnut-brown body on top of the white sheets, oiled and shapely, waiting for him to take her. The clean, neat order of the room danced a sense of purity in his head. *Beautiful, feminine, and angelic.* The green potted plants removed any feeling of the sterile or sanitary which white could often project. In his mind, its reflection of Eve was fertile, ready, ripe for the picking. He felt his manhood stir at the thought.

Repressing the notion because he was still angry with her, he left her bedroom and entered the room next door. A single wrought-iron bed met his gaze. The same white linen. Similar potted green plants. A simple room like her own, only there was a brown box on the floor. He felt no conscience about opening it.

The first thing he saw was a newspaper clipping with the heading CAR BOMB VICTIM DIES AGED 33. He realized the box was jammed-packed with memorabilia, whatever scraps of life Eve felt she had the right to save about her brother. Papers, photographs, and more newspaper cuttings were all unceremoniously scattered and about as organized as a garbage bin.

Theo grew curious. The death of this man had put him in a lot of trouble without their having even met. He began to wonder what he might find. Maybe a peg of what had eluded him so far. He could hear his heart beating heavily in the sudden silence as he dug his hand in and retrieved an armful of stuff.

They were mostly photos, dog-eared and revealing a group of people taken in nightclubs. He put them aside on the floor and skimmed through the box again. He found a cigarette lighter aptly inscribed HONEY BUN. It was charred at one side with a brown stain, like it had been burnt. He put it with the photos and looked again. A spectacle case with the initials P.H.H. Opening it revealed a pair of brand new Calvin Klein sunglasses, never worn. He added it to the pile.

Delving in again, he clutched at a book. It was titled *The Crisis of The Negro Intellectual* with a handwritten notation inside which said: *To Honey Bun. Guard your love, Mabel Syrup.* Theo realized Paul Hamilton had a sweetheart. He dug in again and pulled out U.S. one-dollar bills and placed them aside. Becoming impatient, he picked up the box and upended it, tipping the rest of its contents onto the floor.

It was a waterfall. Credit cards, diaries, keys, pencils, postcards, letters, clippings, snapshots, a tuxedo tie, a driver's license, a contact lens case, deodorant, a bottle of antibiotics, a matchbox, and loose change littered the floor. Junk, most of it, but one thing caught Theo's attention. A snapshot of two passport-sized pictures.

He recognized the face instantly. It was a picture of Dr. Jeffrey Harrison, his first assistant who had now been replaced by Dr. Ira Keplan. Theo felt justifiably confused. He stared at the letters. He sampled a few. They were all written in a fine swirly curl, each beginning with *My darling Honey Bun.* She was obviously the great romance of Paul Hamilton's life. Theo picked up the letters and the snapshot and went downstairs to find Eve.

Eve was in her lounge. No sign of Theo. He had probably gone to the bathroom to have a sulk, she thought. She would give him a few minutes before yelling at him for lunch. She placed her bag on one of the white sofas and went to the answering machine that took her personal calls, reminding herself that she had eggs frying on the cooker in the kitchen downstairs.

It played back the usual mix from old friends, all of whom were concerned about the morning's reports. She made a mental note to call them. The last one made her jolt. It was from Tyrone. His rich baritone explained to her that he was in Sri Lanka on a test match. Someone had tipped him off. He left a phone number. She chose to erase it along with all her other messages.

She picked up the mail at her main door at street level. The door she never used, but where the postman would push her personal mail. Because the studio was at the back basement of the house and had its own entrance from the street closest to it, it fell under a separate post code which allowed her mail to be separated quite conveniently. It meant she could keep some semblance of privacy from her staff and retain a personal life once she left the studio.

To judge by the small load, it was the usual bills, fliers, and an invitation to attend a musical soiree. Eve placed the stack by her bag on the sofa and listened for any sound of Theo. The sound of the toilet flushing alerted her, and she smiled before returning to the kitchen downstairs to continue making lunch.

Theo joined her in the kitchen with a forlorn expression on his face. Eve noticed it the moment she placed two plates filled with eggs, toast, and tomatoes on the dinner table.

"You might at least try to chill out," she snapped, aware that he seemed ready to give her the same silent treatment he had done on leaving his apartment. She turned and reached for some knives and forks in a drawer. "I don't like the idea of being chased by two goons either."

When she turned, Theo threw the snapshot onto the table. "Who's that?" he asked her, his voice very forthright.

"Where did you get it?" Eve countered, suspicious.

"A box in your guest room," Theo bristled. "You didn't answer my question."

"Quiet revenge is it, to search through my things?" Eve mocked. "How childish."

"Just tell me who it is," Theo hissed icily.

"It's my brother, Paul," Eve said, shaking her head to shirk away the emotions which stuck in her throat. "What's the big deal? I told you he's dead."

Theo closed his eyes and sighed heavily before taking a seat at the table. "This gets worse," he murmured almost in a whisper. He placed the letters by his plate and pointed at the snapshot in front of him. "That guy *did* work for me," he muttered, "only he didn't call himself Paul Hamilton. While he worked for me he was a Dr. Jeffrey Harrison."

Eve joined him at the table. "What do you mean?"

"I mean Paul Hamilton and Jeffrey Harrison are one in the same."

Eve shook her head in disbelief. "No. Paul wouldn't do something like that. I know my brother. He just . . . wouldn't."

"Then what was the name of his girlfriend?"

"What?"

"He had a sweetheart," Theo confirmed. "What was her name?"

"I . . . I don't—"

"You don't know," Theo finished. "My guess is that you don't know anything about your brother at all."

Eve was furiously angry, but at the same time, she was riddled with guilt. "Now wait a minute—"

"No, you wait a minute," Theo interrupted harshly. "You've been on a moral high horse since you dragged your dirty laundry through my door. Everything you've done has stuck in my brain like a splinter, and now you expect me to roll over and believe that your brother was some kind of saint. Well he was a con and you're not the only game in town."

Eve's blood ran cold. "What's that supposed to mean?"

"It means . . . Ms. Temptress, that beautiful body of yours isn't going to sway with me." Theo picked up his knife and fork. "You may sashay your way through life on some kind of romantic dream that everything can be stitched together so perfectly, like one of your designs, but I can't. What you stand for is not about glamour so much as creating the illusion of glamour. And we all know what happens to illusions. A man has to ask himself, is it all worth it in the end?"

"How dare you?" Eve jibed, teary-eyed. "What do you

want me to do, grovel all my apologies so that you can take revenge by searching my house? You've got one hell of a nerve." She picked up her plate and her knife and fork and rose to her feet. Eve glared at him, her breathing shallow and erratic in her agitation. "Why not question your responsibility in this?" she attacked head-on. "Did you check this Dr. Harrison's references before you hired him? Did you ask to see his credentials?"

"I didn't think I needed to," Theo interrupted. "He came recommended by—"

"I don't care who recommended him," Eve cut in. "To suggest that it's Paul after me and my mother . . ." Her voice trailed with pain. "If you're looking for a game, I'm good at blood sports, so don't push me. I want to mean more to someone than just some picture in a wallet, so don't flatter yourself. This is your world I'm in, not mine. I happen to know what goes on in my life. Sadly, you don't."

"Where are you going?" Theo yelled.

"To eat in my room," Eve screamed. "And before I leave, ask yourself one more question. How did Dr. Da Costa know that your formula is called Phoebe?" And with that remark, she stormed from the kitchen.

She ate her breakfast on her bed, through her tears. How dare he be so unreasonable. How dare he accuse her of such things. How dare he . . . her eyes blurred. Whatever existed between them had fallen apart. Eve felt the pain stab her in the heart. The feel of his presence having been there between her legs was still with her, even now. The pleasure of it. The aching for it again. How could she reconcile wanting someone so badly when their behavior was so unpleasant?

There was almost something masochistic about it, and she was never a person to purposefully desire pain. But that was always the result when falling for someone. There was always some degree of painful soul searching when the flaws began to show. Eve found herself asking if he was worth it. She had been relegated from Adam's temptress to unscrupulous, scurvy little mercenary all in but a few days. She had done just about every injustice possible in his eyes. He had bruised her head and she had bruised his heel. Now they were even.

She ate slowly, hardly tasting her food. She finished her lunch, then went to the next floor and took a shower. She heard the television at midvolume in the lounge before returning to her bedroom to change into fresh clothing. Eve refused to disturb Theo while dressed in a robe. She would rather he stewed for a while and pondered over everything she had said.

She took her time to don a black T-shirt, fitted black jeans, and a pair of black sandals before applying light make-up to hide the pallor of her face. Rebrushing her hair, Eve swept it up into a single loose braid at the back, allowing a few strands to run down the sides of her face. She looked in the long dressing mirror while passing the bathroom and was satisfied with the result before entering the lounge.

Theo was seated quite comfortably in one of the sofas, reading the last in the pile of Paul's letters. He looked her critically up and down before his mouth twisted in genuine approval. "You're going to need a jacket."

Eve moved forward in long easy movements, glancing across at Theo with cool, brown eyes. "Who's paying for this trip?"

"You don't have any money?"

Eve deliberately gave a careless shrug. "It's not my intention to go to Birmingham." Theo acknowledged her reply by standing. Only then did Eve see that he had been reading Paul's letters. "Those are private," she frowned. "Give them back."

His mouth quirked as he handed them over. "It must be wonderful to love somebody beyond your own un-

derstanding," he said absently. He had not meant his
voice to sound wistful at all, yet somehow it did.

Eve's brows rose as the bundle of letters landed in the
palms of her hands. Exactly what did Theo find in them
to subdue him so dramatically? Her eyes narrowed as
she looked at him. To her chagrin, some inner instinct
wanted to reach out and soothe away the troubled lines
she could see on his forehead. She could see the boy in
him, too. The drooping eyes and vulnerable expression
that seemed to signify the silent demand for a motherly
hug. But she was not a major factor in his life and felt
herself withdrawing from her basic impulses.

"What's the matter?" she asked instead.

"I've been . . . reevaluating," Theo said in bemusement. He glanced at her briefly, then dug his hands into
his pockets. Turning to face the window, he made his
way there. "Moira wants custody of Trey," he blurted
suddenly. "I'm afraid I've been taking it out on you. I'm
sorry."

Eve was stunned and thought back to what he had
told her about Dr. Keltz. "That's why you gave me the
business card of your attorney," she surmised, recalling
his initial distrust of her. "You thought I was snooping
around to pin something on you she could use."

"It's the sort of thing she would do," Theo acknowledged, annoyed. "She threatened as much in her letter.
It had three grammatical errors, two tautologies, and a
false premise. Her use of English is improving, though.
I've written a reply."

Eve sighed heavily, missing the point. "Why are you
telling me this?"

She could hardly imagine it was any of her business
given the circumstances. Before she had gone for her
shower, his arrogant remark about her not being the
only game in town was a blatant reminder he was reluctant to enter into any sort of a meaningful relationship

with anyone. He was in denial of something. Or perhaps he had been fighting some niggling feeling to seek an explanation for exactly what was going on.

Theo turned from the window. "It was just something you said about the picture in my wallet," he told her, his voice filled with tension. "Until now, I never thought to remove it." He gazed toward the sofa where Eve could see he had placed the small snapshot.

When his gaze came back to her, Theo's eyes were so melancholy, Eve felt thrown by his change in mood. What the devil were in her brother's letters to tame Theo in such a manner? Gone was his arrogance. Gone was the harsh tone in his voice. Even his hard, roguish expression had softened to one that seemed more affectionate, like the one he had given her when they were in his bed, making love . . .

Eve shook herself in haughty dismissal of everything that had transpired between them. "Don't," she reproved.

Theo was bemused. "What?"

"Don't try to rationalize this," she swallowed, defending her emotions. "You're only going to tie us both up in knots."

Theo took a step forward, removing his hands from his pockets. "Eve," he exclaimed. "I just felt that I owed you an explanation after—"

"We made love," Eve concluded. She shook her head and turned away from him. "For a man of your education, I expected better," she said. "What do you want me to say? That I'm grateful you're no longer carrying your ex-lover around in your wallet? I am aware you had a life before you met me."

"I know," Theo nodded, his voice strangled with pain. "I just shouldn't have to spend a lifetime paying for one stupid mistake. Not anymore."

"You have Trey," Eve reasoned.

"Do I?" Theo was delving too deep. Eve was not used to this side of the professor. She felt nervous, shaky, and a little out of her depth. His emotional turmoil was too much on top of everything she had endured.

"Look," she said softly, thinking she should perhaps read Paul's letters herself. "Like I've told you before, you're too tactical. If carrying that picture of Moira was some kind of guilt trip, then you were the loser. She's living her life. You need to live yours."

Theo stood motionless as though he had recollected something. "You once said that in this un-ideal world, there are a lot of winners."

"My optimism," Eve said lightly. She looked down at Paul's letters, pondering what was in them. "Love is out there if you want it. It's a choice no one should really deny themselves."

Theo took long strides toward her until Eve found him staring at her head-on. "We're back to the conversation we had in Cramond," he breathed, running a light finger down her cheek. "And since you told me that you hate repetition, I guess I just want to know, do I have a choice?"

"Stop it." Eve pushed his hand away. A wealth of sensations were beginning to churn inside her, but none of them felt appropriate because she had no understanding of what Theo was about. Between lunch and her taking a shower, he had lurked into some kind of emotional territory which was allowing him to question his life. She was inept to deal with it. Her own pool of emotions were rippling with enough problems to complicate her view. "What answer are you looking for?"

His one word shook at Eve's heartstrings. "Love." Theo's hand reached out and touched the bundle of letters in her hand. "The kind that is in these letters." He paused to catch the glistening mirror of bewilderment in Eve's eyes. It touched him with such tenderness, he made another admission. "As much as I thought ill of your brother, he had a heart. In fact, I've come to quite envy him."

Eve was moved. Theo had reached an awareness and it took the actions of her dead brother to do it. "Theo."

He touched her lips. Eve felt the tingle of it run along her veins. "Don't say anything," he objected in a whisper. "Let's just go and sort this mess out. We'll go to the police, then we can talk later."

Eve warily agreed.

But no sooner were they at the door than Theo and Eve froze as if in a tableau. Both stared at the man who calmly stood looking at them. His dark brows were raised questioningly, and Eve wondered who he was. Theo seemed irritated as the man's icy blue eyes suddenly became speculative as he looked them both up and down.

"Going somewhere?" he drawled derisively. He met Theo's contemptuous glare. "You must be the professor the assistant commissioner was tailing." He looked at Eve with a more appreciative gaze. "I take it you're Eve Hamilton."

Eve's mouth tightened in anticipation. "Who are you?"

"Chief Superintendent Michael Neels," he introduced, extending his right hand by way of a general greeting. "And this is Superintendent Abdul Nassiri." An Indian officer poked his head around the door and offered her a smile. "We'd like to ask you both some questions down at the station."

Eve was stunned. To her relief, Theo moved in front of her, his expression reassuring as his arm moved protectively about her waist. He looked at the officers resolutely. "I'm the one you want," he announced.

Touched by his chivalry, Eve caught Theo's gaze. She saw his solid strength and steadfast support. It struck a chord inside her. Theo cared. He was actually concerned about her. About what would happen to her. She hardly knew how to react.

"It's okay," she said mildly. "I need to find out what happened to Humphrey—for my mum's sake.

They were allocated a room with no windows. Only a simple table, four chairs, and a packet of cigarettes occupied it. Theo and Eve sat motionless, weary, and a little frustrated at having been kept waiting, when both Michael Neels and Abdul Nassiri entered. They seated themselves in a leisurely fashion at the other end of the table and smiled politely. Michael Neels decided to offer Theo the packet of cigarettes.

"Ciggie?"

"Not really," Theo objected.

Eve shook her head in her refusal, deciding that on their own territory, both men seemed less imposing than when they stood on the doorstep of her house.

He replaced the packet where he found it. "We would normally interview you both in separate rooms," he began, "but because of the delicate nature of this investigation—"

"You do have the right to an attorney of course," Abdul Nassiri interrupted, his accent quite English as he placed a folder on the table.

Theo raised an inquisitive brow. "Delicate nature?"

"We know you both didn't kill Assistant Commissioner Brown," Neels said suddenly.

Eve's eyes narrowed. Watching models strut their stuff down the catwalk had given her some perception on body language, and right now she considered both officers were giving off all the sort of signals which told her they were withholding something.

"Humphrey Brown was like an uncle to me!" she

blurted out, her gaze roving from one man to the other. "I want to know what's going on."

Both officers inhaled a ragged breath before delving in to tell her the full story. She was amazed to learn that Humphrey Brown had been suspended from duty. He was under investigation by the Police Complaints Authority, which was looking into three charges cited against him, including taking bribes and selling intelligence.

Eve could hardly believe they were talking about the same man whom she had known as a child. The man whose knees she would sit on at night before bedtime, who had sung her lullabies until she fell asleep. Who was once her father's best friend and the rock of her life. It was not very pretty in the telling. She kept her gaze fixed as detail by detail unfolded until the tears fell again as she remembered his cruel death.

"What we don't know is his latest activities before he got shot," Abdul Nassiri finished. "All we know is that it involved you . . ." He stared at the professor. ". . . and seeing as you were on the scene when he died, we figured you could fill us in."

Theo nodded heavily, his face grim. "We went to the park to try and get my formula back," he began.

He explained his work with the UN Drug Control Program, his experiments on a fungus spore that could kill drug crops, how he had to make a presentation of his findings at a UN Summit the following week. Both officers' eyes widened when he told them of the formula having been stolen. He did not mention Eve's involvement, only related how it came into the possession of Assistant Commissioner Brown and that it was his belief it was to be sold on to a drug baron.

Michael Neels was overwhelmed by the information. "So that's what the little squirt was up to." He paused in awe. "The two men who chased you . . ." Abdul pro-

duced two black-and-white photographs from the file he
had carried into the room. "Did they look like these
two right here?"

"That's them," Theo acknowledged, gritting his teeth
as he remembered his own gunshot wound.

"Cantrell's men," Abdul nodded.

"I figured as much," Theo stated firmly. "It's common knowledge at the UNDCP that he's caught in a
bitter feud with Emilio Bogetti over excess drug supply
to the market. He's losing profits because prices are
down. Only now my formula is just the ticket to wipe
out a rival crop. They need someone to decipher it."

He went on to tell them about his concerns for Dr.
Keltz. Eve felt her heart plummet as she saw the wistful
look of fear in Theo's eyes. She wondered just how deep
his feelings went. Did he still harbor any for Trey's
mother?

"We'll get an officer on that right away," Neels reassured.

His gaze shifted to Eve. She had remained silent and
tearful the entire time while Theo divulged enough for
the officers to go on. It seemed like eons since she had
looked at Theo's snapshot and then forced her way into
his life. Now he was protecting her very reputation by
concealing her involvement in what had now become
an international affair. Michael Neels could see it, too.
He saw her shamefaced expression and Theo's wistful
one and knew they meant something more than what
could be taken at face value.

"How did you come to know Professor de Cordova?"
he probed.

Eve winced. Her self-condemnation of her actions
were beginning to expose her as the troublemaker after
all. "I—"

"She attended one of my seminars strictly to lend her
name for a fund-raiser," Theo interrupted with a half

truth. "It's a coincidence of tragedies that she knew Humphrey—"

"I can't believe he would risk everything he'd worked for," Eve whimpered, prevaricating the topic by thinking back to when the assistant commissioner had talked about his career. "He was only two or three years away from retiring and collecting his pension."

Abdul searched her expression, not entirely sure he had been given the full story, but accepting what he had been told all the same. "Sometimes the greatest of co-incidences are mysteries," he said thoughtfully, as though he was quoting an ancient proverb from his mother country.

Eve closed her eyes. The history of what had unfolded about Humphrey Brown was a predicament she could never tell her mother. It would ruin her fondest memories of a man she had always kept in high esteem. This was the man who, as a child, she had hoped her mother would one day take as a second husband. Sadly, that was no longer an option. She clasped her fingers knowing full well that arrangements would have to be made with her church to retrieve his body and bury him.

"He mentioned you once," Neels suddenly recollected, as though he had pulled a single thread of memory from his brain. "Didn't you have a brother who died last year?"

Eve's eyes opened wide and she was unable to speak. She looked at Theo, dread building up inside her. Theo could see every measure of it in her face. The prospect of her brother still being alive, of being under the guise of his first assistant Dr. Jeffery Harrison. He weighed the consequences of divulging this fresh piece of information, then decided in his wisdom against it. He would rather work with the authorities first to have Dr. Keltz placed somewhere safe away from harm than attempt to piece more of the puzzle together.

"Ms. Hamilton is still trying to come to terms with losing her brother," Theo answered for her before glancing at his watch. "She also has a fashion show to—"

Michael Neels overrode his remark. "Didn't your brother die in a car bomb explosion?"

Eve nodded, quite mute as the awful truth flooded to overburden her.

"He was identified by . . . contents found in a burnt briefcase in his car." Neels recalled in sympathy. He shook his head in mortification. "Nasty business." He observed Theo's tight reassuring squeeze of Eve's hand. He committed it to memory, but said nothing of his detection. Nor did he make comment about the slight furtive glances of what he considered to be more than affection pass between them.

"One more thing," Abdul added, his attention on Theo. "You reported a raid a year ago on a warehouse in Piccadilly where you allegedly had a laboratory?"

"I did have a lab there," Theo confirmed, his tone tainted with renewed anger as he remembered also reporting who he thought was responsible. "You never charged Dr. Henri Da Costa, so he still thinks he can throw his weight around."

"The Met didn't have enough evidence," Neels put in.

"Do you think he's involved in what we're dealing with?" Abdul questioned as an afterthought.

Theo's mouth twisted. "I wouldn't put it past him or those ecological terrorists he's dealing with. He's an absolute discredit to my profession. And he knew I code-named the formula Phoebe."

"Then we'll bring him in for questioning," Abdul decided, closing his file and standing. He looked at Theo. "We'll need to run this by the National Criminal Intelligence Service, so we're gonna have to keep you in safe custody until you leave for the UN Summit next week."

"Can I call my son?" Theo asked.

"Of course." Abdul's gaze shifted to Eve. "Ms. Hamilton, you're free to leave."

Eve's gaze switched from person to person as though she was coming out of a daze. Suddenly she realized it was all over. "I can go?" She slowly rose out of her chair. "What about those two goons?"

"If they are Yayo Cantrell's men, then it's likely they were after the professor," Neels concluded.

"They say the only woman he ever cared about was his daughter," Abdul commented.

"Before he killed her," Neels piped in.

"Ah, yes," Abdul conceded suddenly. "Allegedly. But Ms. Hamilton can't read the formula." He looked at her worried face. "We have no reason to think they would be looking for you."

Eve nodded warily, hoping he was right, for at that moment she felt very much like she was on the precipice of the white cliffs of Dover. And she was about to slip.

"We'll give you a minute with the professor," Abdul added, striding toward the door.

The moment they left, Eve looked at Theo. "Well this is it," she said, charting the masculine angles of his face.

Still seated, he raised his eyes to her before standing, his tall frame towering above her. "Yes, this is it."

The finality in his tone felt like a sledgehammer coming down and smashing all her emotions into a million pieces. Mixed with all her strong and confused feelings toward Theo, Eve hardly knew how to cope with finally leaving him. To her chagrin, she felt broody and morose.

"I'm sorry, for everything."

"Sssh," Theo held her wrists, shaking both her hands to force the spirit back into her. "We're here now and it's all going to be fine." He chuckled, but it was faint and strained, and Eve knew the sea of worry that lay beneath it. "By this time next week when you'll have done your show, me my seminar, and Trey is back in school, we'll be laughing at how our lives have become boring again."

She could not smile. Eve knew this would be the last time they would be seeing each other. "Are you in a lot of trouble? I mean with the United Nations?"

"I was hired as a consultant," Theo rationalized, "and found myself a living target. I can hardly answer for every looney tune drug baron out to make a fast buck."

"I just wanted justice for . . ."

"I know," Theo nodded in contemplation. "He's out there Eve. And he's madly in love with somebody."

Eve raised her eyes to Theo's, drowned in the chocolate-brown depth that greeted her. "Theo . . ."

His mouth, as it claimed hers, was warm and deeply penetrating. It came unexpectedly, too, much to Eve's delight. Suddenly, she was enfolded against his chest, against the hardness of his body as he molded her to each sinewed curve, deepening his kiss as the seconds passed.

Eve responded instinctively, feeling reassured, elated that they were parting in this way. It was her last chance to touch him, to run her hands down Theo's spine, the shivers of delight coursing through her body like a burst of fireworks. Her mouth opened to the intimacy of his kiss, a feeling of hard possession sweeping over her. She wanted this man. She needed him. But now, their destiny had an uncertain future. When he finally released her, Eve was shaking and definitely out of sorts with herself. She could see the finality in their act.

"Let's forget this ever happened," she whimpered, knowing they had truly reached the end of their trail. "Forget we ever met."

Theo saw the tears in her eyes. How he would love to see her smile again. "Obviously you can't," he returned.

"I never planned it," Eve told him, her heart begging

that he understand. "I never expected to care about you the way I do."

"I'm sorry it didn't turn out the way you planned," he said, accepting her decision. He would miss her. Terribly. But she had her life in the city and he had his in Scotland. "For the short time we were together, I was the protector of your heart and you were the protector of mine."

Eve glanced at him, finding his words quite touching. She was moved by them. "Why did you say that?"

"Just wishing out loud," Theo sighed. "I'm repeating a line I read in one of your brother's letters." He ran a shaky finger down her cheek, brushing the single tear away. "What I should say is that I'll be thinking of you when you do your show in Paris."

"I'll be thinking of you, too," Eve nodded. It was the last thing she said to the professor as she walked miserably out of his life.

Eleven

It's just as well it ended this way, Eve told herself. It was for the best. She could now return to the normal humdrum of her life without being immersed in the whirlwind of some man's life adventure. At least that was what she had thought when she looked at the photograph of Dr. Moira Keltz that Theo had left on her sofa. It served as an awful memento of how complicated the professor's life was. Only a cruel twist of fate could make her fall so easily for such a man.

Every image in her brain had been of Theo; his well-shaped profile, his broad nose and sturdy build, his generous eyelashes and thick dark brows, and the roguish hard angles around his unshaven jawline. The sensuality of his thick, rounded mouth and the taste of it when he had kissed her were foremost in her mind. It merely added to her stockpile of suffering. The anguish of knowing they were destined never to meet again.

Periodically, while packing her bags for Paris, she would fantasize alternative scenarios of leaving Theo that provided a better salvage for her inner mood. There was the *Gone with the Wind* scene where she would picture herself, strong-willed, defiant, determined to win him back. *West Side Story* provided the scenario of true love dying in one's arms as a vision of permanency. The *Casablanca* setting, where she was weak, tearful, but silently sensible at finding and losing a love, was disturbingly realistic. All three vignettes were painful.

In real life, she told herself, her efforts had to be focused on letting him go. Just as she had done with Tyrone. Though Tyrone had been someone her mother approved of and her friends quietly adored, he was much too selfish for her to love. With Theo, everything felt different. She had a sense of hanging on in there, not that she believed the two of them were destined for a great ending, like riding off into a perpetual sunset, seated in the surrey with the fringe on top, while an orchestra played the tune from *Oklahoma*. Even she was not that surreal. It was more a case of believing she could sustain a . . . friendship with a man more on her intellectual level.

Theo was a good conversationalist. Okay, he rationalized a little more than the average guy, but she had enjoyed talking with him. It gave her a sense of grounding with the man. And when they had made love, even though it was just one time, it felt extraordinarily special because she had saved his life. Still, it did not prompt her to tell him how she really felt when he had asked. A lot could be read into "It was fine."

Eve cursed herself for being so stupid. She had left Theo with the impression she was not all that interested, that whatever had happened between them was simply a flight of fancy, touched with a little intrigue which had now burned its course. They could now wake up to the stark gaze of reality with no harm caused to either person.

It was just as well it ended this way, Eve told herself for the thousandth, and doubtless the final time, as she boarded the plane for Paris with Jasmine. Though she was soon above the clouds and could plainly see them from her window seat, they did not give her the same cocoon effect of being snuggled safely against cotton wool as she had experienced on her previous journeys. It was three days since she had last seen Professor de Cordova and the dawning that life had to go on was beginning to feel like a strain.

"You really should have had some breakfast," Jasmine said curtly, aghast that Eve bore the look of an abandoned woman. No make-up. Her hair, though freshly washed, pulled back into a simple ponytail. She knew Eve had not given her the full story and considered the whole event had caused Eve some trauma. "You can't let everything that happened wear you down."

I do not intend to, Eve thought. It was a phase she would soon knock herself out of. She had succeeded with Tyrone. No doubt she would succeed again and remove memories of Theo from her mind just as easily. "I wasn't hungry," she said, yawning.

"I suppose Professor de Cordova will be returning to hibernation in his laboratory," Jasmine said, assuming the short-lived affair was now over. "Lola tells me he rarely comes out for daylight, and you're a city girl." Again, there was that note of envy.

Eve shot her a dagger stare. The homestead part of her was reluctant to accept that she would always remain in the city. She hoped to settle in the suburbs and plan a family of her own one day. Surely, there was more to life than designing the best innovation in haute couture only the affluent could buy. "I don't think you know me that well," she peeved, feeling the discomfort in Jasmine's remark.

Jasmine heard the sting in Eve's tone and decided to distance herself immediately. "The media were wonderful, don't you think?" she crooned, more spirited. "The moment I released your press statement, you got calls from—"

"Let's not go into that," Eve interrupted, when she thought of the flowers which had arrived at her home and the cards of best wishes and sympathy following the news announcement on the TV and radio prompted by Jasmine.

The simple statement had outlined her distress at having found the body of a close family friend, and her attempts to apprehend the suspects. The news had turned the whole ordeal into an act of bravery on her part, and she had been cited as a heroine against the backdrop of London becoming a more dangerous place, swarming with criminals. It was hardly a tag she deserved, and she wondered whether Theo had seen the coverage.

"Yeah, let's put it behind you," Jasmine agreed, turning to the diary in her hand. "I've booked us into the San Regis, just off the Champs-Élysées. We're due to arrive there at 3:30 P.M. Leon wants to see you right away, so I think we should eat at the hotel first, then go straight to the chateau to check on the models and the pavilion."

Eve nodded her agreement.

"The show starts tomorrow in the afternoon," Jasmine continued, "after the champagne reception. It'll probably finish around 8:00 P.M., then it'll be followed by dinner and networking until midnight. I couldn't get us a room at the chateau so we'll be going back to the hotel."

"That's sounds great." Eve, too, tried to add spirit to her voice, but failed. She stared through the window and tried to conjure up ways of enjoying her fourth trip to France.

The last time she had visited to do a show, she had been accompanied by Tyrone. He had wanted to see the place where Victor Hugo said "the beating of Europe's heart is felt." That meant Paris. The Seine. Monet's house at Giverny. Versailles. A pilgrimage to Chartres. They saw them all. Together. At his expense. Now she was going to the city of love alone, abounded with money problems. The very thought took her back to Theo. Her handsome number-one suspect whom she feared had stolen her heart and left her no closer to finding out what happened to her brother. If only it were he sitting in Jasmine's place right now.

Forlorn, she reached into her handbag and was immediately alerted by the sight of Paul's letters. All the stamps had been removed from the envelopes, and she wondered if he had returned to his hobby of stamp collecting. Eve forgot she had packed them. She picked up the bundle and, as she did so, Theo's words ran through her head. *If you find out how a victim lived, you'll find out how he died.* While bored at thirty-thousand feet, Eve decided to occupy herself by opening the first of the twelve envelopes. She was captivated the moment she read the first line: *My darling Honey Bun . . .*

Paris was just as she had left it; buzzing with excitement. The plane had touched down at Charles de Gaulle airport half an hour earlier and Eve was seated in the hired limousine—another item charged to her business account—glancing through the tinted windows. It was a hot day. The streets were full of people dressed in hot-pants and flowery dresses, short-sleeved shirts, vests, or T-shirts, many seated in chairs drinking coffee outside the many small cafés for which Paris was renowned. She was thankful she had not overdressed, though the car had ample air conditioning.

She asked her chauffeur, who had introduced himself as Anton, for a window to be open wide enough so she could feel the cool warm breeze that signaled the first day of June. The traffic noise was phenomenal. She had always thought that the wide roads of Paris lacked a composite sense of order, and that eight lanes of cars seemed to have the right of way to do as they pleased. Being immersed in it now made her wary of the edge of danger, but it did not take away the sudden wake of excitement which had begun to build in the pit of her stomach.

Eve decided if anything was going to help her to escape the upheaval of the last few days, her trip to Paris would certainly be it. And with that resolve, she asked the chauffeur to take the leisurely route along the Seine so she could take in the sights.

Jasmine was delighted that a smile had formed on Eve's face as they toured a city of arts *par excellence.* The Jardin des Tuileries, Grand Palais. Across the bridge toward the Arc de Triomphe, then down Avenue des Champs-Élysées to where their hotel was located.

A former nineteenth-century mansion with a magnificent neoclassical façade, it seemed aptly suited for the gourmet jet set for whom Eve designed most of her fashion. She placed her suitcase on one of the two single beds in their hotel room and purposefully forgot about the huge expense of putting on the charity show as she ran out onto the balcony. Taking a deep breath, she inhaled the fresh smell of French air. The cool breeze rippled against her white georgette blouse and azure cotton trousers while her eyes took in the superb view of Paris and the Eiffel Tower.

She was alive again. Her mind began to fire up with myriad thoughts about how she was going to make her show a success. Excited about seeing her pavilion, she turned and went back into her room to find Jasmine already emptying her small suitcase.

"Did you arrange a car to take us to the chateau?"

"Anton returns for us in an hour," Jasmine informed her, carefully unloading the black cocktail dress she planned to wear the following evening. "That'll give us enough time to eat downstairs before we go to the chateau to oversee rehearsals."

"Good." Eve nodded, feeling her world was now falling back into place. She returned to the balcony with ideas anew. She would do her show, reap in her orders, which would more than compensate her promotional budget and gross outlay, then get back down to the business of completing her design for next summer's fashion.

The enchanting seventeenth-eighteenth-century Normandy chateau, discreetly restored and retaining its period atmosphere, on the edge of a hamlet seventy-five miles west of Paris, looked wonderfully historic as the limousine pulled into the large forecourt. As Eve departed the car, she could see the house was surrounded by moats and extensive outbuildings, including a barn and a sixteenth-century chapel. Further afield were meadows and woods extending eighteen acres or more. A heated outdoor swimming pool met her gaze. Her heels dug into the pebbled forecourt as she made her way toward the main doors.

Leon Cavalli was waiting impatiently. Formidably dressed in black tight-fitting trousers and a black silk shirt, its neck open to reveal his clean-shaven chest, he eyed her warily as she made her way toward him. She was there at last.

"Hello." She extended her hand for a formal greeting before indicating her personal assistant. "You remember Jasmine Halpern."

Leon nodded. "About time you're here." He sighed. Clutching a clipboard and a pen with both hands he turned immediately and led the way ahead. "It's like a madhouse in here. Only three designers are now showing, including you. P. Diddy pulled out, and everyone's clamoring to get their rehearsals in."

Eve could see that Leon was quite flustered. If she had not been caught up in events of the last few days, she would have arrived sooner. Her show was very important to her, though convincing Leon of that was sure to be another matter. Nevertheless, she felt she owed him more than just a simple apology, for Leon Cavalli was not a man who could be bought easily. His long strides took them through the chateau and down a black-and-white marbled corridor where men on ladders were yelling at men below to be sure they stayed out of the way.

"Electricians," Leon cursed beneath his breath, his feet avoiding all manner of cable that ran along the marbled floor. Eve followed diligently, silenced by the magnificent hallway. Chandeliers delicately hung from the patterned ceiling, huge windows with handmade glass let in the bright rays of light, which bounced off the genuine works of art on the walls, and an imposing stairway led upward to a wide balcony on the first floor.

Eve continued looking in all directions, absorbing the vast wealth of the house, when Leon took them through two more doors and directly into a large ballroom. It was filled with people hustling around: glitterati models, a throng of cameramen, workmen adding finishing touches, florists arranging hoards of orchids on the tables dotted around the ballroom, personal staff taking orders, and chateau staff disappearing in and out through the terraced doors. A lawn outside was beautifully set against the backdrop of a cascading water fountain. As a designer, Eve was suddenly overwhelmed with the enormity of what she had gotten herself into.

"As you can see," Leon remarked, making her instantly aware of the sheer volume he had endured. "It's a madhouse."

He did not wait for Eve to appreciate the elegance of the room itself, with its elaborate ceiling and gargantuan windows draped with wonderfully rare fabric. Instead, he immediately took her through the chaos and out the terraced doors onto the lawn. Eve could see four pavilions ahead of her. She followed Leon as he passed one pavilion that was decorated like a French boudoir, complete with rococo touches. Her own pavilion was just a stone's throw away.

Eve saw her name boldly displayed in the middle with the sponsor's name aptly placed at either side of a colossal hardboard mannequin adorned as a female shrouded with marvelous arrays of ethnic colors. The catwalk was proportionately sized with red velvet gilt chairs lining the perimeter, and a collection of Egyptian and African statuettes were placed prominently to add a blend of the Nile and the Sahara. Eve loved it.

"It's beautiful," she gasped, throwing her arms around Leon, deservedly so.

His smile said it all. He was satisfied with her acceptance of his work. "Queen Makeda. King Solomon's true love," he said of the mannequin. "It was difficult," he did not neglect to say, "because you didn't give me much to go on, but I thrive on challenges."

Eve felt the strain of how unorganized she had been. "I can see why you were worried and wanted me to see it before you added the finishing touches."

"Absolutely," Leon agreed. "Some of the other designers flew in a few days ago to have a preview of their pavilions."

Eve winced. "Did my collection get here?"

"Yesterday," Leon confirmed. He placed the clipboard on the pavilion catwalk and reached into his back trouser pocket for a packet of Benson & Hedges.

Eve faced her personal assistant. Jasmine read her thoughts immediately and followed Leon's directions to the back of the pavilion which he had allocated as the area where the models would be changing.

"And the models?" Eve asked.

"They're here now, backstage," he added, lighting a

cigarette. "They arrived just after lunch. I've scheduled the first rehearsals in half an hour."

Eve nodded again and sighed with true contentment. She was looking forward to her show with more relish than when she had arrived at the chateau. Reaching into her handbag, she pulled out an envelope and handed it to Leon. "I had it drawn up yesterday. And there's a bonus in there, too, for all your hard work. My way of an apology for the uncleared check."

Leon stood back in surprise, softened by Eve's generous nature. "Did you sort out that unfortunate business in London?" he questioned with genuine concern, blowing puffs of smoke into the air as a form of release from his own pent-up anxieties.

Eve's thoughts were suddenly propelled back to Theo. She wondered where he was, what he was doing, whether he had located Dr. Keltz. And with that reminder came fresh thoughts that startled her. She wondered whether the professor had rekindled his love affair with Moira. Whether he was going to turn over custody of his son to her. Were they engaged in a tug-of-love battle? She was troubled to the point that she was forced to blink before she spoke.

"They haven't found who killed the assistant commissioner in St. James's Park," she exclaimed sadly, sticking to what the news had covered. "He was a close family friend." Her lips trembled. "I shall miss him dreadfully."

Leon touched her hand in understanding. "I was very harsh with you. I'm sorry."

Eve acknowledged his apology with a pained smile. "It's just one of those things." She looked around and digested the noise and general confusion outside on the lawn. "I can't wait to do this show. The weather's beautiful and there are so many people. Where's Shola Onyeocha?"

"She and her partner vacated the chateau two weeks ago when the first set of workers arrived to begin removing furniture from the ballroom," Leon explained, inhaling more nicotine. He looked around, approving the venue. "They live well, don't they?"

Eve nodded. "Quite charitable of her to be lending us her home, too." Curious she asked, "Who's her partner anyway?"

"Some Greek tycoon. Yiannis something-or-other. I'm told they'll be arriving tomorrow," Leon said, looking at his watch. "You'll get to meet her and Nelson Mandela."

Eve checked her own watch. "How many rehearsals will we get in tonight?"

"Two, maybe three,"

"That should be enough."

"Yep."

An uncomfortable silence followed as Eve's mind took her back to her recent ordeal. She dismissed it from her mind and made a firm resolve that she would forget Professor de Cordova and his dangerous formula. "I'll just go backstage and check my collection and the girls."

"I'll be ready to go in ten," Leon said, tapping his watch with his cigarette hand, causing burnt ash to fall on the lawn. "We need to time it. The schedule goes up on the main board tonight."

The pained smile returned to her face before Eve followed Jasmine's trail behind the pavilion. The niggling suspicion that Theo could once again strike up a relationship with Dr. Moira Keltz resurfaced to haunt her like a bad dream. She was riddled with jealousy at the mere thought, her head full of doubts and bleak misgivings. Eve could not understand why she was feeling this way.

Hadn't she just gotten her life back on track? She was the woman who had, only that morning, decided it was probably for the best that she and Theo had parted. For a woman who took pride in the fact that she was self-aware, Eve failed to understand herself. What was she hoping to gain by putting herself through such torture? As she cornered the pavilion and saw the bustle of excitement as her models began to handpick from her collection, the answer hit her like a heavy, ironclad sledgehammer. It was simple. Eve wanted Theo's love.

"War is a purification rite," Jasmine said quite objectively as she peered through the curtains at the back of the pavilion, watching the camera crew rushing to stake out the best vantage points, using their tripods as territorial markers. "This must be one of their toughest assignments outside the Israeli battlefield."

"Tell me about it." Eve shrugged, her nerves on edge, her senses aware that true veterans positioned their equipment the night before as precise indicators of their place in the fashion war stake for principality. As in any ritual, proximity to the altar—in this case, her pavilion's catwalk—was paramount. These were photographers who were eager to get a glimpse of her latest collection. It was her second opportunity this year to show her work, and Eve felt some elation that she was giving them a peek.

As the audience flooded the pavilion to the classical rhythm of a string quartet, all she could see were the eyes of journalists and photographers from *Vogue, Tatler, Ebony* . . . They would be rising out of Paris like locusts from a sweet cactus by nightfall to send the image she had created across the world for hard bargaining. Eve had them to contend with, as well as the minor set of celebrities and the European jet set who had flown in to Paris to see the shows that weekend. Nelson Mandela had flown in by helicopter with a pla-

toon of bodyguards and was being directed to his seat
along with his entourage.

She recognized some of the frenzy of fashion emper-
ors, general buyers, and royalty, in particular Princess
Fatima Adjani, who was famous for fainting her way in,
only to recover, causing a nuisance, often over the po-
sitioning of her seat. She was a difficult client. Always
requiring fitting after fitting. And Eve could never see
the point, because only her Saudi husband and the female members of her family got to see the cut and sway
of her design. Princess Adjani would return to her country and completely adorn herself in a black *abaaya* and
veil over her garment, like the Muslim women she and
Theo had hidden behind in London when they tried to
escape the two goons who chased them.

At that precise moment, Eve detested her mood. She
should be happier. An audience had gathered to see
what she, as a British style bandit, had to present on her
catwalk. Her concentration waned from nervous show
presenter to anxious woman-child wanting to run home
to mother. She prayed her make-up would prove deceptive to the churning mass inside. She had carefully ac-
centuated the color of her eyes with dashes of cream
and brown, added definition to her brows and marked
her cheeks with a faint blush of pink for gusto. Still, she
felt very daunted by what lay ahead.

"Ready for your launch?" Jasmine's voice suddenly
bellowed into Eve's ragged thoughts.

Eve looked at her and tried to absorb the worker ants
busily getting into their gowns while sipping a courtesy
supply of Mini Moëts. She felt herself suddenly detached
from her surroundings. She still did not have an answer
to Paul's death. Humphrey Brown was now murdered.
Professor Theophilus de Cordova was in protective custody. And there was the risk that he might rekindle an
old flame with the mother of his son. Eve felt nauseous

and panicked. These were the thoughts which had prevented her from sleeping.

She had tossed and turned in her hotel room with the demons of the night taunting her with images of Theo when they had made love. She had recalled all the small nuances which had given her pleasure. The way his roguish jawline had rubbed against her skin. His gentle touch making a snake's trail down her chestnut-brown body to the one place that caught the breath in her mouth. She was choked with that same breath when Jasmine tapped her on the shoulder, thrusting her back into reality that her show was about to be airborne.

"I said are you ready to launch?" Jasmine hollered.

"Yes," Eve shrieked, girding herself into the profession which kept fashion editors panting for her next seasonal change.

She smoothed the slinky, specially dyed, desert-colored fishtail gown she had created for the occasion. It revealed all her womanly curves and was the perfect accent for her show that evening. Her brown hair was styled into a sweeping cascade around her face and pinned up with pearl clips. If only her mood was as immaculate.

Jasmine was more perceptive than usual. "You're really going to have to put that man out of your mind," she jabbed, shaking her head in annoyance. "This is much more important."

Offended, Eve walked behind the pavilion and tried her best to concentrate on what she was doing. It was not easy. Nervous as ever, the three modestly experienced elongated models of Kenyan and Caribbean origin—Celia, Lena, and Enya—were fiddling with their necklaces, twisting their rings, smoothing their dresses, and drinking more champagne for courage.

The chateau owners, Miss Shola Onyeocha and her Greek partner, choosing to host *Style Paradise* for five hundred of the swankiest, sexiest, and most famous faces, to raise funds for the Nelson Mandela Children's Fund, were seated as though in golden chairs, having already presided over two shows, one after the other.

Eve looked at her watch, knowing timing would be Navy precise. She was the last of the three pavilions to display her signature style. When the last zipper was zipped, hem was checked, and the giggles started, Leon Cavalli stepped out onto the catwalk and announced her show, then blended into the audience.

As the models got in line, she began calculating whether they would give her her money's worth. It had cost her a modest nine thousand pounds to hire them. Only part of the entire cost of her show would be met by her sponsor. And Tia Maria was being overly generous. The rest she had charged on her credit card. It was a risk. What she needed right now was cash register feedback.

That meant appealing to her buyers and to the fashion editors. It meant switching off all her haunting thoughts and sensual musings about Professor Theophilus de Cordova and giving full concentration to her show. With everything hanging on the thread of the fabrics which made up her designs, Eve gave the cue to send out her first model.

With the lights dimmed and the sound of Jay Z thundering through the speakers, the crowd applauded wildly. Pencils leaped into action, cameras flashed, and a wave of cheer echoed throughout Paris.

The theme was the Queen of Sheba. The models were as exotically dressed as Eve herself in colorful patterned lace and organza, silk, georgette, chiffon, and satin embellished with varying tropical shades of découpé. It was an elegant celebration of style which bordered on the right side of eroticism—nothing too revealing of the girls' anatomy—and each material slowly and carefully snipped away to produce figure-hugging dresses inadvertently sexy, but not vulgar.

With Africa as her source of inspiration, the runway was filled with hot, raw tribal costumes: red beaded dresses, embroidered and fringed eau de nil linen slim gowns, some made of python skin edged with chiffon shredded like straw, and an adornment of what Eve considered to be some of her best work.

The cheer at the end, and the flashes of cameras had Eve out on her pavilion, taking curtsies and smiling at the crowd until she melted into the spotlight. After dinner inside the grand ballroom, and while talking with the elite, who had come from far and wide to see her work, Eve began to relax and feel more assured about the progress of her career thus far.

"Chère madame." A Parisian man rushed toward her, placing a card in her hand after Nelson Mandela had addressed the audience with a lengthy speech. *"Au nom de Jean-Pierre Cavelet."* He owned seven boutiques in France, considered himself a devotee of ethnic fashion, and wanted to order an obscene number of her designs.

They talked endlessly, though Eve was loath to admit her French had become quite rusty. Still, she was able to communicate with what little she knew, while drinking *Esprit du Siècle* Champagne and projecting in her head the profits to be made. They cut a deal in euros, the new currency, and Jean-Pierre kissed her hand with a gallant gesture before milling back into the crowd.

"Merci beaucoup," she said, eternally grateful as he waved a hearty farewell.

The Middle Easterns were equally impressed. Princess Adjani was particularly enamored, purchasing the entire collection with an insistence that, because her sister was getting married very soon, she would be requiring everything as a matter of urgency.

And so went Eve's evening. Appearing statuesque in her high heels, buyer after buyer clamored for her attention in her pavilion after dinner, laughing and joking, carefully exchanging business cards, and generally allowing her to build on her *Hamilton Connections* with flair, finesse, and charm. Even Lola Henriques, whom Eve had seen on two occasions while engaged in dialogue, signaled her approval.

"I can't believe how well everything is going," Eve finally beamed at Jasmine while reaching for another glass of Moët & Chandon's rarest vintage, offered by the chateau staff. She had talked with the hosts, met prominent members in her pavilion, watched the charity auction and fireworks display, and was now thinking of winding down preparatory to returning to their hotel. "All money well spent."

In her black cocktail dress with complementary lace shawl, her make-up and hair well presented for the occasion, Jasmine was suitably pleased with the outcome. "Absolutely," she responded, smiling across the room at the Afro-European male models who had especially impressed her. So different from the Delroys and Delvins back home whose subculture of hip hop, jungle, or garage was not the clean-cut image to which she was more accustomed.

Eve, aware of the preoccupation of her personal assistant, decided instead to circle the room one last time before suggesting they head on back to the hotel. Jokingly holding her nose she indicated to Jasmine that she was going to take a final plunge before bedtime. Eve turned and was about to dive back in with the crowd when a hand gently gripped her arm.

She stared at the man who examined her with respectful attention, before her gaze shifted to the young Trinidadian girl—attractive, teeth shining like polished ivory, and wearing a pair of outlandish earrings—then back to the face she recognized. "Tyrone!"

Spellbound, he smiled happily at her. "How ya doing?"

Eve was stunned. He seemed shorter, with more inches on his waistline, and it was evident he was beginning to lose his hair, in contrast to Theophilus de Cordova, who had plenty of hair. Eve could not help drawing comparisons between the two, especially as there were only two years distance in age between them.

"I'm fine," she said, taking another gulp of champagne. "I was going to return your call."

"What, all six of them?"

Eve winced as a vision of their last meeting formed in her head. She had been seated in his MG sportscar, calmly listening while he voiced his misgivings about their relationship. She could still picture the agonized silence which fell between them, during which the only sound to be heard was the patter of rain against the car windows. They had decided it was fruitless to go on. Her last act of salvaging any honor was to place his diamond engagement ring on the walnut dashboard of his car. The simple act said everything. It was over. They were no longer an item.

"It's nice to see you again," she said with moderate courtesy.

"Eve, this is Geraldine," he introduced, carefully omitting her last name.

The younger woman stepped forward to affect a handshake, inadvertently revealing Eve's former engagement ring on her left finger. "Pleased to meet you," she said with a small island burr, her adolescent tone an absolute giveaway that she had very little intellect. "I enjoyed your show."

Eve scoffed at the discovery of the ring, but had little

choice but to attempt polite courtesy, though she knew any conversation with Tyrone Mosley would prove equally fruitless. "I thought you were in Sri Lanka. What are you doing here?"

He shrugged. "Bopping around Paris. Heard about your show."

An uncomfortable silence followed, and Geraldine clung to Tyrone's arm possessively. He seemed quite dismal, or so Eve thought. Not quite the Tyrone she remembered. "It went well tonight," she smiled. "Much better than I expected."

"I'm pleased for you."

"Me, too," Geraldine enthused.

Eve smiled at them both. They were unsuitably matched. Anyone with eyes could see that, despite their poise and very presence at such a glittering event to force their growing acceptance as a couple. Still, it was none of her business. "Well," she concluded, wrapping up their brief conversation upon spotting an alert cameraman showing more than his fair share of interest from across the ballroom. Oddly, no one had mentioned the incident in London, which was a blessing. The last thing Eve wanted was for the paparazzi to apply gossip and undermine the success of her show.

"You should take Geraldine for a dance," she remarked, approving of the younger woman's Italian gown. "I'm told there's going to be a mini nightclub in the empty pavilion with a local DJ spinning the tunes. I hope you enjoy your evening."

She was about to pivot on her heels and leave, when Tyrone delayed her with a simple hand on her arm. "Eve." His face was forlorn. "I'm sorry to hear about Humphrey Brown. I know what he meant to you. I came because . . ." He paused. "I wasn't there for you when you lost your brother. If you need any help, I'm right here."

Eve's body shook at the sudden reminder of Paul and the memories she had pushed to the far recesses of her mind. Tyrone rousing them now was not what she had expected. "Thanks," she muttered without thinking. "But I'm coping. So let me go."

Tyrone's tone lowered to a whisper and his hand still held firm to her arm. "Just because we're no longer together doesn't mean I don't care about you. I've been a heel and I'm sorry." He let go and raised his tone again. "Congratulations on your show."

Eve stared at him defiantly. "Congratulations on your engagement."

Tyrone flinched, but Geraldine basked in the glory. "Thank you," she beamed, thrusting her ring into Eve's face.

She eyed the familiar cluster with a wry smile. This woman was accepting second best and did not even know it. Eve told her how lovely the diamond was, offered Tyrone a forgiving smile and then excused herself without incident. She was applauding herself for having handled seeing Tyrone again, when Lola Henriques, clutching at her red halter-neck gown, came rushing over. Eve failed to see the worry in the older woman's face as she threw her a smile.

"How are you?" She greeted Lola with an extended arm. Amazingly, she was already conspiring how best to quiz her about the professor without showing too much interest

"You haven't heard the news."

Eve's expression was blank. "What news?"

"Of course you haven't." Lola immediately pulled Eve by the wrist to a discreet corner of the room. "You wouldn't be throwing yourself around in such a party spirit if you had known."

Eve grew alarmed. "What is it?"

"It's the professor," Lola said bleakly, her face distressed. "I got a call on my mobile from a colleague in London. He heard it on the news. His laboratory in Scotland has been raided."

"What!" Eve's mind swam. "Is anyone . . ." She thought of Trey. "Do they—"

"I don't know," Lola interrupted, shaking her head. "I just got word five minutes ago. I'm leaving for London tomorrow."

Eve did not need to think. She was adamant. "I'm coming with you."

Twelve

It was one of those peculiar coincidences of fate that only falls into place after you have had a few days to blessedly appreciate how beautiful it was while it was happening. That was how Eve felt when she heard Theo's familiar voice through the intercom allowing her into his Mayfair apartment.

It was Sunday afternoon. The sun was shining brightly. She had arrived from Paris two hours earlier, taking the first flight. At home, she deposited her suitcase, called her mother, changed from her travel clothes into a suitable pair of blue jeans, demi boots, and a mauve, front-zipper jersey, her brown hair brushed around her face and falling loosely to her shoulders, before catching a taxi.

A squad car was parked across the street. Eve saw the customized Mercedes Benz with Chief Superintendent Michael Neels and Superintendent Abdul Nassiri behind the wheel. They watched her enter the building and did not detain her, but Eve's mind was racing with worry when she finally knocked on Theo's door.

His eyes widened slightly—approvingly—on seeing her in front of him. It had been five days since they had last seen each other, yet it felt like an age had passed. For Theo, so much had happened. He felt his whole life bordered on a roller coaster ride. While coming to terms with it all, Eve had never left his mind. Even now, seeing the perfect picture in front of him: her well-placed cheekbones, doe-shaped brown eyes, the rounded face that was forever implanted in his brain, made him comprehend just how accurately his memory had harbored its image of her.

Forever young. That was the first thought which flung through his head as he opened the door wider to let her in. Eve entered without hesitation. Theo closed the door, and she turned to face him. A silence enveloped them both as each took in the appearance of the other.

Theo was dressed in a white robe, his hair still wet from an interrupted shower. He seemed rooted to the spot. Eve was unsure whether he was pleased to see her, because his expression remained stolid and bovine. Eve wondered whether Lola Henriques had told her the truth. She had expected to see the older woman at Charles de Gaulle airport, hoping they would share the same flight back into England. But Lola had failed to meet her there.

Naturally, Jasmine thought it was a bad idea for her to be returning so quickly. She had earmarked Eve for several interviews on French television to commemorate *Style Paradise*. It was of some alarm to her personal assistant that she had chosen to return to England the following morning. With prudence, Eve chose not to tell her what Lola had disclosed. Instead, she related that her mother was not well and needed her attention immediately.

It was only when she had boarded the plane did it occur to Eve that she was not sure she would even find Theo in London. All she could recall was that he was expected to give a presentation seminar at the UN Summit, which gave her a hunch he would not be at his laboratory in Cramond. Still, with what Lola had told her, she could not be sure. It was simply fate that Theo was in London, that they were predestined to meet again.

The silence claimed more precious seconds before Theo spoke. "Eve."

He took hold of her wrist and suddenly words were no longer needed. Theo kissed each side of Eve's mouth, then planted a more lingering one dead center. Eve was thrilled. She threw her arms around his neck and inhaled the fresh scent of him. His hard body pressed into hers, his arms molded themselves around her waist, and he pulled Eve off her feet and kissed her again more tenderly.

Together, they held each other. The kiss lingered on and on until Theo had to finally place Eve on her feet and release her for air. She gasped and pressed her cheek against his chest, hearing the fast thud of his heart through the softness of his robe.

"I came as soon as I could," she whispered. "I saw Lola Henriques."

"In Paris?"

"She heard about your laboratory from a friend," Eve explained. "And I saw Michael Neels and Abdul Nassiri in a car downstairs."

"I know," he nodded. "They're making sure I stay in one piece until I leave for the UN International Antidrugs Summit."

"Your presentation," Eve acknowledged. She had not forgotten he was scheduled to give his talk the following day. She clung to him closer. "I didn't know if I should come after what I told you before leaving for Paris."

"You were trying to be realistic," Theo surmised. "You've been hurt in the past. It's not easy."

"I know." Eve sighed. "I just needed to see that you were all right."

Theo stroked her hair with shaky fingers. He could not believe Eve Hamilton was with him again. "I haven't stopped thinking about you," he admitted, enjoying their serene, magical moment. He did not want to break the ambience, though he knew it would be cruelly severed. "Everything's been chaotic. I have to leave for Vienna in an hour."

Eve pulled away and stared at him. "Vienna?" She was aghast.

Theo sighed, his face becoming grim. "We need to talk."

He turned and invited Eve into the kitchen, offering her Brazilian coffee as he looked at his watch. It read 10:44 A.M. Eve seated herself on a stool and contemplated his troubled stance as he leaned his tall frame against the refrigerator. Starting with Dr. Moira Keltz, who had been in a fighting mood when she was picked up outside her place of employment in Birmingham by local police, he explained how she wanted to negotiate custody of Trey. This was told to him in a well prepared speech on her arrival into London, with the added information that he was not Trey's biological father.

"What?" Eve was mortified.

And that was not all. Theo stiffened when he continued that Moira had gone on to cite none other than Dr. Henri Da Costa as the boy's true parent. Theo laughed coarsely. "They had begun an affair when we were all at Oxford," he told her disbelieving. Moira, rebuffed by Dr. Da Costa, had used Theo instead.

"Oh, Theo," Eve gasped.

He snorted. "She's been making secret visits to see Trey at his school in York."

"Yes," Eve acknowledged. "Trey told me."

Theo's eyes widened. "You knew?"

"I didn't know it was some kind of secret," Eve whimpered, amazed at the startling news Theo was unfolding. "And I can't understand why he would tell me and not you."

Theo waved her off. "She said that's how she found out about Phoebe. Trey told her. She told Dr. Da Costa and the slimeball's been trying to discredit me ever since." He paused. "Of course, neither I, nor those two cops at the Met believed a word of it," he added.

Eve was about to agree with him. The whole thing sounded too fantastic to be real. Theo had been a father to Trey from the age of three years. What could Dr. Keltz have to gain by inventing such an elaborate story using an innocent child?

"So . . ." Eve anticipated the worse.

"Dr. Da Costa was located and brought in for questioning," he went on. "Moira didn't seem the least bit worried that she could be endangered by my formula. In fact," he scoffed, "she made a point of telling me and the officers present that it was another impediment to the well-being of our son. She made *me* look like I was some kind of mad scientist who wades knee-deep with the mafiosa."

Eve closed her eyes. This was all shocking news. Scandalous. "What did Dr. Da Costa say?"

"He confirmed everything she said," Theo snorted, shaking his head in complete denial. "Everything. Even that they'd been part-time lovers since Oxford."

Their gazes intersected, and to Theo it was like being hit in the head by a laser beam. Despite seeing his joy at her being there, Eve could also see that Theo was still quite stunned. This was obviously not what he had expected when he had sought to find Moira Keltz for her own safety. Instead he was to discover a dark secret which she had hidden from him for nine years.

Eve had read things like this in women's magazines. It was not uncommon—women becoming pregnant and duping someone else, mostly for financial means—but she never thought she would actually *know* someone who had been used in this way. Least of all Professor Theophilus de Cordova.

"Do you believe him?"

Theo's expression changed to one of sheer annoyance. "I think that black eye he's walking around with is answer enough."

Eve's mouth dropped open. "You thumped him?"

"It's what he deserved."

She grew alarmed. "What about Trey?"

"Moira and Trey were placed in safe custody two days ago," Theo informed. "By the following afternoon, my laboratory was raided. Three guesses who's responsible for that."

"Dr. Da Costa?"

"And his merry men," Theo finished, his eyes blazing. "He took great delight in telling me that Dr. Ira Keplan was his more than enthusiastic accomplice, which explains how they got in. His way of intimidating me again."

Eve was moved. Her body quaked at everything she heard. It all had to be some kind of mistake. She could imagine nothing worse than discovering that the things held dear in life were all a fabrication. An elaborate lie. She thought about Paul. "You're having dreadful luck with your lab assistants."

"Tell me about it," Theo thundered, his Brazilian accent holding a saddened tone. "And your brother came recommended. What I'd like to know is how long Dr. Da Costa knew about Trey."

Eve had never seen Theo so angry. When she thought back to the snapshot Humphrey Brown had showed her of this man, she never dreamed his life could be so mixed up and plagued with all manner of complications. One thing was certain, she need never worry that he may rekindle his love for Dr. Moira Keltz. Eve was equally amazed that the face she had first seen in Theo's wallet could harbor such deception and chicanery.

She was reminded, also, that she was not so far removed from the artifice herself. Her initial motives for meeting Theo was a guile to ultimately steal from him. Had she not done so, he would not be in this predicament. The pang of guilt shot through her with such force, Eve was moved to standing on her feet. She was unable to repair the damage. A man so forgiving of her motives must be a fool. The very thought roused her to tears.

"I shouldn't be here," she floundered, her lips pursed hard with remorse. "This wouldn't be happening to you if I hadn't taken your formula."

"Wait a minute." Theo restrained her as he saw Eve head for the door. His swift pantherlike strides ate up the distance with such speed, Eve did not stand a chance. "You're not responsible for my history with Moira," he told her firmly. "Who knows what goes on in the heads of women like her. Maybe Trey, being the way he is, has made her realize something. Maybe . . . I've thought about it since this nightmare began, that I'm going to find out something I don't want to know. But I can't hold you responsible for that."

"If I stay, I'm going to remind you that I began this nightmare," Eve implored, her eyes glazed with heartfelt sorrow. "I mean . . ." she paused. "I did it for Paul and all the time, the answers are in his letters. He's been in love with somebody for a long time. Maybe he *is* out there like you said." Eve paused as a contrite tear fell. "Someone should guard your love, too, Theo, and all I've done is prove that I'm incapable of doing that."

Theo stood back, seeing the shame in Eve's eyes. He did not have the time to explain that he had long since forgiven her for her actions. If one of his sisters or his brother had been murdered, he would do the same thing. He knew Eve was conscience-stricken from the moment she had left his home in Cramond. It was this pure basic trait which had touched him so. Eve did not possess one cold bone in her body. She was a warm person, alive and fiery with her emotions. She was creative and spirited with every word that fell from her lips, and he had long ago decided this was the sort of woman he deserved in his life.

He did not know how to convince her that whatever had occurred was just some sort of fluke that, in all honesty, began with her brother working for him under the guise of Dr. Jeffrey Harrison. Eve's mention of Paul's letters brought his mind back to their content. Divine love. A rarity to be found. Looking into Eve's tearful face, Theo's loins were stirred with the belief that he, too, had found such rarity.

He glanced at his watch and grimaced. Time was moving on, and there was still so much he wanted to tell Eve. Theo took firm hold of her wrists. "Come with me to Vienna," he drawled, his tone full of promise.

"Didn't you hear what I just said?" Eve breathed, her eyes widening at his suggestion.

"I heard, but I want you to put it behind you. Behind us," Theo urged. "Let the United Nations sort out Yayo Cantrell. I'll go and do my talk, and then *we* can talk."

"Theo." Eve paused on a ragged breath of disbelief. "I've just come back from Paris early this morning. I knew I had to see you, but—"

"That's it," Theo pressed. "You said you *had* to see me. You're here." He raised his hands into the air. "What more do you need to see." He took a hold of her wrists again. "You saved my life, Eve. In my country, when someone saves your life, you owe them your life."

Eve chuckled away her tears. "Another proverbial Brazilian aphorism like what you said about Paul?"

"I like it when you talk dirty," Theo said, chuckling.

Eve laughed, too. "I don't know."

She saw the funny side, even though their situation bordered on the unreal. It was too much of an adventure for any one woman to find herself in, but she was the one who went along with what the assistant commissioner had wanted. This, staring into the deep chocolate-brown depth of Theo's eyes, was the dire consequence. Eve had two options. She could see it through all the way or leave. And this time, not be swayed to return.

Theo saw the seriousness in her eyes and chose not to push the issue. He stepped back and again glanced at his watch. He wanted nothing more than to have Eve with him by his side on his journey to Vienna. It would be one less worry on his mind since the Met had not located the two men who had chased them through London, though he felt certain his apartment was still being watched. Her being in Paris had relaxed him a little, but now that she had returned he was aware of how uneasy he felt.

"I have to go and change," he exclaimed, his face clouding over. "Think about it."

Theo opened the kitchen door and went to his bedroom. Eve heard the tone of acceptance in his voice of whatever decision she made. It was not a happy tone. She knew he had already prepared himself for her negative response. This was not what she had expected on seeing Theo again.

Eve was somewhat amazed that the raid on Fairafar Mill, which was so heavily protected, seemed less worrying to him than his personal troubles with Moira. Judging by the seriousness of his work there, she was perplexed that he had not already taken out a restraining order against Dr. Da Costa and his group of troublemakers. Still, he had said he would leave it to the United Nations Drugs Control Program to sort out the dangers his formula presented. That, she told herself, did not resolve the problem. Someone out there, owing to her stupidity, had a copy of the deadly strain.

It was this single thought that had Eve following the wet trail Theo's feet had left on the carpeting to his bedroom. He turned to unexpectedly find her standing at the doorway, a glimpse of concession mirrored across her face. He was dressed in a pair of gray tailored trousers and was plunging his arms into a clean white shirt. Eve could see the simple Elastoplast which covered his healing gunshot wound.

"How's the shoulder?" she asked.

"Doing fine." Their eyes locked and Theo felt the fire of passion run through his heart. "You've changed your mind?"

"I was wondering," Eve said, even while thinking that it would be so easy to board a plane to Vienna with Theo. "About your laboratory. Did they steal anything?"

Theo shook his head, musing at the question. "Whatever they were after, it isn't in Scotland."

Puzzled, she sat at the edge of his bed, recalling the last time she had been here. She had dressed his wound before they made love. The heady recollection caused her body to stir with longing, a movement she realized did not go unnoticed by Theo as he wrapped his blue tie around his neck and safely positioned it over his top button.

"What do you mean?"

Theo briefly glanced at her as he pulled on his socks and slipped into black leather shoes. "The evidence," he said. "For my presentation." He tied his shoelaces. "It's over there." He pointed at a silver cold-storage capsule on the bed which was flashing a green digital code-sequence lock.

Eve turned and stared at it, the pieces of the puzzle

in her head falling into place. "That's what was in your incubator at the lab?" she ventured.

"The prototype," Theo explained. "Which I will hand over in Vienna tomorrow and see what decisions they arrive at from my research."

"That's it?" Eve said simply.

Theo gazed over at her. She looked adorable. Within seconds, he found himself across the room, crouching at Eve's knees. "That's it," he nodded. "And if you come with me, we'll be able to spend some time together. Properly."

Eve sighed. She had her order book to sort out, bills to collect, a whole host of other chores that needed doing. And, of course, Princess Adjani's entire collection was required within a few short weeks before her trip back to Saudi Arabia. Then again, her passport was still in her handbag from her visit to Paris. She did not require a visa to enter Austria to its capital. At best, she could stay a day and return by Tuesday.

"C'mon, Ms. Temptress."

"Ms. Temptress!" Eve chuckled.

"You were the woman who told me that love is out there if you want it," Theo cajoled. "A choice no one should deny themselves."

So I did, her brain confirmed. It was a belief she still held dear as she recognized the olive branch Theo offered. Eve chose to accept it.

One of the attractions Theo liked about Vienna was that it was a city of legends. Part of the attraction of going there was in discovering how much was true and how much was fantasy. That was how he felt about Eve Hamilton. He likened her to the character of the Viennese—charming, witty, and worldly. Her appearance to the palaces and churches—grand, elegant, and graceful.

The core of her being to be as complex as the noble façade of the Stephansdom cathedral itself.

This time, on his second visit to what was officially one of the three UN cities, he was more than happy not to be in his habitual status of traveling alone. It was not customary for him to be taken to the airport in an unmarked police car, but Michael Neels and his partner against crime, Abdul Nassiri, had been more than accommodating, their brows raised on seeing that Eve would be joining him. It would be her first trip. He noted that she had become quite excited on their arrival into Austria.

He glanced at her staring through the taxi window as they headed toward their hotel, seeing, but not looking at her own reflection. Instead, her eyes were in awe of the beauty the city presented her. He himself had stared in wonder his first time in Vienna. The ebb and flow of folk along the baffling medieval lanes, the Gothic designs of the buildings around them, the Danube river which they had passed on leaving the airport. It was all captivating, he imagined, to someone creatively minded as Eve.

"Beautiful," he approved, seeing the smile on her face.

"I know," Eve agreed. "I thought it might be like Paris, but it's so different."

"I wasn't talking about the city," Theo corrected.

Eve turned and glanced at him, a demure smile broadening her lips. "Are you really going to be doing a presentation tomorrow, because you don't sound like you're on a professional trip at all?"

"That's because you're here," Theo said. He looked to the side of his seat in the taxi to check that he still had the cold-storage capsule. Finding it safely snuggled by his briefcase, he turned his attention back to Eve. "How was Paris anyway?"

"Brilliant," Eve announced. "Not a hitch in the whole operation. And, for once in a good while, a healthy order book."

"That's good," Theo nodded.

"There was an unexpected face I didn't intend to see though," she added quite candidly. "Tyrone was there."

Theo was surprised to find his body reacting with a slight twinge at hearing the news. "Say anything?" he queried, dubious.

"He introduced his new fiancée," Eve announced with an icy note in her tone. "She wore the same ring he had once given to me. It looked better on her I think."

Theo homed in on her sardonic remark and grew curious. "How did it end?"

"Between Tyrone and me?" Eve sighed, shrugging her shoulders uncaring. "I told him I didn't want to be messed about. He must have decided that was what he wanted to do, so he ended it."

"Just like that?" Theo was sure the man needed glasses.

"Yep," Eve nodded. "I gave him his diamond ring back and that was the last I saw of him until France."

Struck by her sense of nonjudgmental acceptance, he asked, "You sound very brave about it, but are you really?"

"Me?" Eve chuckled. She paused for reflection. "Tyrone didn't love me the way I needed to be loved. I think he had his own way of loving somebody. Sadly, it wasn't my way."

"Which is?"

Eve giggled. This was clearly a peculiar conversation to have in a car on her way through a city which looked so romantic. She feared what thoughts could easily jump from her lips. "You ask too many questions," she said, as the taxi slowed and finally parked outside a postmodern glass building opposite a park. Dipping her head, she looked through the car window. *"Vienna Marriott,"* Eve read out loud. "I think we're here."

She was right. Theo had little option but to shelve the subject, but he had it in his mind to pick up the thread of their conversation later. He unloaded his briefcase, the storage capsule under his arm and carefully followed Eve in. She only had her handbag. Her decision to join him at such short notice was impulsive and without care for luggage.

Eve's rash decision served only to deepen Theo's attraction toward her. Any other woman would have worried about clothes, a hairbrush, and, particularly, make-up. Not Eve. Whatever means for survival kept her appearance so vibrant and youthful, he was sure would always remain a mystery to him.

Their room had an impressive view of Stadtpark where he remembered the statues of Schubert, Bruckner and Johann Strauss provided a musical route for joggers. He had visited the park before and thought about taking Eve for a leisurely stroll to see the many monuments to composers that were located there. Perhaps later they could walk along the riverbank promenades and pick up on that conversation still dabbling around in his head.

"I love the room." Eve was overjoyed as she threw her handbag onto the bed. It was a very elegant art nouveau-style, not what she would expect for a recently built hotel. "I expect there's probably a shop downstairs."

Theo turned from the window and faced her head on. "You're shopping?"

"It's still daylight," Eve told him. "Besides, I fly back to London after tomorrow." She looked at her Cartier watch. It read 2:33 P.M. "Let's go and see some of the city."

"What, now?"

"Yes, now." Eve immediately picked up her handbag.

Theo looked nervously at the cold storage capsule. He did not want to leave it unattended, even though it was electronically locked with a sequencer. Perhaps if he took it with him, he thought. He suspected the hotel room was probably quite secure, but decided he would not take the risk, and he did not want Eve to go out on her own, either. Until he formally handed it over after he made his presentation at the Antidrugs Summit at the UNO-building, he felt justifiably keen to keep it within sight.

Eve noted Theo's possessive hold on the storage capsule as they left their room. She was immediately thrust into the reality of their trip to Vienna. A cloud formed over her head as a picture of Humphrey Brown muzzled her mind. Her mother, Marlene had probably now claimed his body from the city morgue ready for a burial service at their local church. She would be back in England in time for the service. It was a troubling thought that momentarily shook her as they went out on to the street.

"Did you need to bring that?" she asked, looking around them as though his very possession of it posed them some harm.

"I can't very well leave it unattended," Theo explained to her. His gaze traveled across her features. He could see Eve had become annoyed with him. "What'd I do?"

"Nothing." She shook her head. Her voice lowered. "It's Humphrey's funeral this week."

They were silenced. Theo slung the capsule over his shoulder. He took a hold of Eve's wrist. "C'mon."

"Where are we going?"

He lead the way ahead toward the park. "You want to see the city, so let's go in a *Fiaker*."

"A what?" Eve's eyes widened as they approached a

line of horse-drawn carriages. A charming Viennese coachman smiled happily at them. Dressed in a black bowler cap and traditional garments, a gray velvet jacket and black-and-white check trousers, he helped Eve into the front carriage, allowing her to seat herself comfortably before Theo deposited himself beside her. "This is a *Fiaker?*"

He looked at the pair of brown horses that would be taking them along. "Best way to tour Vienna."

Eve smiled. Her spirits were back with her. She leaned into the carriage as the professor negotiated the price and duration of their ride. He was told they would just be seeing the Innere Stadt and all the wonderful pieces of history the inner city had to offer. They were treated to the Stephansdom with its soaring spire, the opulent fountains and statues which punctuated the city, a trip around the pedestrianized square of the Stephansplatz where Eve was able to do some shopping, and finally the Hofburg, the old palace once synonymous with the Hapsburg dynasty, but was now taken over by various state organizations, museums, and conference centers.

All the while throughout their trip, Eve realized Theo never once took his eyes off her. It seemed he was quite enamored by her bursting enthusiasm to see and touch and buy everything that came into contact with her gaze of wonder. He talked casually, too. Nothing too heavy. His subjects light and breezy, delving into architecture, art, music, and the opera, all the things Vienna had to offer, but which would be impossible for her to see in a few short hours.

By the time they returned to the hotel, Eve had a boutique shopping bag. She had quite exhausted herself and was ready to take a hot shower. The dress and sandals Theo had bought at the Stephansplatz were beau-

tiful. Not a design she would normally wear, but nonetheless Eve was eager to slip into it for dinner.

"Nice day?" Theo asked as he closed the door to their
room, closing out the world. They were alone again.

Eve was moved. "Wonderful day."

Theo placed the storage capsule onto a dresser with
a small bag containing a new shirt and tie he had purchased for himself. He pulled Eve into his arms and
held her close. He had wanted to do that all day, from
the moment she had agreed to travel with him to Austria. "Happy you came?"

She nodded. Their eyes locked and again that laser
beam hit him dead center, right in the chest. Theo was
mesmerized by its intensity. He dipped his head and
took Eve's lips with his own. Her immediate surrender
weakened him completely. His eyes closed and he was
lost to the world. At that precise moment, they were
both lost in each other . . .

They kissed and kissed. Their naked bodies were entwined between the fresh sheets in the oversized bed.
There was room enough to accommodate them both;
outstretched arms, extended legs, the breadth eaten by
their tossing between the sheets. The flurry could only
be likened to two cubs pouncing on one another. She
was like a wildcat, he her predatory lover.

Theo circled Eve's tongue with his, heard her whimper as he felt her legs clamp around him. Her eyes were
soft, misty, brandy-colored. Her lashes fluttered at the
scrape of his jaw beneath her chin. He felt himself throb
beneath the condom. He stretched her arms over her
head and laced his fingers through hers. She was shiv-
ering with passion. Her skin was as hot as his.

"I'm making you sweat," he whispered in her ear, nipping her earlobe.

Eve laughed. He kissed her forehead, leaned up on his elbows, and smiled at her. She smiled back and touched his chin with her fingertips. Their eyes locked. Eve was swept away by the depth of fire in Theo's gaze. "I can't believe I'm here with you," she murmured softly. "After everything—"

"Ssh," Theo whispered, rubbing his hardened rod against her. "Believe that I want you."

It was all Eve could stand. She kissed Theo until he could not breathe, until what small fraction of air Theo could suck into his lungs was trapped in his throat. Her heart was thudding faster as he pulled up for air. She took the opportunity to slither closer to him, opening wider to take him in. He let her. Theo was unable to stop himself. He buried himself into her velvety fire and felt himself lose it.

It was his intention to go slow, to seal the first serene day they had spent together by savoring every magical moment, but Eve would not let him. She wriggled beneath him, tightened her legs, and arched herself for him to thrust deeper. His primitive, animal instinct took over. His fingers still laced through hers, he dug hard and deep to the very core of Eve's being.

Their sheer unadulterated act was fast and furious. Heated passion was whipped into every movement and tousle until the fire seared them both. He murmured her name. She gasped his. Her fingers clutched his so tight her nails bored into his skin. He felt her spasm lock around him, hard and convulsing, until it made her legs shake behind his back. Theo felt choked tears in his eyes that it was he who had jiggled her to such heights of ecstasy. A moment later, he shuddered with her, his heart pumping in motion until he laid his cheek against the top of her forehead, spent, exhausted, and complete again.

His last thought as he held her were the words ingrained in his mind on reading her brother's letters. *Guard your love.* Theo felt Eve's sated breath against his neck. He moved his body down until her gaze met his. He wanted her love. With that on his mind, he kissed Eve again.

Thirteen

"I've been thinking about Paul's letters," Eve began as she seated herself across from Theo at the table in the hotel restaurant. "They're very poetic."

"Indeed," Theo agreed, placing the storage capsule by his wineglass to join her. He fixed his tie and gray jacket and sucked in a breath of warm evening air as his eyes appreciated the picture of Eve in front of him.

She looked immaculate in the sequined gold dress and plain white sandals he had bought her at the Stephanplatz, with her hair finger-tossed around her shoulders, her fresh face clean of make-up. Not quite as she was two hours earlier; body wet, limbs exhausted from a wild romp of raw sex.

Eve flashed him a smile as he picked up the menu. "She must love my brother very much," she went on, aware of how Theo was carefully scrutinizing her.

"She sounds like a nice girl, but I think she's suffered." Theo said without much curiosity. He was hungry, and after the workout with Eve, he was just about ready to eat anything the Viennese chef had on offer.

"Really?" Eve queried, reaching for her menu. "It's a surprise to me that Paul would correspond with anyone, but to write to someone who has such command with words . . . I never saw my brother as the romantic type."

"Her pseudonym, Mabel Syrup, isn't very original,"

Theo reasoned, looking at the menu. "And she always closed each letter by telling your brother to guard his love, as though she were in constant danger. Makes me wonder what was gong on. I still envy your brother, though. He must've made her feel quite special."

Eve's brows rose marginally. "You make me feel special, too." She was being truthful. For the first time since meeting Theo, Eve decided to be honest about what her true feelings were saying.

It brought a deep smile to Theo's face. "Wow."

"I know," Eve sighed a little unsure. "It's scary. I always said I wouldn't justify my feelings, hunches, or intuitions, and here I am, telling you how I feel."

"That's not scary," Theo said, his eyes revealing how touched he was by her admission.

"Yes, it is," Eve proclaimed. "Before Tyrone left, he told me that I was too analytical. That I complained too much about everything—sex, clothes, my work . . . He said I was fussy. Too much of a perfectionist. I decided he was messing me around. But maybe it's me. Maybe I want too much."

Theo gazed at her. The depth of his emotions reached her eyes. "You're being ridiculous," he said. "You want the same things we all want, and that is to get it right. Consider that maybe Tyrone just couldn't handle a woman of your status and importance. Maybe he just wanted a pretty face and nothing else."

Eve thought about Geraldine. How small a threat she posed to someone like Tyrone who mirrored his own self-importance. The professor had a point. "You really believe that?"

"If you were having to complain about sex," Theo chuckled. "The man was obviously doing something wrong."

Eve's face reddened beneath her fresh-faced, bashful expression as she thought back to two hours earlier.

Theo had been beyond her wildest expectations of what she demanded by way of male performance. She would be a liar to have any reason for concern there. Not only was he extremely fit and set the pace which kept them both working, she felt annoyed she could ever have considered him over-the-hill at forty-two.

"I have something to tell you," she said with a wry, shy smile.

Theo's brows raised.

"When you asked how I felt after our first kiss and our first time making love, I did want to tell you how wonderful you were. But, like I said, I didn't want to question it."

Theo's smile widened further. He took a hold of Eve's hand and pressed it to his mouth where he planted a kiss into the palm of her hand. "You make me believe in a certain theory I once told you in Scotland doesn't work."

Eve's heart thundered in anticipation and understanding. "What happens now?"

"What do you want to happen?" Theo countered.

"There'll be no fallback position," Eve told him, thinking they were destined to walk the full length of their path after all. "If you want to test the option that we're falling in love, then you'll have to accept the weaker position it's going to put you in. We're both going to be quite vulnerable, but personally, I'd like to see the determination pay off."

Theo clasped her hand tightly. "I guess I'm in for a learning experience then."

Eve nodded, accepting that he had lived through enough lies and deceit. "I'm not Moira Keltz," she reminded him. "I know I made a mistake, and I'll do whatever it takes to make it up to you. And whatever happens about Trey, I'll help you get through it."

Thoroughly shaken, Theo kissed Eve's hand again,

thinking back to his first views about her while she had stayed at his cottage in Cramond. He had wanted to know everything about her. He was going to tap her brain to reach some semblance of truth to allay his fears. What he discovered was more than he ever dreamed possible. His one conclusion was paramount. *Genuine or fraud?* He decided genuine.

He smiled. "Let's eat."

The food was stupendous. Theo and Eve had eaten their fill and were halfway through a bottle of chardonnay. They had exhausted most subjects and were giggling about the next movie classic she wanted to see on her return to England.

"Showboat," she told Theo as a shadow approached their table. "The original black-and-white version. I love that song 'Old Man's River.' "

"It just keeps rolling along," a deep Latin American baritone added.

Theo and Eve looked up. A harsh hand placed itself over the storage capsule on the table. Time froze for three awful seconds. Theo might have known it was too good to be true that he could enjoy a full day with Eve without complication. The other man who approached and stood behind Eve's chair was the second face he suddenly recognized. They were the two men who had chased them in London.

Theo's eyes turned to black slits. "How did you know?" he asked, tight-lipped. A short woman was instantly pulled from behind the larger man and thrust to the side of their table.

"Lola!" Eve gasped.

She looked slightly dazed with a good measure of alarm etched into every line on her face. "I'm sorry,

Professor," Lola whimpered sorrowfully. "They forced me."

"You were supposed to meet me in Paris," Eve pounced, about to hurtle from her chair. The man behind her placed a firm hand on her shoulder, keeping her in her seat.

"My alarm clock stopped," Lola gushed, apologetic, protectively pulling her brown jacket around herself. "I caught a late plane. I went to Theo's apartment and—"

"Found us," the larger man finished.

"If you're thinking about the two cops back in London," his accomplice added in a thicker accent. "They're wasted. All we want is the girl."

Eve looked at Theo. He looked at her. They had obviously missed an important point. "What girl?" they chimed simultaneously.

"Yayo Cantrell wants his daughter back."

"His daughter?" Theo looked around the restaurant. He could see the other diners did not suspect anything was amiss at their table. "We don't have his daughter."

"She disappeared with your assistant, Professor," the larger guy sneered, picking up the storage capsule. He weighed it in his hand as though it were a bar of gold. "Until you find her, I'll keep a hold of this." He shook it. "I figure it must be something important. You've been carrying it around with you all day."

"You've been watching us," Eve snarled.

"My assistant?" Theo mused, drawn back to the subject. He suspected they could not be talking about Dr. Ira Keplan. He was just some idiot mixed up in the fanatical activities of Dr. Henri Da Costa. So that meant they had to be referring to Eve's brother under his guise as Dr. Jeffrey Harrison. "You mean Jeffrey?"

"That's him," the shorter one acknowledged. "He made a deal with Cantrell to steal a formula you were working on. He said it would gross millions. Then he short-ended the deal by disappearing with Cantrell's daughter.''

Eve's blood ran cold. *Dear God,* she thought. They were talking about Paul. Her voice trembled. ''What's her name?''

''Theresa Maria,'' the larger one informed.

Theo eyed Eve and decided to stall. ''My assistant died in a car bombing.''

''He should have,'' the shorter man shot back, ''but he didn't.''

Eve gasped and fought back the choking constriction in her throat. She reached for her wineglass and downed a large gulp, throwing a panicked gaze across at Lola, before swallowing her emotional shock with the wine.

The shorter man looked at her before continuing. ''One of our men bungled the job when he planted the bomb. *He* went up in smoke instead.'' He eyed Eve suspiciously. ''You look familiar.''

Eve was too moved to say a word.

''She was in the park with the professor, you moron,'' the larger man told his accomplice, aware that her glamorous appearance was proving deceptive. He looked at Theo. ''We were supposed to meet that kingpin from the Met you murdered.''

''We didn't kill him,'' Theo insisted.

''Yeah, right.'' He did not sound convinced. ''He said he would get Theresa and the formula, only we turned up at St. James's Park to find you two over the dead body.''

''We didn't kill him,'' Eve yelped, aware that Lola was shaking miserably, not from cold but from fear. ''He was—''

''Let's continue this talk upstairs,'' Theo interrupted, noting a diner gazing at their table. If there was going to be any trouble, he would rather it be somewhere which presented the least number of casualties.

"Good idea," the taller man agreed.

He pushed Lola forward while the man behind Eve dragged her from her seat. Eve thought about causing a scene to alert some stalwart citizen to their aid, but that was before she saw the gun the larger man discreetly held poked against Lola's ribs. As Theo slowly rose from his own seat, the gun did not escape his attention either. He knew the two men could not have boarded the plane out of Britain with the pistol. That told him they had contacts in Austria and probably a hideout, too.

He looked into the older woman's face, silently acknowledging with his eyes that he had seen the weapon. He stepped forward and walked by Lola's side, touching her arm ever so slightly in reassurance that she would be fine.

As they walked toward the elevator, he felt some annoyance with himself for having not taken care in looking around him while he had gone on the town with Eve. Perhaps he would have seen the men earlier. Maybe spotted Lola held captive and forced into divulging where he could be found. Only she and a few close friends knew he was scheduled to be in Vienna. And, as before, he had stayed in this very hotel because he loved the view of the park.

The elevator car arrived quickly. The two men cautioned with the gun that they all get inside, giving Theo no time at all to plan a strategy on how they were going to escape. He thought about alerting the tall stranger in a tweed jacket standing across from him, rubbing his long nose and pretending that he did not exist. He considered that the man looked African in appearance, probably from one of the Mediterranean borders on a work permit and visa. Lean-looking, toned rather than flabby, with a real crowd face, not as notable as his own. A panama hat positioned at an angle so no one could really see his eyes.

He had hoped the stranger would approach their elevator, giving him the diversion he needed to do something. Anything. But when he felt the gun poke into his back and saw his missed opportunity when the doors closed, Theo's heart fell.

They traveled in silence. Eve and Lola were in the middle, the two men and Theo on the outer edge. The silence was fraught with anxiety. He saw the blood had drained from Eve's cheeks, making her chestnut-brown complexion lose its healthy glow. He did not want her to come to any harm. The very thought of it seared his heart. He felt her life held more importance than his own. *She has people to dress,* he told himself. He, on the other hand, was responsible for inventions that often had a danger element attached.

He saw his capsule under the heavier man's arm, his work concealed within. His frantic gaze fell on Lola's face. She deserved to see the eleven orphaned children in Brazil she loved so dearly and whose futures she was working very hard to keep with projects such as the one his foundation had sponsored. Theo was struck with the notion that he had to do something. Even if it meant . . . his death.

When the elevator bell chimed softly and the steel doors slid back, Theo's heart skipped a beat as he considered making a move. In anticipation, he was hoping to find an empty corridor so that he could attack without the worry of hotel guests. But the first thing that struck him was the stranger from the ground floor facing the elevator. The second thing that registered in his tormented mind was that he was holding a Colt .45 revolver with a black silencer seated at the lethal end of the long barrel. Their eyes locked and he saw the look of death. Then he saw the man's mouth open.

"Duck!"

Theo only needed to be told once. He flung his body

over Eve and dragged Lola down with him as they hit the floor. The sound of a gun being discharged twice rung through the air, making a clanking sound like the broken chain on a bicycle wheel. A waiter or hotel guest would hardly be distracted by either meager sound. Only the hard thud as two bodies slumped to the ground vibrated in the air.

Theo dared to raise his head. The Latin Americans were slugged out on the elevator floor. He caught sight of Lola covering her mouth, smothering a scream. But Eve's eyes were fixed on the stranger who was removing the silencer from his gun. He seemed to have no interest in them until he removed his panama hat.

Her voice trembled when she spoke. "Paul?"

Lola raised her head and her eyes widened. "Jeffrey!"

The stranger reached into the elevator and pulled the cold storage capsule from beneath the dead man's arm. He glanced at Theo as he stood. He recognized the face.

"Hello, Professor."

Eve stared aghast. Her brother was alive.

If she had thought that Theo looked like the kind of man you knew only existed in dreams and, by the sheer will of God, was fortunate one day to meet, it was daunting to Eve to now find her brother standing in front of her in Theo's hotel room.

Standing five-ten barefoot, his height marginally higher in his shoes, little had changed about him except he had a shaved head and looked like he had become a dangerous adventurer. He was still mildly handsome in an introspective, scholarly kind of way, of average build and wearing plain brown corduroy trousers with a tweed jacket over a camel-colored sport shirt open at the throat.

Her eyes glazed with tears at seeing him again. She

was almost too choked to speak when she thought back to his memorial service back in England. "Paul, what are you doing here?" she gasped. "And what are you doing with a gun?" Eve felt a scream suspended in her mouth. "Those two men—"

"I haven't time," he interrupted, impatient. He had jammed the elevator car circuits, but that would only buy him sixty minutes tops. "A service waiter is going to suss those two bodies in about an hour, so listen up."

"No, you listen up." Theo's eyes narrowed icily. "Whatever you have to say, it'd better be damned good."

They both tried to outstare each other. While their gazes held steel, Lola Henriques was moved into sitting down on the edge of the bed. She saw immediately the tousled sheets and followed the trail they left from the bed to Eve's pair of jeans and mauve jersey on the carpet. Her gaze moved from Eve's demiboots to her sandaled feet, traveling up the sequined dress to Eve's teary face. Lola's eyes flashed with a tinge of something that was surely not usual for a woman of her years.

Eve clasped her hands together, recognizing the simple trait of a woman caught in the throes of envy. She was sure Lola could smell the raw sex in the room, too. For an Old-World Brazilian woman who loved to wear her exotic designs, Eve realized that beneath Lola's façade lay a passion that had never wilted with age. Lola may have wished she were twenty years younger as she had made plain at Theo's seminar, but in her soul she had never left her youth. Theo would never know how much this woman admired and adored him.

"He thinks I played a double cross," Paul's voice infiltrated Eve's thoughts. He threw Theo the capsule he had picked up in the elevator and placed his gun in a black plastic bag he pulled from his trouser pocket. "This is between me and Yayo Cantrell."

"The drug baron?" Theo exclaimed, squeezing his

fingers around the capsule. The digital sequence lock was still intact.

Paul nodded and paced the floor. "Two years ago, I met his daughter Theresa, unconventionally, in an Internet chatroom. We talked. We e-mailed. Suddenly, we were arranging to meet." He glanced at Lola's disapproving countenance as she remained seated on the bed, and he ran an exasperated finger across his forehead. "It was love at first sight."

Eve stared at him, shocked. "This is about you and a woman?"

"Cantrell's daughter," Paul declared harshly, as though the point needed to be made perfectly plain. He paused to wipe his hands with a tissue he had pulled from his jacket pocket.

Eve saw he was sweaty and nervous and wondered exactly what he had gotten himself involved in. "I read your letters," she revealed, doubtful of what he was saying. "This woman—"

"Theresa," he piped in. "She lived in São Paulo. We wanted to be together, but I didn't realize that no man can just walk off into the sunset with Yayo Cantrell's daughter."

Eve folded her arms beneath her chest, finding it hard to grasp what Paul was telling her. "Where did you meet her?"

"In Miami," he explained. "The letters were not enough. She wrote beautiful letters." A wistful smile briefly crossed his face. "We met in a shopping mall when she arranged to stay at an aunt's house."

"And hatched a plot," Theo announced, his perceptive tone harsh and stern.

"I just wanted her . . . us to be happy," Paul crooned, struck by the professor's cool attitude toward him. "When she went back to Brazil, I thought about getting a job out there. I saw an ad on the Internet and applied for it."

"You were not qualified," Lola suddenly threw in, recalling when Paul had attended an interview at the offices of the South American Ecological Project in São Paulo. "And you couldn't speak Portuguese."

"Wait a minute." Eve was confused. She glared at Lola. "You saw him?"

"I recommended him to the professor," Lola breathed, throwing her hands into the air, helpless. "He was looking for a student medical researcher, which was not what we wanted."

"Only I now know you came to me as Jeffrey Harrison," Theo chimed, his chocolate-brown gaze hardening like cocoa. "You were never in that car bomb. So what happened?"

Paul noted the strain of agony in Eve's face, but persevered nonetheless. "I didn't want anyone to find out I was unqualified, and *he* was dumb enough not to check." He indicated the professor.

The masculine angles in Theo's jawline hardened. "Don't push it," he mustered, his teeth clenched. "You're walking a very thin line."

Paul shrugged, not taking the threat seriously. "It didn't take me long to figure out what you were working on. I saw your formula as the answer to everything. So I arranged to see Cantrell. I flew into Brazil and told him I could get it as long as I was allowed to marry Theresa. He agreed."

"You—" Theo lunged forward to grab hold of Paul, but Eve immediately restrained him with a hard tug at his jacket.

"Don't," she pleaded. "Please."

"You made a deal," Theo thundered, wanting to fight Eve off. "With *my* work." The urge to knock Paul off his feet was too strong.

"The deal didn't go down," Paul chided loudly. "It couldn't, not even if I wanted it to." He paused. "When I got back into England, your lab had been raided. I was surprised because you had all this state-of-the-art stuff. I couldn't get a thing without clearance. Then you decided you were going to relocate in Scotland."

"And I offered you a job up there," Theo responded raucously. "Two days into it, you disappeared. I had to get in a replacement who, I've now discovered, happens to be as looney tunes as you. Jesus wept." He sighed heavily, his voice deep as thunder. "When I heard about a car bomb on Edinburgh TV last year, I had no reason to link it to you, because I had never heard of Paul Hamilton."

"I know. I'm sorry," Paul quipped, annoyed. "How was I to know Cantrell wanted me dead?" He reached into his jacket pocket and nervously pulled out a packet of cigarettes. Pacing the floor, Paul struck a match and lit one up. He puffed with agitation as three pairs of eyes stared murderously at him. "I got rational," he said sadly. "I panicked and called the only person I knew who had the right sort of connections and would help."

"Humphrey," Eve whimpered. Her gaze seared into Paul with such intensity, he shrieked back from the force of it. "He died for you thinking Theo was responsible."

"It was a mistake," Paul raged, self-contempt cutting him to shreds. "It was Humphrey's idea that we should have everyone believe that I was dead. He said he would get the formula and sell it."

"To Cantrell's archenemy," Theo concluded, shrugging himself loose from Eve's restraint. His eyes were simmering with rage. "Idiots. Both of you. Didn't you realize you were living on the sharp edge the moment you let any of those drug gangsters know such a formula existed? Your uncle used Eve to get close to me and steal it."

Only then did Paul's eyes shift to survey what he had not noticed earlier about the room. About Eve. In a flash, he saw it all. The flicker in his eyes revealed that he had become fully aware that they were lovers. "Humphrey wanted revenge against Cantrell," he said lamely, unable to look into Eve's eyes, "for wanting me dead."

Eve was angry. This was not the brother she knew who was ambitious, a hard worker, and someone their mother was proud of. "You and Humphrey lied to me," she wept. She could not hold back the large, sad tears of pain that fell down her cheeks. "I believed everything he said about the professor. I thought he was responsible for your death. I'm not proud of what I did to try and get justice for you."

"It wasn't supposed to be like this." Paul swallowed, his shoulders shaking.

He glanced at Lola, who had adopted the cynical expression often seen on women of her years who had heard and known of such wild male behavior. With it came a more tangible trait of perception which marred her face.

"What happened to the girl?" she asked.

Paul dipped his head and took a long drag from his cigarette. "I don't know."

"All this and you don't know?" Theo gushed, throwing his hands into the air in disbelief. He paced the floor, his voice becoming harder. "We heard she was allegedly killed by her ruthless daddy until those two goons you just switched off in the elevator told us they wanted her back. They thought we had her. Cantrell wanted you dead because he thinks you've disappeared with his daughter."

Paul's head rose with renewed hope. "That means she's alive somewhere." He accidentally burnt his finger with his cigarette. "Ouch."

"Just tell me what happened to the formula Eve stole and gave to your uncle," Theo snapped harshly.

Paul feigned innocence. "I don't know that either." He glimpsed Eve's sense of betrayal and knew she hated herself for it. "I was supposed to meet Humphrey Brown at St. James's Park, but when I got there, police were all over the place like a bad rash. I later heard on the news that he was found dead."

"We got to him first," Theo drawled, leaning by the window which overlooked the park. "I went there with Eve to get my formula back. I think he arranged to meet one of Bogetti's men to sell it and they backhanded the deal."

"Bogetti?" Paul pondered the name as though a wheel had begun to turn in his head. "We need to get out of here."

"What is it?" Eve panicked, wiping her wet cheeks with the back of her hand. One thing she remembered about Paul was that his lips always twitched when he got nervous. "What's wrong."

"Counterterrorism," Theo responded, his fists tightly clenched. "You brother, for the love of one woman, has just started a drug war like nothing we've seen before." He glared at Paul while taking swift strides toward him. "I ought to knock you on your ass."

Eve gasped. "Let's keep our heads," she ordered, bridging the gap between them. As much as she respected the professor and was happy to see her brother again, she did not want to see them fighting over what had happened, though she knew it was impossible they could ever be friends.

"You don't get it do you?" Theo shot back. "Where else can you pick up a competent scientist on plant pathology and who may have enough knowledge to decipher a genetically coded antidrug crop formula?"

"The UN International Antidrugs Summit," Lola appended, switching her gaze from Theo to Paul. "Biologists from all over the world will be coming to see the professor's presentation."

Eve's body weakened.

"Get your things," Paul instructed, glancing at his watch. "I know a place we can stay tonight."

Eve never thought she would have to one day contemplate that for the love of one person there would be so many casualties. Added to losing the assistant commissioner, the one man who had been the closest thing to a father in her life, two police officers in London had been struck down in their careers, two foreign assassins in theirs, and now there was the very real danger of Theo being taken out in his.

She sought solidarity by lacing her arm through Lola's as they sat forlorn in the backseat of a car, Paul at the wheel, and Theo in the passenger seat staring at the darkened sky which enveloped them.

The streets of Vienna were busy. The *Wiener Festwachen*, one of the city's main cultural festivals, was alive with noise while people, making their way to the opera, music, or theater, laughed and giggled as they ambled along.

Eve would have loved dearly to have been a part of the revelries, to have sealed the day with Theo as it had begun; appreciating the arts, making love, enjoying dinner and hopefully seeing the night through lost in each others arms. As it happened, she was instead cowered in the backseat of a car, inappropriately dressed in a sequined dress, keeping her head down as the vehicle slowly worked its way out of the Innere Stadt.

"I'm frightened," Lola whispered. "One minute I am on a plane from France, the next I am in Vienna."

Eve squeezed her arm tight. "I bet you didn't expect to be accosted by two men either."

"At my age," Lola taunted, trying to calm herself. "As long as he has his own teeth and hair, a woman can't be too choosy."

Eve chuckled with the irony in Lola's humor, though it was tainted with pain. For the first time, she saw the shadowy expression of a woman who was evidently lonely. "You'll be fine," she urged, knowing her tone was not encouraging. "We all will."

Lola patted Eve's fingers. "I can tell you're in love," she whispered, her voice lowered as though she had uttered a great secret. "It's one of the greatest things in life to love somebody. Your brother is suffering a great deal."

Eve tried to smile, but felt nothing other than sympathy. "Were you ever in love?"

"Oh, yes," Lola admitted wistfully. "He was my gentle giant, Theo's godfather."

"The ambassador?" Eve gulped in shock.

"I was his first wife before he became ambassador," Lola began to relate. "Sadly, we could never have children. We divorced, and he remarried. His wife is a very charming woman and has given him the children he deserved. But I miss him still. The love we had. All my life, I only found it the one time."

Eve had heard a lot of stories since walking into Theo's world, but this one towered above them all. "Theo's like a godson to you, isn't he?"

"He's a wonderful man," Lola proclaimed with a faint smile. "I hope you make him very happy, and he you. His work, especially the projects like Green Light, must continue. I could never do it alone. He is a very generous person."

Eve nodded in agreement. That was the truth after all. Professor Theophilus de Cordova was remarkable.

He had absorbed Paul's troubles with a much better reserve than anyone else she could name caught in Theo's position. If he had been some one like Leon or even Tyrone, Paul would not have seen the next light of day.

She wondered where he was taking them. The journey was not long. About an hour going east, she guessed. Eve's only awareness was that they had crossed a tram line and had entered a small suburb. Soon they arrived at a small building that had the appearance of an old café, of the type she often saw in France.

"We'll be staying with a small group of students," Paul explained carefully. "They're nice people, but don't get into any heavy subjects with them." His tone was a warning one as they all departed the car. "They're not your regular kind of students."

Paul immediately knocked a series of sharp, nonofficious raps on the worn oak door. Theo was alert enough to know that they were an encoded password to gain entrance. He instantly restrained Paul by firmly grabbing his wrist as footsteps from within could be heard.

"Who are these people?" he demanded, his paranoia in the red zone. He had the sudden awful premonition he would be finding himself facing a group who were the sort to target his work.

"Don't worry," Paul assured, knowing old habits died hard. "They're friends. They helped me keep my head down when I rolled over and played dead. In fact, it was a member of this group who gave me the tip-off about you, Professor. That's how I knew to come to the hotel. We underground students, researchers, and scientists have a grapevine of our own out here."

Eve did not like what she was hearing. She was hard pressed to recall any endearing qualities about her brother. He had hardened, like steel. He was uncompromising in his actions. He was a man possessed with an agenda of his very own. A man who carried a gun.

She gingerly walked over to Theo and took hold of his hand. It made her feel like a little girl again, seeking the protection of someone strong, powerful, and firm.

Eve stroked his fingers as the sound of bolts being yanked back rung through the air. The door opened. Paul smiled and urged them all in. As the door closed behind them with a deathly thud, Eve could see that they were in a small, smoky room. Candlelight dimmed the interior, the air was yellow with the stench of hashish, and she estimated that up to fifteen people were huddled around the seven tables, drinking what smelled like strong coffee, smoking joints, and talking in conspiratorial tones among themselves.

Paul took them boldly through the smoke and up a short flight of stairs into a much brighter room at the top. It was carpeted, with a number of empty chairs dotted about. A small, white table was in the center with several ashtrays cluttered with cigarette butts. He invited them in and proceeded to take off his tweed jacket. Hanging it over the back of a chair, Paul clasped his hands together.

"We'll be safe here," he said. "I'll get us all some coffee."

He left the room and Lola looked around carefully before depositing herself in a chair. Eve felt uneasy as she turned to Theo. He could see how frantic and exhausted she had become. Without make-up, her face seemed even paler, but the sparkle had not left her eyes. He placed his storage capsule and briefcase onto the same chair Paul had draped his jacket over and rubbed his warm hands along Eve's arms and shoulders.

It felt so good to touch Eve again. She was shaking from the slight chill in the room due to a window open to diffuse the smoke. Ever lovely in the dress and sandals he had bought her, it left Eve's arms and neck exposed, and she had no jacket or shawl to cover herself.

"Here, take this." He was about to remove his gray jacket when Eve stopped him.

She moistened her lips to distract her attention from the feelings which, like a snake gone loose, was beginning to run up and down the length of her body. "I'll use Paul's."

Stepping back, she reached for his jacket, denying herself the comfort of being snuggled in the warmth and luxury of Theo's natural scent. As she did so, an item fell from the inner pocket to the floor. Lola was the first to reach for it. She picked it up and held it limp between her fingers before offering it to Eve for safe return to her brother's pocket. But Eve's hand became motionless. She could not take the creased yellow folder Lola held out to her.

"Theo." Her voice was shaking.

He took the folder immediately and opened it up, seeing his formula fully intact. He gazed at Eve, then heard a noise behind him. Paul was returning to the room. Impulsively, Theo bent the folder and placed it in his own jacket pocket just as the door burst open.

Eve no longer knew her brother as he walked in with a tray of coffee, the man whom she had seen kill two people in cold blood. She had duly replaced his jacket and he did not seem to suspect a thing as he placed the tray on the small, white table, allowing them all to pick their own mugs. All she knew was that for the night they were expected to stay in the small café together, in the middle of God knew where, she wanted to stay as far as possible away from him.

Fourteen

They slept in sleeping bags. Something tickled the back of Eve's hand. She dazedly flicked her wrist back and forth, clinging to the bliss of her dream. When she felt the feathery brush on her hand again, she yawned and awoke to find Theo staring from his position next to her on the floor. He wore a faint smile as he admired her rounded face. Eve felt self-conscious that he should be seeing her hair so disheveled and her eyes puffy from lack of sleep.

There had been many noises and low voices chatting throughout the night, and at one point there was a heated argument that had prompted Theo from his sleeping bag to investigate what was going on downstairs. He had been told to return to their room as the students were simply debating a political issue which did not concern him. Paul had tried to stop him from leaving, but the professor had been unable to settle until he knew what sort of people were sharing the building with them.

While huddled in their sleeping bags, Eve recalled Theo whispering an explanation that they were discussing staging a protest outside the UNO building in the morning. The UN International Antidrug Summit was to be held in the same building. Theo explained they were the type who drifted in the Bohemian demiworld, where capitalism was considered corrupt, western-ization criminal, socialism and all manner of equality strived for, and given the absence of all values, *they*, the educated, were destined to take control.

Their protest would be seen as a precursor to the G8 Summit due the following month. They were part of a much larger umbrella organization consisting of church groups and unions, scientists and students, environmentalists and peace activists, and the so-called *Black Bloc* of unaffiliated anarchists who gathered on occasions such as this to demonstrate against the power wielded by the most successful economic nations of the world.

The nature of the summit, where it was likely that border controls and law enforcement would be an issue, and the legalization of drugs an even bigger controversy, would attract prodrug hardliners from far and wide. Theo whispered that she should not sustain any illusions about getting help from these students.

Eve was to realize that Theo was an unusual combination of cynic and idealist. He was committed to fighting the war against drug crop cultivation at its source and did not seem to concern himself whether prodrugs activists would be staging their hatred against the purpose of the summit. What mattered to him was the ultimate change which would result from his seminar and how it would affect world safety.

It was everything he had told her when she had first arrived in Cramond. Maybe she did have a sense of dressing the world to her tastes as he had accused her. Somehow, that one thought made her feel naive. Theo had told her that concepts have to make sense to someone. He had a sense of how the world should be and in his mind, there was always an alternative view.

It was all this which forbade Eve from sleeping. On occasion, reluctantly tearing her own gaze away from Theo, she had looked at Paul huddled quietly in his own sleeping bag caught up in a malaise of his own. She did so again now. The only time he had stirred was to repudiate Theo from leaving the room. Paul mentioned about the toilet two doors away and expected it to be the only place they should visit. Now, at 5:20 A.M., his body was motionless, lost in dreaming.

She guessed Theresa was the only thing in that dream. His endless journey to be with her touched Eve in some way. She could not imagine such determination existed. It did not excuse what Paul had done, and she was thankful he had not yet searched his jacket. *One less confrontation to deal with,* she mused. In some ways his life had become a tragedy because so many lives had been lost leaving him none the closer to being with the one he loved. When her gaze returned to Theo to find him still staring, she was suddenly alerted to actually believing they were in love.

"Get used to it," she breathed, gazing at the roguish, unshaven angles of his jawline. "This is how wild my hair looks in the morning."

"I know," Theo whispered, his faint smile still holding. "The morning after we made love the first time, remember?"

Eve felt the hot flush beneath her skin. Of course he had seen it before. So much had happened since then, it was hard to correlate everything even though she had not forgotten how much she enjoyed his tender touch. Naturally, Theo seemed unruffled, or so it appeared to her. His cornrow-braided hair was still neatly intact, there were no bags beneath his eyes. Only the fine lines that was evident with age were slightly more pronounced around his forehead than previously. She imagined it was stress due to wondering what pitfalls were facing him that day.

"What time is your presentation?" she asked, lifting her head slightly to see where Lola Henriques was camped. She was two feet away, between Theo and Paul. "Are we allowed to go with you?"

Theo lifted his head and delved to unzip his bag. "My talk begins at 9:00 A.M. but I'm expected to be in the building before 8:30 to brief members and consultants of the UN Drugs Control Program."

"What are you doing?" Eve whispered, as Theo began to unzip her own bag.

"I thought I'd give you a big hug to make up for last night."

She smiled and snuggled closer. Eve placed her arms around Theo's neck and melted into his hardened frame. It was bliss to feel his heart beat again next to her own. To run her hands along his jawline to his neck, to be embraced by strong, soft hands which pressed her into his rigid frame. Together, they held on. The reacquaintance brought back heady memories of just how good they were together. It was an understanding of minds Eve knew she wanted to keep.

"What are we going to do?" she murmured.

"I know what I'd like to do," Theo muttered.

Eve chuckled softly. "Down, boy. Down."

She pulled away in his arms to survey his face. All the softening features she expected to see were there. The smothering in his deep chocolate-brown eyes, the desirous tilt of his brows, the swelling of his pink rounded lips braced ready to kiss her. She obliged. Eve took Theo's mouth into hers and tenderly moved it in time with her own.

The kiss kindled an assortment of feelings anew. Wonderful, thrilling emotions which put her in an immediate fluster. She gasped and pulled back for breath. *What was that?* a voice in her head screamed. The overwhelming shock of such commotion flapping around inside her had Eve wide-eyed and momentarily confused.

Theo did not wait for the shock to catch up with her. Within seconds, he pulled her back and tasted her lips again with another onslaught on her emotions. The pulsating ripples deepened. Every fiber in Eve's body quickened with the feel of Theo's kiss. His body movements told her he felt it, too. It was as though she had turned on a switch and all the rage of a night of passion denied was let loose.

They kissed until Eve became conscious that they were losing control. "Theo," she whispered, pulling away. "I just saw Lola move."

Theo stilled himself and grimaced in annoyance. "We're getting out of here," he murmured. "I need to get us to a bed."

Eve wanted to laugh at his joke. How she would dearly have loved that. "We can't." But she wanted to leave anyway.

"We can," Theo insisted. "C'mon."

"Theo!" Eve panicked. "What about Paul?"

"I don't trust your brother," he admitted, gazing tenderly at her. He was not going to be fooled. "And I trust them even less downstairs. We need to go."

Eve's eyes widened. He was out of his sleeping bag in an instant and was already tackling the zipper on hers. Eve looked down, finding herself still in her sequined dress. "I have to change." She saw the boutique bag from the Stephansplatz at her feet. It contained her bag, jeans, jersey and demiboots. "Unzip me."

She turned her back and Theo examined the wonderful sculpture of her slender neck as he pulled the zipper down on her dress. It stirred his manhood to see such a sensual work of art. Eve stood, stretched, and rotated her shoulders, feeling the stiffness in her body, much of which was the result of too much tension. While Theo carefully put on his shoes and tucked his shirt into his crumbled trousers, Eve went to the bottom of the room and quickly changed into her jeans and jersey. She was slipping into her boots when Theo roused Lola.

Lola awoke with a start. "Theo!"

He had to gently place his hand over her mouth to prevent her from speaking. "Get your shoes on," he whispered. "We're leaving."

She immediately looked at Paul. He was still asleep. Lola slowly sat up and allowed Theo to unzip her sleeping bag. He had to help her out of it for she felt as though all her joints had stiffened. "My back is hurting," she complained.

"We'll find you some painkillers on the way," Theo assured her, bending to his knees to help her into her shoes.

"Where are we going?"

"To UNO-City," he told her. He glanced across the room at Eve. She was fully dressed. "I don't know what Paul has planned, but I think we'd better leave without him."

Lola nodded and similarly allowed Theo to help her into her brown jacket. Eve threw a quick glance at Paul and thought she had seen him stir. They all stood still. She was reminded that they had found the original formula she had stolen from Theo in his jacket pocket, but it was now safely tucked away in Theo's. Paul had said he did not know what happened to it. If he had taken it from the assistant commissioner, he had to have done so before he was killed. Her heart trembled as she thought the worse. Eve could not rule out her knowledge that Paul carried a gun.

Her eyes closed for brief seconds as her mind spun with awful torment. Cowardly, she decided she did not want to know the truth. All she wanted at that precise moment was to leave with Theo and Lola and be somewhere perfectly safe. Her worried eyes bounced off the chocolate-colored ones she had grown to know so well. Theo nodded and picked up his briefcase and cold storage capsule containing the live fungus of his deadly strain.

It was proof of his formula. Proof that it worked. Proof that it could be made. Eve saw the importance of him getting it to the UN building more than ever. They could not risk it being illegally used by drug traffickers in a war against each others' deadly crops. Without the relevant field tests the repercussions, as Theo so rightly considered, could be devastating. She nodded as he indicated with his head that they should leave through the door.

They descended the stairs, relieved Paul was not alerted as they left the room. Taking one step at a time, Eve saw that the room below was occupied by a handful of people, remnants of the hoard that had been there throughout the night. They had heavy-lidded eyes from smoking hashish and drinking. The students paid little attention as they passed by, though she threw one—a burly Moroccan—a smile so he would not think a dawn escape was in progress. They had reached the same oak door they had entered through, when suddenly someone approached from her side.

He spoke in French. *"Comment vous appelez-vous?"*

Eve froze and saw that it was the Moroccan. Thankfully she understood him, something she had learned on her recent visit to France. The trip had licked her into shape somewhat and so she was able to know he had asked her name.

"Eve Hamilton," she told him truthfully.

"Mode Styliste!" He grew excited.

Eve turned and indicated Theo and Lola. *"Voici mon mari, mon mère,"* she told him, aware that he recognized who she was by name. It was intriguing, almost comical, to know her fame had stretched to the furthest reaches of mankind.

He nodded and gazed more intently at her. *"Vous allez où?"* he inquired, curious as to where they were going.

"Stephansplatz," Eve returned, thinking up the only

place she had heard of in Vienna, only because she had shopped there with Theo the day before.

He understood and even offered her a smile. *"Qu'est-ce que vous désirez?"*

"What does he want?" Theo whispered at her annoyed, nodding and throwing the Moroccan a discreet smile.

"He's just asked if I'd like something," she told him in a murmur.

"A car would be nice," Theo interjected.

Eve kept her gaze fixed on the Moroccan and widened her smile. *"Je voudrais une voiture."* She was amazed when he nodded his agreement and disappeared into the room from where he had come. Eve turned to Theo perplexed, finding that he was already releasing the bolts to the door. He had just yanked back the final bolt when the man returned, holding up a key to their view.

"Voilà"

He held out his hand. Confused, Eve looked at Theo. He looked at Lola. It occurred to them almost simultaneously that the Moroccan wanted money. Lola instantly dipped into her handbag and pulled out a wad of English sterling. She handed it over. The man checked it without counting, simply holding some of it in the air to authenticate it was real money. Then, without question, he handed Eve the key.

"Vous voulez autre chose?" he inquired.

Eve shook her head. She did not require anything else.

"What did you say to him?" Theo gasped in amazement, as he delivered himself to the street outside where the fresh dawn revealed the thousand-and-one creases in his gray suit.

"I told him you were my husband," Eve applauded herself, glimpsing at the clouded sky. "And that Lola was my mother."

"I see."

He did not pass comment, Eve noted, but simply followed the Moroccan to a wreck of a car parked nearby. It was an obscene, murky green color with rust spots scattered from the bonnet to the boot. Within spitting distance of it, Eve could smell gasoline. Only the wheels looked tenable. The rest of the vehicle was doubtless condemned for the junkyard.

"We are not going in that," Eve said, disbelieving Lola had parted with good money for them to be faced traveling in a death trap.

"Give me the key," Theo ordered. "If it'll get us to UNO-City, then let's use it."

Reluctantly, Eve got into the car with Lola and Theo. The Moroccan threw them a farewell *"Au voir"* and a wave as Theo reversed the car. It spat out an unhealthy cough as he pulled away. Eve's heart fell as she looked back at the café and remembered her brother. She knew when he awoke, he would be moved to scream at his Moroccan friend that their departure was totally without his knowledge. He would know that his sister no longer trusted him, he would realize that her allegiance was steadfast with Theo, and he would find that the written formula was gone.

Eve had no idea where they were, but guessed that Theo perhaps had a better sense of direction. His face seemed to express he had conjured up some sort of recollection as to where they were located. "Know which way you're going?" she asked, gazing through the dirty windows where she saw trees and woodland.

"I think we're on the border of the city," he wavered, unsure. "I remember the *Wienerwald*—the Vienna Woods. I think that's where we are."

"Is that good or bad?" Eve inquired.

"It's not bad," Theo summarized. "If I head back toward the city and follow the road signs for UNO-City, I can't miss."

But miss he did. Within an hour, they were lost. Eve was exasperated. They seemed to have gone further into the woods than away from it. Theo succumbed to the knowledge that he had made a wrong turn and doubled-back on himself. Finally, they seemed to be on the right road. Two hours had been wasted by the mishap, but soon Eve found herself staring at the United Nations number-three base after New York and Geneva.

As the clapped-out piece of metal they were in approached the six Y-shaped, glass-fronted high-rises on the left bank of the Danube, Eve decided it went against the architecture so customary of Vienna. The monstrosity that faced her seemed intimidating and essentially ugly in comparison, and the entire area was cordoned off with wire fencing, bristling with armed police and CCTV cameras.

The UN functionaries who were once housed at the Hofburg were now based here among the bureaucracies of the International Atomic Energy Authority, the Commission for Infectious Diseases, the ever-busy High Commission for Refugees, and a number of other international bodies. Its new role as a cultural link, bridgehead between east and west, and meeting place for summits was the final destination for Theo to launch the results of his work.

Raised brows by the armed police as they approached the gateway in their wreck of a car brought heavy-handed scrutiny before Theo was able to display his entry pass. When he killed the engine, they were all relieved to stretch their legs in the rising sunlight before Theo led the way ahead into the building.

"They have a hospitality suite for guests," he told Eve. "You and Lola should be fine in there until after the summit. You can both get some rest."

Eve nodded, knowing she could kill for a cup of coffee.

"I'll take you there, then I need to go freshen up and register us all in. Fire and safety precautions," he added. He considered he probably had the appearance of one of those fuddy-duddy professors often seen in black-and-white movies, judging from the state of his suit. He had no means of pressing it, but he had an electric razor in his briefcase and the clean shirt and tie he had purchased at the Stephansplatz.

Eve was pleasantly surprised to find that the interior of the building was generously sprinkled with works of art by contemporary Austrian artists. Soon after taking two elevators and walking what felt like the full stretch of the building, they arrived in the area where Theo wanted them to remain. Eve seated herself in one of the dralon chairs and smiled when Lola joined her. The older woman looked tired and in need of a glass of water.

Theo left and returned a short while later absent of his briefcase and the cold storage capsule. He came with coffee, sandwiches, orange juice, and painkillers for Lola. He explained that he had found where he should be and would be leaving for his briefing with the members and consultants of the UN. He would pop by to see them before the summit actually began. Relieved that they were on safer territory, Eve relaxed and sipped her coffee.

The next time Eve looked at her watch, it was just seconds before she heard a loud bang. It shook the building. She hurtled herself out of her seat immediately.

Lola had been leaning lopsided in her chair, fighting to catch what little slumber she could get after failing to sleep comfortably the night before. She was awoken by the small pellets of debris that fell from the ceiling. Eve, who had been reading one of the magazines spread across a courtesy table, bored, but content that at some point that day she would be returning to England, became instantly aware of the noise outside.

A second, much larger, bang had Lola rising to her feet. The floor beneath them shook slightly, and she gazed nervously at Eve. "What's happening?"

"It sounds like a bomb," Eve said slowly. Her heart began to beat in sickly anticipation. She was unsure whether it would be safe to leave the room. Suddenly, she heard the sound of rapid gunfire. She stood still to decide what to do. She ran to the window and stared outside.

Carnage faced her. A battle between protestors and police struggling to contain them had ensued while she and Lola had been comfortably relaxed in the hospitality suite. She took in the infernal scene of a water cannon truck cleaving its way through clouds of tear gas as scores of extremist troublemakers began to throw gas bombs. Some were wielding hammers, axes, knives, catapults, and other devices with their faces hidden behind the thick Perspex of their masks.

Eve knew they were an amalgamation of small pressure groups like the students she had met in the café the night before. They wore T-shirts and baseball caps emblazoned with logos of their causes, many appearing to be in their teens and twenties, sporting beards, dreadlocks, combat trousers, and dirty trainers. She could discern from her view that many were attempting to penetrate the outer zone that protected the UNO building from protests such as this.

Unsure whether they would succeed in penetrating the outer zone, Eve turned to Lola with one question on her mind. "Do we stay here and wait for Theo?"

"No." Lola was firm.

Eve left the window and threw down the magazine she had been reading. Picking up her bags, she followed Lola toward the door. They looked down the corridor. It was cluttered with people of all nationalities, running in one direction—the exit. Eve could see there was a lot of confusion, hysteria, and general mayhem. She gave Lola access to go first, following quickly behind. They were two minutes into their journey when another bang jolted them, causing Lola to fall over.

Eve used all her energy to drag Lola to her feet. She heard screaming behind her and yelling in front. More gunfire echoed down the expanse of the corridor, and Eve felt herself panicked by the commotion. She did not know what was going on, but suspected that somehow, some of the protesters must have gotten inside the building.

"Let's find Theo," she advised Lola. Eve was concerned whether he was all right. The fact that neither Cantrell nor Bogetti had the formula eased her mind a little. If they did not have it, there would be no need for either one to hunt a scientific interpreter. Still, if the protesters were on the hunt to cause real problems, they could indiscriminately target just about anyone.

She took hold of Lola's arm, intending to pull her along, but was dismayed when Lola slowed her pace. "I can't run any faster," she said, tired and having taken much beyond her normal endurance. "You go."

Eve was alarmed. "I can't leave you." She tried to add spirit to their malaise. "Think of all those wonderful garments I have yet to make for you."

"You find Theo," Lola puffed, short of breath. "I'll come along."

Eve was not swayed. When she heard more gunfire, she took hold of Lola's wrist and yanked her across the corridor and through the doors of what she thought was an empty room. Inside, Eve saw a face which looked vaguely familiar. Behind the rectangular frames of his steel-rimmed glasses, brown eyes were fired up ready to pounce.

"Dr. Henri Da Costa," Lola shrieked almost madly. "I might have known you would be staging trouble here."

He was flanked by six men, two of whom Eve recognized. The first was the Moroccan she had seen earlier that morning, the other was Dr. Ira Keplan, Theo's lab assistant whom she had met in Scotland. He looked shame-faced when he saw her. Dr. Da Costa and his men were dressed in military garb; Da Costa with a balaclava on his head, his stance and demeanor like that of a soldier. Eve could only imagine he had changed his clothes after brandishing his entry pass to gain access to the building when she saw the white overalls they must have been wearing littered across the chairs in the room. He was freshly shaven, his hair trimmed, though he was sporting a black eye which she recalled was caused when Theo had thumped him.

"We are here to make a statement for the peoples of the world," he told Lola Henriques, impassioned with his beliefs.

The Moroccan tapped Dr. Da Costa on his shoulder and whispered something in his ear. A smile rose to his face. "He says your name is Eve Hamilton," he told her with a demure smile. "You're a famous fashion designer. My friend here was very pleased to help you. He says your brother, Paul, is looking for you."

Eve was at a loss as to what to say. Her mind was more captivated by the large glass window behind Dr. Da Costa where she could see a large conference hall with delegates seated facing a large podium. A man was talking into a microphone and his voice was amplified by a speaker hung above her head, his language foreign to her ears.

"You arrived here with Professor de Cordova," he

went on. "I heard he was at one of our safe houses last night. He had a little trouble back in England. I told your brother all about it."

"To which trouble are you referring?" Eve asked, strengthening her allegiance toward Theo. "The one about his son, Trey, or his work?"

Da Costa flinched. "You're very close, I see, to have known that."

Eve didn't comment. Her gaze shifted from Dr. Da Costa to the conference hall where she had a clear view of Theo walking toward the podium. He was holding the yellow folder and the cold storage capsule in his hands, and she was moved by how handsome and composed he appeared in his white overalls, even from her distance.

"You should stop this now," Lola ordered, her tone chastising and firm. "You are not achieving anything by staging a protest here."

"The whole world will take notice today," Da Costa ranted, "and know we have struck a blow for mankind against corruption."

"What are you going to do?" Eve asked, alarmed.

"We're going to take the conference hall," Dr. Da Costa proclaimed. "And keep it under siege until the world listens to what our groups have to say."

Suddenly Theo's voice could be heard through the loud speaker. It instantly diminished the noise outside the room. Dr. Da Costa's eyes rose as he alerted his comrades. Everyone immediately turned and faced the glass window, captivated as Theo spoke. He introduced himself and launched straight into his presentation.

"We can no longer protect our borders," Theo firmly told the seated UN delegates and scientific consultants, all of whom were dressed in white overalls and seated close to the podium. "The price of coca leaf has been falling as a direct result of overproduction. This means the number of lab sites along the Brazilian borders have tripled for turning coca leaf to paste and ultimately to cocaine."

Eve watched as he reached for the cold storage capsule and revealed it to the audience. "It is time we killed the source," he announced, none the wiser to the protest that was going on outside. "Welcome the new fungus spore prototype to wage green warfare against coca and opium poppy crop cultivation. I give you Phoebe."

"Phoebe!" Dr. Da Costa croaked, as applause shook the conference hall. He seemed surprised at the discovery. "So, that's what it is. I thought . . ." His voice trailed.

"You thought he was conducting illegal experiments," Eve finished. "For what aim, I don't know. It was hardly worth trying to discredit him just to find out whether Trey is your son."

He turned and faced her, thunder marked across his face. Eve saw the fire whip into his eyes. "He's known all these years," Dr. Da Costa reproved, quite harshly.

"He's never known." Eve proclaimed his innocence.

A silence enveloped them. Eve could see that Dr. Keplan looked quite embarrassed by what was being said. He had been part of Dr. Da Costa's plans to raid Theo's laboratory in Scotland and had done so without full knowledge of the motives involved. Theo's voice could still be heard above her head when Henri Da Costa interrupted.

"You tell the professor that—" He was instantly disturbed by the commotion outside.

Eve turned as UN security suddenly stormed the room. Seeing Dr. Da Costa and his men dressed in military uniforms, they raised guns, trigger-happy, and without hesitation, fired. Eve caught only a glimpse of Lola running to her rescue before the room disappeared. The last thing she could remember was a loud scream ringing like an echo in her ears . . .

Eve came to in a pristine bed, blinked, and saw walls painted white. Her eyes widened, and she saw an open window letting in the breeze of a warm day. She thought she was dreaming when she saw white, puffy clouds, but as her gaze moved sideways, Theo was seated in a chair. He sprang out of it the instant he saw her awake and pressed shaky fingers against her cheeks.

"Try not to move," he whispered into her ear. "You caught a bullet. It nipped the side of your face."

"Oh, my . . ." Eve's eyes swelled with tears. "Am I going to be all right?"

"Fine," Theo smiled reassuringly. He kissed her forehead as Eve raised her hand and gently felt the swelling just above her left temple.

"I must have fainted," she declared, trying to think back to what happened. "Where am I?"

"Hospital," Theo gently told her. "They've given you the all clear. You're going to be fine."

"What happened?"

"I'll tell you later," Theo sighed, his tone sounding as though he was holding a number of things from her. "Paul's outside. He was among the group of scientists who came in with Dr. Da Costa. He used a false ID. He wants to talk to you."

"The protestors?"

"They're under control."

"Does he know about—"

Theo nodded. "I've turned in my work and . . . I'll wait and see what they decide to do with it."

Eve closed her eyes. At last it was all over. She felt Theo's soft hands stroke her forehead, soothing her as wet tears squeezed through the sides of her eyes. She had marginally dodged a bullet. She could have been killed. It was such a traumatic experience to know that the self-centered nature in some people could cause her harm. When she opened her eyes, Paul was standing over her. His body was slouched like a man who had accepted every form of failing in his life.

"I know you think I'm some kind of monster," he grated bitterly, "but I never intended any of this to happen to you."

"Sure you didn't," Theo jibed sardonically.

Eve's tear-filled eyes bore into him. "What do I tell mum?" she cried, unable to believe he had changed so much, certainly beyond all her fondest recognition.

"Nothing." It was a lie, adding tenfold to his pain.

"You can't mean that," Eve harangued.

There was a strange flexion in her voice which bought his head—which had been hanging down in shame—abruptly up to look at her face. For a second, Eve saw his dark pain before the cynical mask slid into place. This was the Paul Hamilton the world was now faced with—cold, cruel, and dangerous—their childhood a distant memory. Then, in a flash, she saw the truth.

"*You* wanted to sell the formula, didn't you?" He was silent. "*You* wanted to know Cantrell's archrival's name, and Theo made the mistake of telling you it was Bogetti."

Theo's brows rose, failing to see the revelation.

"Humphrey didn't believe me when I told him I didn't know where Theresa was," Paul whimpered. "Yayo would use her as part of his operation to deliver coca paste to mobile laboratories. She hated the work. We only wanted to be together. She disappeared, I think with a large supply of his stash, and he thinks I double-crossed him."

"So why still try and get the formula?" Eve probed tearfully.

"I didn't know she had escaped. When Cantrell tried to kill me . . ." He paused. "Humphrey was supposed to help me find her. Instead, he had done a deal with someone who was willing to pay one million and five for the professor's formula."

Theo shook his head, pent-up anger welled in his face.

"And you thought it was Bogetti," Eve concluded. "You wanted the money all to yourself." She was so saddened, her heart felt heavy. "Was that enough to kill him?"

Paul refused to answer. "I needed money to get to Cantrell. I need to find her," was all he could say. His voice was deep and rough, devoid of any outward emotion.

"Paul?" Eve's voice was shaking as she spoke his name. "Revenge is not justice."

He refused to look at her. "Good-bye, Eve."

He left the room. His tone was final. Eve did not know whether she would ever see her brother again. When she turned and faced Theo, he took her into his arms and crushed her body to his chest.

"He's lost," Theo told her. "Don't try and understand him."

Eve leaned her cheek against him and cried. The bond between her and her brother was broken. He no longer needed her, and she no longer needed him. She was with Theo now, and that was where she would remain.

Epilogue

One year later

If you wake up one morning and find that your heart wants to head north for a break from London, you'll always be welcomed here.

Eve was seated in one of the brown leather sofas in the cottage in Cramond, dressed in a white robe, her hair pinned up, watching Trey as he played with the tiny toes of her newborn baby. Her little boy, Adam, was sleeping quietly in his cradle on the floor, and Eve glanced at the two brothers before swiftly returning her gaze to the postcard in her hand.

It had arrived at her new London studio, redirected by the new owners of her Fulham house. Though the Royal Mail had been instructed to reroute all her current mail, there would always be one to slip through the system showing up weeks, even months later. This was one of them. Eve had not yet shown it to Theo. He was at Fairafar Mill, working on his latest experiments with his qualified, fully authenticated staff. She did not want to disturb him. She had wanted a few days first to absorb the implications of it.

Eve recognized the handwriting immediately. It was from Paul. Just seeing his name brought back the flurry of everything that had happened the year before. Fresh in her mind, as though it were yesterday, she remembered leaving Vienna with a heavy heart on the trip back to England. Two days later, she was attending Humphrey Brown's funeral.

Her mother had handled it well. They were later to discover that there would be an inquest into how he had come to his death in a pubic park near the Prince of Wales's residence at St. James's Palace. Witnesses were saying they had seen him talking to a man in a panama hat. The inquest was still ongoing.

The following week, she was joining Theo in Brazil at a church in São Paulo. She was moved by the burial service given for Lola Henriques. She had died from a fatal gunshot wound, one of seven victims, during the disturbance at UNO-City. Her fondest memory of Lola was that she had never ceased to contribute so much to the causes held dear to her heart.

"It should've been Da Costa," Theo had seethed, pained by the loss of his friend.

Dr. Da Costa had been arrested on five charges and was awaiting trial at the European Court, along with several denomination group members, comrades of the ever-growing trend of plaguing world summits. It was likely he would receive a custodial sentence for violation offenses and demonstration activities dating back ten years.

Dr. Moira Keltz was quite distressed at hearing the news. Gone was her part-time lover who had been a mainstay in her life from their early days at the University of Oxford. She had accepted the results of a DNA test which proved Theo to be Trey's natural father, and had openly admitted instructing their son never to tell his father she had been making secret visits to his school.

Moira agreed to joint custody of Trey and seemed content with the decision that he should live half the year with her. It was a matter Eve did not involve herself in, though she had the opportunity of meeting Moira at a parents' evening she had attended with Theo at Trey's school before it closed for the summer. She was surprised to discover how attractive Moira Keltz was, and equally so the other woman of her.

Moira was everything the photo in Theo's wallet had revealed. They had eyed each other with feminine curiosity. Eve decided she seemed very insecure for a woman of her vast education and knowledge, and slightly troubled at the news that Theo was going to be married.

Eve smiled when she remembered their wedding day. It was at St. Giles Cathedral in Edinburgh. Her mother, teary-eyed, had given her away to the groom in the wake of the loss of her father, Humphrey Brown, and her brother. She was never to tell her mother that Paul was alive. That was a bridge she would cross one day.

Dressed in white, from her own sketch pad, Theo's father Augustus was immediately swept away by her, as was his entire family. The Brazilian Ambassador had also been present with his wife and saddened by the news of Lola Henriques's passing. He lit a candle for her at the end of their wedding service, when the cathedral was empty and he could partake of some silence alone.

Their marriage had taken place three months after the Vienna summit. Deciding to give their relationship a chance, they had begun to make regular visits to each other, excited as flights to London or Scotland became little excursions and excuses to have their wicked way with each other.

Even now, Eve recalled the late August evening in London, when the sun was setting and she had been curled up comfortably on the sofa in Theo's Mayfair apartment, the sound of the professor's voice as he said those three little words to her.

Having committed to, tendered, and nurtured their newfound love, which had become more intense on Theo's presentation to her of a bouquet of flowers to commemorate, as he had put it, their lives becoming normal again, he picked up the thread of a conversation they had discarded on their arrival in Vienna. She was surprised he still remembered it.

"I can't decide if you'll make an old man feel very happy or a young man feel very old," he had said, recalling his initial impression of her.

"That's an odd thing to say," she chuckled. "Are you the young man or the old one?"

"I'm the happy one who is wondering whether he is loving you the way you want to be loved." He smiled. "You never did tell me."

Eve was touched. Of course, it meant he was analyzing their feelings, as he had always done. "A genuine hug, kiss, or cuddle when I need it," she began in all honesty, no longer shying away from the subject. "Deep emotional attachment." He nodded. "A sexually fulfilling love life." He gave a big nod. "And an understanding that we want to spend the rest of our lives together." She gazed into his eyes. "I'd say you give me all those things."

Those were the only words that needed to be said. Theo hugged her close, ensnared her with his molten, chocolate-brown eyes and told her what she had waited a lifetime to hear.

"I love you," he uttered, his voice trembling.

They kissed, passionately, and so came her own declaration. "I love you, too."

He believed her enough to propose marriage. Their wedding night was spent in the cottage at Cramond, their honeymoon on one of the Greek islands, and, on her return, Eve was able to complete her order book of commissioned designs to the satisfaction of Princess Adjani, Jean-Pierre Cavelet and the number of buyers *Style Paradise* had provided.

She was able to put on an autumn and spring show

at two London Fashion Weeks before their baby was born. Theo had been swept by a fresh bout of love for their son, so tiny and immensely perfect. His face was bathed with tears when he told her how intense his feelings were, not so unlike how it had felt when Trey had been born.

"I'm forever blessed to love somebody beyond my own understanding," he told her.

It was what he had said about Paul on reading his letters from Theresa. Eve remembered those letters now as she looked at the writing on the postcard. The stamp and postmark indicated Bangkok. It was short and sweet. *Honey Bun has found his Mabel Syrup and is happily guarding his love.* Eve smiled, tears welling in her eyes.

He would never know that their mother was now engaged to a wonderful Caribbean man, that Theo was now her husband, and that she had given birth to a son. That Phoebe, the formula which had caused so much commotion between them, was now under the control of Viotac International who were soon to embark on field tests in Afghanistan as a way forward to begin cleaning up the country, and would be voting at their next board meeting to begin production for active green warfare.

Her eyes were still filled with tears when Theo entered the room. His tall figure, dressed in denim jeans and a blue sweater, walked over and knelt on the floor, kissing both his sons before he threw himself on the sofa next to Eve. He absorbed the scent of her perfume, the clean smell of her freshly washed hair, and kissed her on her cheek like a man grateful he had such a wonderful wife.

He was exhausted. The heavenly aroma of roast chicken came from the oven. Dinner would be served in an hour. He surveyed her flawless, youthful face, detecting from the tears in her eyes that something was wrong.

"Eve?"

She handed him the postcard. He turned it over, observed the picture on the front which, and after flipping it back over, explained that it was the moon rise at Maenam Beach, Samui Island, Thailand.

"He's never coming back," she whispered.

"They're together," Theo said quite simply, taking Eve's chin in his hand, his finger wiping away the few tears that escaped her eyes. He looked at his two sons and smiled deeply at her. "And so are we."

Theo was right. There was no alternative but to get on with her life. "Do you know something?" she said, snuggling against his chest as she looked tenderly at the boys. "We never did discuss my fund-raiser."

Their eyes met. Locked. Her heart skipped a beat as she leaned forward and planted a kiss on the professor.

ABOUT THE AUTHOR

Sonia Icilyn was born in Sheffield, England, where she still lives with her daughter in a small village, which she describes as "typically British, quiet, and where the old money is." She graduated with a distinction level Private Secretary's Certificate in Business and Commerce and also has a Master's Degree in Writing.

SIGNIFICANT OTHER, Sonia's first romance novel, was published in 1993. Since then she has added five titles to her name. She has been featured in *Black Elegance* and *Today's Black Woman,* and her work has appeared on the *Ebony* recommended books to read list.

Sonia is the founder and organizer of the African Arts and Culture Expo and the British Black Expo in Great Britain. She is also CEO of the Peacock Company. She loves to travel and realistically depicts her characters based on the fine tapestry of the African diaspora.

Sonia would love to hear from her readers. You can write to her at P.O. Box 438, Sheffield S1 4YX, ENGLAND, or visit her Web site at www.soniaicilyn.com.